Acclaim for *Thieves*

"A chilling portrait of a psychopath on a murderous rampage. One hell of a debut for Steve Russo."
—James Hayman, *New York Times* bestselling author of *The Girl on the Bridge*

"Kudos to Steven Max Russo. I read *Thieves* in one sitting—it's propulsive, absorbing, and all too plausible. I warn you, these thieves will steal an entire day or two from you—and you'll love every minute of it."
—Jonathan Stone, author of *Moving Day*, *The Teller*, and *Days of Night*

"Gripping and powerful, *Thieves* is a dynamite read. Definitely a book you won't be able to put down."
—Andrew Grant, author of *False Witness*

"With *Thieves*, Steven Max Russo works the rich tradition of American heist fiction like a pro."
—Wallace Stroby, author of the Crissa Stone series

THIEVES

OTHER BOOKS BY STEVEN MAX RUSSO

The Dead Don't Sleep (*)

(*) – Coming in 2019

STEVEN MAX RUSSO

THIEVES

Down and Out Books
3959 Van Dyke Road, Suite 265
Lutz, FL 33558
www.DownAndOutBooks.com

Cover design by Chuck Regan

ISBN: 1-948235-40-4
ISBN-13: 978-1-948235-40-2

This novel, my first, is dedicated to my mom and dad, and of course, my beautiful Susan.

PROLOGUE

Miami, Florida
Six weeks ago

He came to slowly, as if drifting out of a dense fog. His whole consciousness was focused on his right hand, which throbbed with an intense pain like nothing he had felt before. His throat was parched and swollen, so much so that he couldn't swallow and had trouble breathing. He was afraid that he might begin to gag and choke. His tongue was stuck to the roof of his mouth. He knew something bad was happening but couldn't quite remember what had caused him to be here, his arms and feet immobile, duct-taped to this plastic chair.

His hand was burning, emanating heat as if it were on fire.

Someone grabbed hold of his hair and jerked his head violently upward. It wasn't exceptionally painful, but it was a shock, and he blinked trying to clear the tears out of his eyes so that he could see a little more clearly.

"Hey, are you awake? Good, I thought we lost you there for a minute." The voice sounded low and calm, almost kind.

A face suddenly appeared right in front of him, very close, eye-to-eye, their noses almost touching. Even in his dazed and confused state, he could still smell stale tobacco on the man's breath. The man's eyes were bright and sparkled with what could have been amusement, or perhaps a rush from something recently smoked or snorted, his hair slicked down on his head, held firm and tight with some sort of glistening hair gel.

1

Paul Diggardy tried to speak, but no words came out, just a dry croaking sound.

"What? What did you say? Do you know where he is? Where he is right now?" The face in front of him turned quickly to look behind, one hand pointing and then his fingers snapping as he said with some urgency, "Alejandro, agua!"

The face turned back and looked intensely into Paul Diggardy's eyes. A second later, a young man appeared carrying a plastic bottle of Poland Spring water. The man with tobacco breath reached behind him, this time without turning his head, and took the bottle. He reached his hand around and pulled Paul's hair back so that his face was pointed to the ceiling and put the bottle to his lips, then poured the cool water into his mouth. It was heaven on his dry, swollen tongue, and he sucked and slurped the water down trying hard not to gag.

"There, there, that is enough." The man stopped the flow of water and let go of his hair.

"Now, back to business. Do you know where he is? Where he is right now?"

Paul was not sure what the man was talking about and looked at him blankly. He was trying to focus on what the man was saying.

The man let go of his hair, took a step back, and smiled warmly. Then he raised his right arm and slapped him hard, openhanded across the face. The blow was totally unexpected and snapped his head to the right. It stung his face without doing any real damage.

Paul's left cheek burned where the open hand had hit, and his eyes immediately teared up again. A sob escaped him from somewhere deep inside, a feeling of almost overwhelming dread and hopelessness engulfed him as he suddenly remembered what had happened to him and why he was sitting in this empty warehouse, taped to this plastic chair.

"Your friend. The one who broke in where he didn't belong. Where is he?"

Paul cried freely and tried to talk to the man with tobacco breath between great heaving sobs. "I told you already," his voice was low and hoarse, almost unrecognizable to his own ears, "he lives in Bonita Beach. He's got an apartment, right there near 41 and Bonita Beach Road. I don't know the address." He took a long, gasping breath. "There's a motel, like a Motel 6, right across the street. Christ, I can't remember nuthin'. Can I have some more water? Please?"

The man didn't say anything for a few seconds, and then slowly he began pouring the remaining water from the Poland Spring bottle over the top of Paul's head. Paul leaned his head back and opened his mouth, desperately trying to catch some of the water as it dribbled through his hair and down his face.

When the bottle was empty, the man began again.

"Your friend. Where is he now?"

"He ain't my friend no more, that was a long time ago. We just growed up together is all. I heard he might'a been involved. It was just a rumor, see? I want to help y'all. I told you everything I know. Jesus, my hand, what did you do to my hand? Man, it hurts like hell. What'd you do?"

"Here, let me show you."

The man grabbed Paul's hair again and gently pulled his head down until his chin nearly touched his chest. His feet were taped to the legs of the chair so he could see the ground between his knees. Paul squeezed his eyes tight, and tears ran down his cheeks. He didn't want to see what was below him but felt compelled to look. He opened his eyes and saw the man's polished red cowboy boots. They were beautiful, the supple leather gleaming to a high shine. The man gently moved a small pile of bloody red stubs around with the pointy toe of one boot. Paul could see dirty fingernails on the ends of the stubs.

A low moan escaped his throat. He wasn't even aware he was making the sound as he was totally focused on the small bloody pile between his legs.

"Small pleasures gone." The man's voice was soft and soothing, like he was telling a bedtime story. "Things that we take for granted every day—never even think about them. Scratching an itch, the tender caress to a beautiful woman's breast, picking a particularly annoying booger out of your own nose. What a shame."

Paul was crying hard. He could hardly talk, the words coming out in a harsh, quiet whisper.

"Those are my fingers, man, you motherfuckers cut off my goddamn fingers."

The man stood up. He reached into the pocket of his expensive sport coat and pulled out a phone. He hit the speed dial, put the phone to his ear, and waited.

On the second ring, he heard a voice with a pronounced Hispanic accent answer. "Did he give you what we need?"

"We will work with him a little more, but I think he has given us all that he has. I will need to go across to the gulf coast, make a surprise visit, see if our friend is at home. We will have more business to conduct when we meet him."

There was a minute of silence. Then, "Good. Stop by the office first. And bring me something."

"Yes, of course," he said. Then the line went dead.

"Alejandro," he said, addressing the young man who had handed him the water bottle, "los otro dedos." The other fingers.

"Todos?"

"Si, todos."

He watched the young man walk over to the worktable and pick up the bolt cutter with the long, blond wooden handles now spattered and stained dark with blood. Two other young men who were standing a few feet away eating sandwiches dropped their food into a trash barrel and then made their way over to where Paul Diggardy sat taped to the chair, each grabbing hold of an arm and shoulder to keep him steady.

The man with the tobacco breath and shiny-red cowboy boots continued walking toward the door, which led out to the parking lot. Paul screamed, but the scream was cut off suddenly as one of the young men cupped a hand roughly over his mouth. The man continued to the door, opened it, and stepped out into the bright sunshine and intense heat of the Miami afternoon.

He didn't mind the heat; he had in fact grown up with it in his home country. It was truly a beautiful day. He opened the trunk of his 8-series BMW, reached inside, and pulled a single sheet off a battered roll of paper towels. He then put his right foot up on the bumper and carefully wiped the blood off the toe of his boot. That done, he placed the soiled paper towel in a plastic bag, then grabbed a large glass jar filled with formaldehyde that was held secure in an elastic net attached to the inside of the trunk. Amazing what they come up with for their cars these Germans, he thought absently. He then opened a hidden compartment and extracted the sawed-off Remington 870 pump-action shotgun.

His boss wanted him to bring something back to the office.

The jar was only large enough to hold the fingers.

But that was okay.

He didn't expect there was going to be much left of the head anyway.

ONE

Mendham, New Jersey
Friday

As a rule, Skooley did not like beaners. He grew up in a small town in south-central Florida and though the area where he lived was fully integrated, he was taught early on to stick with his own kind.

His father worked, but only intermittently, and quite often in the fields right next to the illegals. He always thought of himself as better. Better because he was white. Better because he was born in Florida and a true American.

But Skooley had always known that his old man was just trailer trash and no better than anybody.

Still, he found that as a rule, he just didn't like beaners.

But Ray seemed all right. He was actually pretty smart, for a Mexican. It was Ray's idea to steal the bikes from his busboy buddies instead of taking Skooley's car. It was a long bike ride from the town of Bernardsville, NJ, where they were both staying in a rooming house, to this driveway in Mendham, but he would have had to find a place to put his car, the stolen Toyota Camry, for a few hours unnoticed. He hadn't even gotten around to stealing a new set of plates, and that could very well have posed a problem. This way, they just rode the bikes with their six-pack of beer in the rusty metal basket right up to the private drive—that actually looked more like a goddamn street than somebody's driveway—and walked the bikes into the woods. There were plenty of other bicyclists on the road, though most of them were wearing spandex and sleek plastic helmets. Still, nobody paid him and Ray any mind. They laid the bikes down, then sat in the dirt and started drinking beer, smoking cigarettes and watching the house.

"Hey, Skooley, what you think, man? I don't see nobody."

Skooley turned and looked at Raymundo. Ray was a small, dark man, about twenty-three years old and maybe five-three with a thick build and unruly, bushy black hair that fell over one eye. This caused him to twitch his head every so often to get the hair out of his face, which for some reason just annoyed the hell out of Skooley. He was wearing white painter's pants that had turned a dull gray, and a dingy New York Mets T-shirt with what looked like a faded yellow mustard stain just to the left of his navel. On his feet was a pristine pair of white Nike sneakers.

Skooley squinted his eyes and looked at the Mexican.

"Shit, Ray, take it easy. We only just got here." He gave him his best friendly smile. "Let's give it a while. We got beer, the sun is shining, what more can you ask for? Hell, where I come from, days like this are few and far between. I can't tell you what a pleasure it is to sit in this here woods and just enjoy the day."

"What, you don't got woods in Florida?" He pronounced it Flor-eeda, like he was still in Mexico.

Skooley held his smile as he looked at Ray. "Where you from anyway, Ray?"

"Bernardsville, man, you know that."

"No, I mean before."

"Before Bernardsville? I live two years in Newark."

"No, no, where in Mexico you from?"

"I from Guatemala."

"They got woods like this in that part of Mexico?"

Ray looked back at him for a second, puzzled, then shook his head.

7

Skooley nodded, then leaned back against a tree with a beer in one hand and his cigarette in the other.

"There you go, amigo. Where I grew up near Okeechobee, we got mostly just brush, maybe a scrub pine here or there, but there ain't no hills or mountains and certainly no trees the likes of what we got surrounding us here. I feel like Robin Hood in Sherwood Forest. You ever hear of Robin Hood?"

Ray turned away from Skooley without answering and watched the house.

They sat in silence for a while and worked on finishing off the six-pack of beer, which was just starting to get warm. It was pleasant in the shade under the trees, and Skooley closed his eyes and felt himself drifting off for just a second.

He awoke with a start, dazed and unsure of where he was. Someone or something was crashing through the woods. He jumped to his feet and saw Raymundo walking toward him from the direction of the house.

Ray flicked his head to clear the hair out of his eyes. "Man, you should see the pool they got back there. Is beautiful."

Skooley wiped off some spittle that had accumulated on his chin with the back of his hand and then ran his hand under his armpit to clean it off.

"Anybody see you?" he asked.

"No, man, is like I tole you, nobody home. They away. They away for a month, maybe more."

"You go into the backyard?"

"Yeah, the backyard, the front yard, all over. I even knock on the door. "

"I told you we was gonna wait, check it out first."

"We did wait, man. You fell asleep, Skools. I got to pee. I walk back over that way, you know, to take a leak. I right there so I take a look around. I don't see nobody. I come back, you still snoring. We got no more beer. I go out to the road, walk up the driveway in case someone home, you know, looking out the window, they don't see me sneaking around. I

8

walk up to the front door and knock. No one answer. I ring the bell. Nothing. I walk around, yoo-hoo, anyone home? I go into the backyard. Nice pool. It got a cover, but you can still see, you know. Little waterfall, hot tub too, man, is beautiful."

Ray stood there looking at Skooley with a smug, self-satisfied smile, and it took every ounce of self-control for Skooley not to sucker punch him. Instead, he beamed back to his best friendly smile.

"Suppose someone answered the door, Ray. Suppose there was some old lady in the backyard, you know, laying out by the pool thinking she's all alone getting a tan, maybe even naked with her titties sticking out. What then, huh?"

"Someone answer the door, I say I looking for work, you know, clean the yard, cut the grass. Not sneaky, real polite. But no one answer. Is like I tole you already, they not home. They go away for like a month. They go every year. My friend, Esmeralda, she say every year, same time, they go away to California, Arizona, someplace like that."

Skooley rubbed his chin and thought about it. They were there because Ray had heard about this house from one of his beaner girlfriends who cleaned houses. She had told Ray that there were only two people who lived here: an old rich guy along with his wife. She said the guy was loaded, owned a paving and construction company, and had a big motor yacht they kept docked somewhere on the Hudson River. Skooley could see a small backhoe parked on the far side of the house next to some construction debris. It had to be the guy's machine. And his wife was supposedly some sort of famous artist. Esmeralda said that she had her own art studio over the garage, and there were expensive paintings hung up all over the house. One room on the main floor she described as being like a gallery in an art museum. She told Ray that their three kids were grown, married, and out of the house.

But Skooley was cautious. What kind of dumbass would just leave a big old house like this sitting empty for so long?

Guy was rich, and he didn't get that way by being a dumbass. It wouldn't hurt to take their time and look things over. See if anyone was house sitting. Maybe one of his kids decided to stay over for a few days to make sure that everything was locked up good and tight. Shit, maybe this was the year they decided to just stay put and not go to California or Arizona or wherever the hell they went. Maybe right now, this very minute, they were just leaving the local supermarket or their neighbor's house and heading back home. Skooley certainly wasn't afraid of breaking the law, but he didn't see any need for being reckless.

"C'mon, man, let's go check it out, see if we can get in," said Raymundo, and with a flick of his head he started out of the woods toward the house, "I bet they even leave a door open for us, Skools. Maybe they got some beer in a big Viking fridge, huh?"

Skooley scratched his chin and thought about it for just a second, then figured what the hell and followed the little Mexican from Guatemala into the yard.

TWO

The front yard was the size of a football field, easy. It wasn't a nicely kept trim lawn, but more of a sparsely wooded tract. The land had been cleared, but a few big trees were kept intact for shade. There was a row of bushes and hedges that blocked most of the view from the street. Dried leaves and downed branches were littered all about, not making the place look unkempt so much as just rural. All the houses in this area were large and set back off the main roads. The properties were huge, couple of acres each with woods all around. This house was large but not of mansion proportions. Skooley had seen some real money palaces in his travels, particularly in some of the resort areas of coastal Florida. After he left home for good at fourteen, he bummed around working wherever he could, mostly in restaurants as a busboy or dishwasher. He worked a while for a landscaping company in the Fort Myers area that had some rich clients in Naples. Talk about big money. Man, some of those houses were the size of fucking museums. And the cars, shit, everyone in that town drove a Ferrari or Maserati or Bentley. Not the little shit-box BMWs and Audis he saw all over this part of New Jersey. Hell, he'd also been in some sections of Miami and Fort Lauderdale that took rich to a whole other level.

This house wasn't even new. It was old. Parts of the foundation looked to be mortared rock at least a hundred years old. Shit, probably more than a hundred. You could see several additions and alterations that had been made at different times. The windows on the front part of the house were single-paned, looked like they could be thirty or forty years old. Guy still has to put up storm windows. The whole place needed work. Not major work, just maintenance type work. Skooley wondered why a guy who owned a construction company didn't fix up his own house. Maybe the guy was too busy making money. Then again, maybe he *was* just a dumbass.

They strolled up to the front door, real cool and casual. The door was dark blue and appeared new, but the trim around the frame looked like it should be replaced, or at least painted up a bit.

"What you think?" Raymundo flicked the hair out of his eyes and looked at Skooley. His bravado had disappeared. Hell, thought Skooley, the little fucker seemed nervous, maybe even scared.

Skooley motioned with his finger around one corner of the doorframe. "This here whole section should be replaced. See how the wood is pitted?"

"The fuck you talkin' about?"

"At the very least, it could use some paint."

"Yeah? You think we should paint? Hey, maybe they got brushes in the garage. You know what I think? I think maybe you should paint the fucking door while I bust a window and go see what they got inside."

Skooley ignored Ray and rang the doorbell, then tried the doorknob. Locked. There was also a serious-looking deadbolt directly above the knob.

"I thought you said they left the door open for us, Ray." Skooley cupped his hands and peered into the foyer through a small glass window next to the doorframe.

"Sure looks a lot nicer on the inside than it does the outside." He could see a chandelier hanging over a wide staircase leading to the second floor. He craned his neck to see if there was any type of electronic security panel next to the door, but the window wasn't wide enough to provide a good view. He didn't think the place was alarmed. The windows were old. Doorframe was old. He didn't see any signs or window stickers intended to scare away burglars. Usually, if someone has an alarm system, they advertise it. Stops most break-ins before they even happen. That's the whole point. Would most certainly have stopped him. Maybe there was some kind of a setup that he didn't know about. Could be the guy just never replaced the wiring in this old section of the house. Or maybe they lived here in Sherwood Forest for so long without incident, they just didn't feel threatened enough to invest the money. The house was nice enough, but it was old and not even close in size or luxury to most of the other houses on the street. Probably worst thing ever happened was they got some drunken neighborhood kids skinny-dipping in the pool at night.

"Let's find a rock, break the fucking window." Ray was starting to get agitated.

"Hold on there, amigo." Skooley reached into his shirt pocket and shook out a Marlboro Light. "You ever done a B&E?"

"Done what?"

"B&E. Breaking and entering. Ever broke into a house before?" He lit his cigarette.

"Shit, Skools, we ain't broke nothing yet."

"You know, Ray, you can be a real turd sometimes. A fucking Mexican turd."

"What you mean, Skools?" Raymundo squinted the one eye that Skooley could see, the other hidden behind thick black hair. The little Mexican got a look that Skooley didn't like.

"What I mean is the shitbird that owns this house is stupid enough to just up and leave for a month, right? I don't see no security cameras, no electrical panels near the door; them old windows don't look like they got no alarms on 'em. Hell, ya think he might be stupid enough to scuttle away a spare key in some little ole hidey-hole, ya know, just in case?"

They didn't find a key to the front door, but about a half

hour later, they did find a key to a door in back that led into the garage. It was hidden in a fake rock that lay in a flowerbed right next to the door. It was the only rock in the flowerbed. The owners had pushed it far back against the house and partially covered it with dirt and leaves. Skooley found it pretty easily. He had entered several homes in Florida in the same manner. Of course, for most of those homes, it was a bit more challenging as the fake rocks were usually tucked away amongst a pile of real ones. But still, they were usually pretty easy to pick out. Of course, he had also been surprised quite a few times to find a key under a mat or sitting out of view on a doorframe or window ledge or under a pot or taped to an air conditioning unit. Thinking back, he only ever had to actually break into about five or six houses in his life. Same thing with cars. The key to the Camry he drove up from Florida was in a magnetic box that was stuck inside the left rear bumper. Hell, people were stupid all over.

The door into the garage was in the back of the house. This door was certainly not new. It was old and flimsy. He probably could have just forced the door open with his shoulder if he had to, but the key slid easily into the keyhole of the loosely set knob, and with a quick turn and a twist of the knob, they were in.

The garage was oversized and could have easily fit three cars, maybe four. There was a 2010 Mercedes E350 Coupe parked on one side. For a car that was already a couple of years old, it was in almost showroom condition. The black pearl finish gleamed with fresh wax, and the tires, though a little worn, were well-coated in tire shine. Her car, he thought. Right next to the Mercedes, in the middle of the garage, was a dark green 2013 Range Rover. This car had a light coating of dust. There were spatters of dried mud along all the wheel wells, and it was obvious that this car was used for more than just driving around town. His car. Geez, the guy probably paid sixty or seventy grand for this thing. All so he could drive in style to his dirty job sites. Skooley looked in the passenger's side window. The interior was immaculate. Guy probably sits on a towel or something. Fucking rich people.

The last bay of the garage looked more like the garages Skooley was used to. It was jam-packed with all sorts of shit. He saw a riding mower that was more like a small tractor; two weed whackers, one was partially dismantled, the other brand-new; a spreader for fertilizer; two mountain bikes; several red plastic gas cans in assorted sizes; a relatively new Honda 9000-watt portable generator was sitting conveniently right below the house's main electrical panel; hand tools and garden tools were hanging off pegs on the walls; a low shelf with bags of grass seed and grub control chemicals and Scott's fertilizer; a yellow box of rat poison with a drawing of a big old rat with a red circle and an X drawn through it; old sports equipment like a deflated football and baseball bats and tennis racquets; engine parts; hell, stuff was just piled up upon more stuff. The whole place had a familiar odor that could best be described as a mixture of gasoline, motor oil, and old sweat with a slight undertone of dried manure.

Ray had made his way to the door that led to the house. He looked at Skooley and pointed to the door silently. The door was another old piece of crap that needed paint. There were two rickety wooden steps leading up to it.

Skooley tiptoed over to the door and put a finger to his lips in a shushing motion. Then he pointed to his own chest. Ray shrugged, then nodded to Skooley and put both hands into his pockets. Skooley figured the little Mexican was nervous about going in first, and so he slowly reached for the knob, turned back to Ray who was close behind him, nodded back solemnly at him, twisted the knob and opened the door.

A harrowing scream pierced the silence. Skooley threw up his hands and Ray fell back, tripped over a bucket, and landed heavily on the floor. Skooley turned to look at Ray on the floor and began laughing hysterically. He was laughing so hard he actually doubled over. Ray was scrambling on the garage floor, legs kicking wildly. His hands had been in his pockets, and the shock of the scream must have made him lose his balance and fall over backwards. His face was red, and he freed one hand from his pocket but the other must have been stuck because he seemed to be wrestling with it. Skooley slowly lowered himself to a sitting position as he belly-laughed at his partner scrambling on the garage floor.

Suddenly, Ray's stuck hand emerged from his right front pocket with a small, black snub-nosed revolver, which he pointed at Skooley's nose. His face was red and his eyes were wild, and the hand that was holding the revolver was shaking like mad. Skooley saw the gun pointing at his nose but still couldn't stop laughing. He held up one hand and through his laughter tried to talk.

"Easy there, amigo, take her easy. I was just foolin' with ya, that's all." His laughter was ebbing, but his eyes were watering and he couldn't see Ray too well.

The shaky gun hand stayed where it was.

"Don't shoot, Ray, geez, put that thing away. It was just a joke. You were right, there ain't no one home, man. I was just having a little fun is all."

He wiped at his eyes with his hands to clear away some loose tears. The gun in Ray's hand was definitely moving less erratically, but Ray's face was getting redder and there was sweat forming on his brow and just above his lip.

The laughter had just about passed. Skooley wiped at his eyes some more and then ran a finger under his nose. The gun was steady now, pointing at his face.

Skooley wasn't a big man. He was just over five-foot-ten, or as he liked to think of himself, just under six feet tall. He was thin and wiry, maybe a hundred and seventy pounds or so, but with arms that were tightly corded with veins and muscle. He was wearing a black T-shirt and faded blue jeans cinched tight with a slightly frayed, black canvas belt. He had on dark brown boat shoes that had seen better days and dingy white sweat socks. He was thirty-two years old, but from far away, could have passed for twenty-two. His skin color could best be described as somewhere between tan and burnt. His teeth were yellow with tobacco stains, the bottom row just slightly crooked. He had longish, stringy blond hair with a hairline that was not yet receding but looked to be right on the verge. His most notable feature was his eyes. They were a clear, bright blue, but almost expressionless. It was those eyes that Ray looked into right now.

Skooley was smiling, but it was not his best friendly smile this time. Skooley had several smiles that he had practiced over the years. The smile he used now was what he termed his "shit" smile. This is what he used right before he kicked the shit out of someone. There wasn't much that scared Skooley, and he wasn't scared now. "Well, amigo, what you planning on doing? You gonna pull that trigger, then go ahead and pull it. If not, get that gun outta my face or I'm gonna shove that thing right up your ass."

The gun hand started shaking again.

Skooley wiped his eyes one more time and slowly stood up.

"Let's get us inside and see what we got here, Ray."

Ray hadn't moved. The gun was still pointing at Skooley.

Skooley bent down on his haunches and placed his face inches from the gun. He gave Ray a wide smile.

"You should'a seen your face when I let loose that yell, Ray. I swear, you looked like you was just about to shit a brick."

Ray slowly lowered the gun. He was dripping sweat.

"You pretty cool cracker, pendejo. But you fuck with me again, no shit, I pop you ass."

Skooley slowly rose and then reached a hand down to help Ray up. Ray ignored it, scrambled to his feet, and then motioned with the gun toward the door.

"Let's go inside," he said.

17

Skooley went up the rickety stairs and into the house with Ray and the revolver following close behind him.

The door led to a hallway, which opened into a small mudroom. There were wooden benches along one wall with all manner of footwear below—several pairs of work boots, sneakers, rain boots, women's shoes—all arranged in a neat row. There were pegs hanging from the wall over the bench and one or two coats hung on these. Skooley looked behind him. Ray was still holding the gun pointed at Skooley's back. He also noticed that right next to the door from which they had just entered hung a small pegboard with the word "Keys" decoratively painted on it. Hanging on hooks were what looked like keys to the two cars parked in the garage. Skooley smiled. Ray waved the gun in a "get going" motion, and Skooley turned around and made his way further into the house.

There was a half bath directly to his right: just a sink and a toilet with some hand towels hanging on a rack. He poked his head in. The room smelled heavily of one of those room deodorizers and sure enough, sitting there on the toilet tank, was a cone with its blue gel center slowly wasting away.

He turned back toward the hall hoping that Ray had passed ahead of him into the next room, but Ray was waiting in the hallway.

"Ray, if you ain't gonna shoot me, why don't you put your gun away."

"Who says I not gonna shoot you?" He wasn't smiling when he said this.

"Okay, amigo, but at least point it at the floor until you're ready to shoot me, okay? I don't want to get shot in the ass just because you ain't looking where you're going and you trip over something, you know, like you did in the garage." Skooley gave him a great big nice-guy smile to no effect.

They kept walking and could see the kitchen down at the end of the hall. Directly to the left, just past the half bath, was a closed door. Skooley opened it and walked into a small office.

It was a bit messy, obviously well-used. There was a desk with a computer on it. It looked relatively new, though computers weren't really something that Skooley was overly familiar with. There was a tower under the desk. The monitor was pretty large, and flat like a TV. The desk had a plush, high-back leather chair. Skooley felt the cool, smooth leather. Definitely leather, not vinyl. There were filing cabinets against every wall and on top of those sat cardboard boxes that looked like they were filled with files too. In the center of the room were two waiting-room chairs on both sides of a glass coffee table. The table had what appeared to be half rolled up blueprints on it. There was also a coffee mug with a dried coffee ring stain at the bottom. The guy had family photos on his desk and also hung up on the wall over his desk. He was a short, pudgy-looking fellow. Not someone Skooley would have imagined as head of a construction company.

His wife, though not particularly beautiful, had a handsome, intelligent face. There was something elegant about her, almost regal. There were also various shots of the kids at different ages, two boys and a girl. The guy was definitely into boating. Spaced throughout the family shots were photos of the guy standing next to various watercraft, motorboats, yachts, sailboats. One showed him sitting in the cockpit of one of those high-tech cigarette racing boats like the ones he used to see running up and down the beach at Fort Lauderdale, roaring like thunder. Skooley noticed that he looked happier in that shot than in any of the family pictures.

Ray pushed past him and started opening desk drawers and filing cabinets. Skooley watched him grab handfuls of paper and fling them onto the floor.

"What's the matter with you, Ray?"

"The fuck you talkin' about, Skooley?"

Skooley entered the room, pulled out the high-back leather chair, and sat down.

"Man, this is nice. It's got that cushion for your back, you know. Right down there, just above the crack of your ass. Fits your back the way a fine leather glove fits your hand. And check this out: it rocks, you don't hear a thing. Not a squeak." He closed his eyes and rocked gently.

"You one fucked up dude, Skooley."

"Yeah, amigo, you're right about that. Look, Ray, I'm sorry about yelling out there like that. I shouldn't a done that, no sir. I know this is serious business we're on here, and I know, too, that you brung me in on this, not the other way around. But if you don't mind my sayin', you seem strung just a bit tight. Now, I know you got reason to be pissed, and I don't blame you for feeling that way, but waving that gun around like you been doing and makin' a mess of this place when there really ain't no reason to, well, I gotta admit, it's a course of action that pretty much borders on the peculiar."

Skooley got up. "Here, Ray, sit here. Go ahead; just sit down for one second. I ain't fooling with you now."

Ray looked at Skooley, then walked over to the chair and sat down. He still held the revolver in his lap.

"There, that's nice now, ain't it?"

Ray rocked the chair slowly but didn't say a word.

"Ya see, my point is, you was right, Ray. You was right all along. There ain't no one here. There ain't no one coming home today, not tomorrow, not for a couple a weeks I reckon, just like your friend Esmeralda told you. So, we don't have to hurry and rip open stuff and throw it on the floor like we had to get the hell outta here. We got no reason to hurry at all. We can just sit here like you're doin' right now in that very chair and rock easy and take our time and let this lovely ole house give up her secrets in her own time." He beamed his nice-guy smile.

"Remember outside, when you was wanting to bust the window and I told you to take it easy? Well, we found a key, didn't we? I ain't saying I'm smarter than you, Ray, it's just that I done this sort of thing before. I done it lots a times. And it's the same inside as outside. If we just rush around and bust the place up, we're gonna find some things, sure, but we're gonna miss some things too. People hide their treasured valuables, and they think long and hard on where they gonna put 'em before they put 'em anywheres. We'll find the stuff they want us to find easy, and it'll be nice stuff too, I bet. But if they got something real valuable, we got to take our time and learn about this house and study on the folks who live here before we find out where it's hid. Am I making sense, amigo?"

Ray continued rocking slowly in the high-backed chair. To Skooley, he looked like a little kid sitting there, his feet barely touching the floor. "Okay, Skools, but just remember what you said: I brung you in. We go easy. But we look together. No more of your fucking shit, man, you hear?"

"Understood, Ray. Let's go out to the kitchen and check out that Viking. I bet you was right about them having some beer for us in there too."

THREE

Esmeralda climbed the narrow staircase carrying the bag with the now quickly softening chocolate-flavored Shop Rite brand ice cream. It wasn't melting yet, but it was close. She was lucky; work had gone smoothly today. Usually, Fridays were the toughest day of the week. Everyone wanted their house cleaned on Friday, get their home ready for a grand weekend of entertaining.

She could hear the TV through the thin walls, the children yelling at each other in the cramped living room.

When she opened the door, the kids all came bounding over to her, jumping up and down with their hands in the air trying to reach the bag containing the ice cream, which she was forced to hold high over her head.

"Emi, Emi, Emi," they all shouted, "what did you bring us?"

"Get away from me you little animals! You're yapping like puppy dogs!" she said loudly, with a smile in her voice. "This is ice cream, but it's not for you! It's all for me! Nobody eats my ice cream! It's all mine, and I'm going to eat it until I get as fat as a house!"

"Ice cream, ice cream!" the children yelled.

"Okay, okay," she said, "maybe I'll share, but only after dinner."

"Tranquillo por favor!" The voice came from the kitchen. The children quickly lost interest in their older sister and headed back to the TV.

Her mother was in the kitchen frying something on the

stove. The entire apartment smelled of cooking, but it was only partially from what her mother was working on in the kitchen. The apartment where the family lived was just down the street from the Morristown Green, a small park that was the center of town. Their apartment was one of two on the second floor of an old commercial building that housed a sandwich shop and a Hispanic-owned diner below. Across the street was a bar/restaurant called The Grasshopper. Just down the street were several other restaurants and eateries, including a Dunkin Donuts and a Burger King that added the smells of coffee, cooking meat, and burnt vegetable oil to the cacophony of odors. And of course, her mother's cooking: fried onions and peppers and chicken. Esmeralda often felt like she just couldn't breathe in the small, cramped apartment.

She shared the space with her mother, her two younger brothers, and a baby sister. The children were all much younger than she, the boys being eight and ten and the girl only five. Esmeralda was twenty-two and since her father had left for parts unknown a year and a half earlier, she had become the primary breadwinner for the family. She was a pretty Colombian girl with dark, luxurious hair that she grew past her shoulders. She was slim yet shapely with a slightly-round face and a small, upturned nose. Her features and skin coloring were obviously Hispanic, but anyone who didn't know her would be hard-pressed to guess in what country she was born. She had glistening brown eyes that for some reason always looked sad.

Esmeralda worked two full-time jobs; her day job was working as a house cleaner for a local company, and she also worked nights at a separate commercial office cleaning company. On weekends, she waited tables for a restaurant in a neighboring town or, if they were really short of help, worked as a hostess. She spoke English with only the slightest hint of an accent and tried always to be helpful and pleasant.

She also helped out in a beauty salon on the other, shadier

side of town whenever she could find the time. A friend of hers named Maria had actually gone to beauty school and earned a cosmetology license, and it was Maria who got her work at the salon on occasional weekend afternoons. It wasn't much, just sweeping and answering phones or getting coffee or doing whatever needed doing. Sometimes she even did shampoos. They didn't pay her much, but she was really just there for the experience.

Esmeralda had ambition and was working to save enough money to attend beauty school, get her license, and eventually open her own salon. But not like the ratty little place she sometimes worked in the Hispanic section of Morristown; she was going to open a high-end salon like the ones that lined the ritzier South Street section on the other side of town. She had driven past salons and spas in nearby towns like Summit and Millburn and Short Hills on her way to clean houses, classy businesses that looked like they belonged in midtown Manhattan or Paris or London. Shiny wood floors and dramatic lighting and hair stylists who looked like runway models and make-up artists to add sophistication and flair to a new haircut and dedicated nail girls who gave foot massages to beautiful, rich customers dressed in expensive outfits.

That's what she was working toward. That's what she was saving for. Of course, that was after the rent and food and other bills that had to be paid, got paid, so she hadn't saved much.

She kissed her mother on top of her head and put the ice cream in the freezer. She looked at the clock and decided that she just had time to freshen up, eat a quick dinner, and then head off to meet the van that would take her and few other girls to her second job: cleaning offices in nearby Parsippany.

She stole a quick look at her phone.

Still no message.

FOUR

The kitchen was a large room loaded with super high-end appliances, yet still seemed bright, airy, and uncluttered. The cabinets were finely crafted with a lot of beveled glass and expensive hardware. Large, double stainless-steel sinks sat on both the regular counter and set into the large island in the center of the room. Two side-by-side ovens with burners were built into the counter, and the island also had four stove burners beside the sink. Shit, thought Skooley, that's twelve burners in one kitchen for just two people. He ran his fingers gently along the smooth marble countertops. The refrigerator was a behemoth stainless-steel side-by-side with two sets of drawers along the bottom that Skooley was pretty sure would be freezers. He opened both doors, stuck his head inside, and came out with two beers.

"Well, I guess they just couldn't afford to get themselves a Viking. Ya ever hear of a Northland fridge before? I can't say as I have. They ain't got no buds either, but they got beer and it's cold."

He handed a Stella Artois to Ray, then began rummaging around in various drawers until he found a bottle opener.

The kitchen opened up into a sunny breakfast room, and they walked over and sat down at the table with their beers.

Skooley noticed that Ray still held the gun in his right hand while he sipped his beer with his left.

"Well, Ray, seein' as this is your deal, I guess that puts you in charge. So, big jefe, how you wanna go about doin' this?"

Ray looked at Skooley, then sipped his beer slowly. "We finish these beers, then we look in every room, man. We find money, we find watches, rings, whatever."

Skooley nodded his head slowly and said, "Might be better if we split up and take a fast look around the whole place first, you know, just to get our bearings so to speak, then we can pick the rooms that look most promising and go through them together."

"Why you wanna split up, eh, Skools? We're in no hurry. We got us lots of time—days, maybe weeks, no one come home. We look together, we go in every room, see what we find." He gave Skooley a smile, then flicked the hair out of his eyes and took another sip of his beer.

"That sounds like a good plan, amigo. Hey, I'm gonna see if they left us anything to munch on. You hungry?" He set his beer down on the table, got up quickly, walked back into the kitchen, and started opening up cupboards. "Man, this is all plates and glasses and stuff. Wonder where they keep the good stuff at? I bet rich folks like this gotta have some Ritz crackers or Velveeta or something."

He walked over to a smallish door and opened it. "Bingo, Ray, we hit the mother lode! Man, you should see this!" The pantry was a small room stocked floor to ceiling with all manner of food—canned goods, pasta, jars of sauces, snacks, sodas, bottled water, you name it.

"Jeez-zuz, only two people live here? Ya could feed a friggin' army with all this stuff. They got more crap in here than most a the restaurants I ever worked at." He came out with a bag of Fritos corn chips and a box of Ritz Crackers in one hand, and a blue can in the other. Then he walked over to the table where Ray sat with his beer and his gun. He dropped the chips and crackers on the table, then held the can in his hand and looked at it lovingly.

"I can't believe this, Ray, I mean a can't fucking believe this. You know what I found in there? Spam! I ain't had this since I left home when I was just a kid. Hell, we used to live on this stuff." He held the can of Spam out so that Ray could see it.

"Don't know where my old man got so much of it, but he musta got it free from somewheres or stole it because it was Spam for breakfast, lunch, and dinner. I got so I couldn't even stand the sight, nor smell of it. For a while after I left, even just thinking about it could set my stomach to whirling."

Ray was looking at him as he gazed at that can of Spam.

"Ray, we ain't in no hurry, right? I'm gonna cook us up a can. You gotta taste this stuff. Hell, it's been so long, I can't wait to try it again, see if I can still hold it down, you know, bring back some old-timey memories. Why don't you open up them chips and that box of crackers. They say everything tastes better on a Ritz, I wonder what the hell Spam will do to one?"

Ray slammed his beer down on the table. Foam started coming out the top like a little beer volcano. "What the fuck is it with you, Skools? Why you messing with that stuff for, man? We got work to do.'

Skooley sat slowly back down at the table. He put the can of Spam down and picked up his beer. He took a sip and looked at Ray, right into his eyes.

"Wow, man, I can't believe it took me so long, but I do believe I finally got you figured out."

"What you talkin' about?"

"You, Ray, I'm talking about you."

"What about me?"

"It's your attitude, dude. All of a sudden you start coming on like you're some kinda gangsta from LA or Dee-troit. We doin' this Skools, we doin' that Skools, shit, like I don't know what the fuck I'm doing. I gotta tell you, Ray, I was starting to get fed up, you know, just plain fed up."

"Yeah, and what was you gonna do about it, Skools?" Quick flick of the hair. Ray was starting to get that look in his eyes again that Skooley didn't like.

"Well, Ray, I was gonna leave. Just walk out that door yonder and get back on your buddy's bike and pedal my ass back to Bernardsville. This is your deal, Ray, it weren't mine until you asked me along. Now don't get me wrong, this is a pretty nice setup and I'm glad to be here. We can make some money, you and me, and I for one sure could use it. Or you can make some money all by your lonesome. But there was a reason you asked me along. You know, like knowing where to look for that key outside so we're sitting here nice as you please without having to bust a window or break down a door. But now you come on with this tough-guy shit, and you pulled that gun outta your ass and start bossing me around like I was your bitch. I just ain't gonna be told what to do all the time, you hear. I really ain't, Ray. And what are you gonna do about it? Shoot me for not taking nothing and getting on my bike and leaving?"

"So, what's stopping you?"

"Well, a couple a things, Ray. First, like I said, this is a nice setup and we can both make some good money. And second, I believe I finally got you figured out."

"What you got figured out so good, pendejo?"

"You're hangry."

"You bet I hangry when you act like such an asshole."

"No, Ray, not angry, 'hangry.' It's when someone seems to get mad at nothing, but he's really mad because he ain't ate nothing in a while and he's hungry. See, it's a combination of hungry and angry—hangry. I knowed lots of people like that; hell, I'm one of 'em myself. Some little girl I used to know taught me that word and you know what? She was right. That's why one of three things is gonna happen next, and since you are the jefe on this job, you are going to decide what that's gonna be. One, I'm gonna walk out that door empty-handed, get on the bike, and go back to Bernardsville. Two, you're gonna shoot my sorry ass right here and put an end to this comedy. Or three, I'm gonna cook us up this delicious

28

can of whatever kinda meat they make this shit out'a and we're both gonna enjoy another Stella beer and eat Fritos and have our Spam on a Ritz cracker and maybe even add some Velveeta as I bet dollars to donuts they got some hidden back there in that gigantic fucking food closet."

Skooley held up his beer to Ray, smiled, took a long pull, and just waited.

Ray looked at Skooley. Then he put his gun down on the table, picked up his beer with his right hand, wiped some of the foam off the top with his left and said, "What that shit taste like?"

Skooley popped the top on the can, put it up to his nose, and took a deep sniff. "Well, even when it's cooked just right, it still tastes a lot like dog food, Ray."

"Hell, Skools, I worked in some places they cook up real dog food and them stupid customers don't even know what they eat."

"Cool, man, then you're gonna love it." He got up and went to the kitchen. He put the Spam down on the island counter, then disappeared into the fridge again and came out with two more beers. He put those under his arm, reached into a cupboard, grabbed two plates, and then walked back to the table. He put the beers and the plates down. "Why don't you open all this stuff up and I'll get the Spam going. Only gonna take a few minutes. Just gotta fry it is all. I seen some butter in the fridge. Now I just gotta find a good fry pan. Probably in one of them cupboards on the bottom. Hey, lemme have some of them Fritos before I get started. Won't do to have both a us being all hangry at each other." He took a handful of Fritos and went back into the kitchen.

"Where you think we should start at, Skools? You think we go back to the little room back there, the office with the desk? Maybe he got some money hid there? Maybe in one of those drawers. I bet this guy, he got lots of cash, you know, pay people who work for him."

Skooley was bent down peering into a cupboard looking at a wide assortment of pots and pans. He was looking for just the right pan. "We could start there, sure, if that's what you wanna do. But we could also go right to the room where most people hide their very best stuff, see if we hit a jackpot real quick. If we do, it'll make anything else we find like biscuits and gravy." He reached back and found an old cast iron pan, just like the one his old man had used. It was black, seasoned with age, and heavy. "Hey, Ray, they got a fry pan just like my old man's. This is unbelievable." He brought it out and set it on one of the burners. He puzzled on figuring out where the controls were to turn the damn thing on, then got one burner sparked and moved the fry pan onto it.

"How you know where they got their best stuff hid?'

"Well, I don't. That's why we gotta take our time and look around real good. But, you know, if we didn't have all the time in the world and we hadda get gone outta here real quick, the very first place I would look is their bedroom. Probably got a big walk-in closet, maybe two. Lady's sure to have jewelry, probably lots of it. She'll leave a few things lying around, easy to find, maybe even a jewelry box, but she'll have the good stuff squirreled away somewhere she thinks we'll never look. That's what we gotta find."

He pulled the Spam out of the can. There were slimy gelatin globs stuck to the edges of the meat. He laid the meat square on the counter, pulled out a paring knife from the knife rack and began slicing. "Course, you want, we can save that for later. Maybe this guy keeps some cash in his desk drawer. You never know. But even if he does, it probably won't be more'n a few hundred. Course, that's not bad either."

He went back to the fridge and took out a tub of butter. He took the knife he had just used to cut the Spam and scooped out a large glob of butter, which he set to sizzling in the pan.

"Maybe he got a safe." Skooley heard Ray pop another beer open. "Hey, you know how to open up a safe, Skools?"

Skooley picked up the slices of Spam and set each gently into the sizzling butter. The meat hissed and spat in the pan. "I'd have to see the safe. But if he's got one and it ain't too big, we'll probably have to haul it outta here. I can't pick a lock like they do on TV, and he probably ain't got a key hid out in them rocks. And if it's a combination lock, well, I can't do them either. But we get that sucker into the garage, we take whatever money we find and we get us a blow torch, I'll get into it sooner or later." He lowered the flame under the pan and turned each slice over, one after the other. The smell of butter and frying meat started filling the kitchen. An exhaust fan turned on of its own accord, momentarily startling Skooley, and started drawing the smell toward it.

"That smells pretty good, Skools."

"Wait till you taste this, Ray. Why don't you put a few a them Ritz crackers on those plates. I'll see if they got some ketchup and we can make us little Ritz and Spam sandwiches." Skooley went back into the fridge and grabbed a plastic bottle of ketchup.

"Here, catch." He tossed the bottle to Ray who caught it and set it on the table.

Looking around in drawers again, Skooley found a spatula and a dishtowel. He turned the flame off from under the burner, wrapped the dishtowel around the handle of the cast iron pan, which had become hot from cooking. He grabbed the handle with his right hand and the spatula with his left and headed toward the breakfast room. Ray had both plates heaped with crackers.

"Watch yourself, amigo, this shit is hot." Skooley scooped up slices of Spam and divided them evenly onto each plate. "Damn, this friggin' pan is heavy."

He dropped the spatula down on the table and grabbed the pan with both hands. As he turned back toward the kitchen, he angled the pan so it was perpendicular to the floor and just kept on turning, swinging the pan with all his might. There was a dull, sickening thud as the pan connected with the back of Ray's head. Skooley didn't let up on his momentum at all, knowing that it was the follow-through that made all the difference when swinging for the fences. Ray's head hit the table and the plates bounced with a loud, rattling clang and both bottles of beer fell over, one of them rolling off the table and landing on the floor. The pistol that was sitting on the table next to Ray also clattered to the floor. Skooley's momentum almost caused him to let go of the pan. His grip had loosened and slid a little because of the dishtowel, but he managed to keep hold of it even though he just about fell over from the effort. As he caught himself, he felt his fingers start to burn and saw that the dishtowel had slipped some more and two of his fingers were touching bare metal.

"Ow, ow, ow." He hurried back to the kitchen and set the hot pan down on one of the cold center island burners. "Damn, Ray, I just burnt two of my fingers on that damn pan." He put the burned fingers to his mouth. Then reached over and turned on the cold water spigot in the center island sink and let the water run over the burns.

"Bet you didn't see that coming, huh, amigo? Cooking Spam, sometimes it can turn out to be dangerous business. Hell, just look at your head and my poor fingers."

Skooley turned off the water spigot and dried his fingers on the dishtowel that now sat on the island counter right next to the fry pan. He examined his fingers and saw a faint red mark where skin had touched hot metal. He walked back to where Ray sat hunched over in his chair with his head facedown on the table. Skooley leaned in close to look. Ray was making a combination gurgling/wheezing sound that seemed to be coming from somewhere deep in his throat. The top back of his head appeared to have caved in somewhat and was matted slick with wet blood. There was also blood dripping out of one of his ears and a pinkish-yellow mucus oozing from his nose onto the table. One eye was open wide, but it was glazed and bloodshot. The other eye was almost closed, and his cheekbone, where it had hit the table, was red and beginning to swell.

"Damn, Ray, you don't look so good."

Skooley slid one of the plates with the cooked Spam over to the other side of the table and sat down. He cut a small piece of Spam, placed it on a Ritz cracker, and took a bite. He chewed blissfully, then popped the rest of the Spam and cracker into his mouth.

"Wow, that ain't as bad as I remembered." He studied Ray from across the table. "Sorry about this, Ray. I mean, I wasn't planning on this, no sir, not at all. But you sorta forced my hand. Really, what the fuck was that with pulling the gun and all? No need for that, no sir, none at all." He cut another piece of Spam and this time ate it without putting it on a Ritz. "You brung me in on this deal and I certainly do appreciate it. But I did my part; I got us inside. And, Ray, I shit you not, I done this before and I do know what the fuck I'm doing. But I don't take kindly to my partner, my amigo, walking me around pointing a gun at my ass. Now, how can I trust a guy like that? What happens we find something big, then what? You got a gun, you got no problem pointing it at me for no more reason than I was fooling with you a little, you know, just to loosen you up some. Look it how high you jumped when I let out that holler in the garage." Skooley smiled at the memory. "Hell, you fell over and I thought you shit your drawers right there on the floor. I thought that was pretty funny, and I thought you'd have a laugh at it too. But then I saw your eyes in there, Ray, when we was in the garage, I was looking right at 'em and I know you was close, Ray, you was just this close to pulling that trigger. Not because you're some kind of bad-ass gangsta, Ray, but because you're a pissant Mexicali that was scared shitless."

He finished all the Spam and crackers on his plate.

"So, I figure it's just best to part ways now, you know, before we find anything and start to arguing one way or the other. Makes sense, don't ya think? Say, Ray, you gonna eat any of that?" he asked as he reached over and dumped the Spam slices from Ray's plate onto his own.

FIVE

Loretta was disappointed. No, she was angry. Eight weeks! Two months she had invested in that Ross couple, showing house after house. She was sure they were going to buy, damn it, she was positive. They called her almost every day. They had been renting a small house in Morris Plains. The husband worked at Novartis, right there on Route 10. The guy had money. Was pre-approved for a mortgage and everything.

Finally, she showed them that beautiful colonial, right there on the border of Denville and Randolph. Beautiful home, four bedrooms, new kitchen, large deck. She actually watched Katherine Ross' face light up like Christmas tree. It was perfect for them. Each kid could have their own bedroom, a two-car garage, one-and-a-half acres on a quiet, tree-lined street. And it was going for a song. The owners couldn't afford it any longer. They just wanted out. And then that asshole, Mr. Jonathan-fucking-Ross calls her up as happy as could be and tells her the great news—he just got himself a big promotion. Only now (so sorry, I know how much hard work you put in for us Loretta) he has to make another move.

To Georgia!

Georgia, for Christ's sake! There simply isn't enough money that could make me move to Georgia, she thought. Why would anyone move to Georgia?

Loretta put her head down on her desk. Her shoulder-length hair, dyed a deep reddish brown, was splayed around her like a mop head.

"Hey, what's up, girlfriend?" It was the voice of her friend and co-worker, Robin: a light-skinned black woman of about forty or so, right around Loretta's age. Robin was tall and shapely with a gregarious personality. She was fun to be around and always a big hit with the men they met when they went out together. She must have been walking by and stuck her head in the door.

Loretta didn't move. She spoke into the desktop. "My big sale, that couple I've been working on for months. It just blew up."

"You mean the scientist? Guy who works over at Novartis?"

"Yep."

"What happened? I thought that was a done deal."

"It was. You should have seen the wife. She was beaming like a headlight when I showed her that house. And it wasn't just because she's pregnant. She just kept carrying on, you know, actually couldn't help herself. 'Oh, this will be Emma's room and little Tyler can sleep in that room and we'll make this the nursery for the new baby. Oh, this house is perfect, Loretta. Just perfect.' I actually felt good about all the work I did for them. I was happy to do it even, find that perfect house. It wasn't like I was just trying to close a deal, you know? And I need a sale, Robin. I really need one. And I had one. The perfect house for the perfect little family."

Robin came into the small sales office and sat in one of the chairs that the clients usually used.

"So, what happened?"

"Well, Mr. Ross just called to let me know that he got a big promotion."

"That's great! Look, if this house didn't work out, you'll just find them another one. A big promotion usually means more money. Maybe they think now they're able to trade up. Bigger house, bigger commission! Cheer up, Lor! Got to see the opportunity in every situation."

"Robin, they're moving to Georgia."

"Georgia? No shit. There's not enough money on earth could get me to move to Georgia." She got up and patted Loretta gently on the shoulder. "Cheer up, girl. This too shall pass. I gotta run, I'm showing a townhouse in Morristown. Intercepted a message for Phyllis a few days ago. Poor girl was out to lunch, missed the call. Was going to tell her, but what do you know, it just slipped my mind. By the way, I can't make it to happy hour tonight, so you be good. And seriously, cheer up. This business is peaks and valleys. Things are getting better. Really. Traffic is improving every day. Just gotta hold out for little a while longer. The next Mr. and Mrs. Ross are just a phone call away."

"Yeah, they're probably calling Phyllis right now."

"I'll talk to you later." Robin began heading out of the office. When she got to the door, she turned around and said, "These people are actually moving to Georgia? Why in God's name would anyone want to move there?"

Loretta didn't answer and her head never left the desk.

Georgia peaches, clean air, warm climate, friendly people, the beautiful historic city of Savannah—why indeed?

SIX

It didn't take long to find the first stash of cash. It was in the little office just off the garage. There was a small closet crowded with boxes and files and old, dusty work boots. Way in the back, on the floor, in an old shoebox held closed with several rubber bands was an oversized envelope with fifty one-hundred-dollar bills in it. Five thousand bucks, and that was just the very first room he checked!

Skooley sat at the desk in the oversized leather chair and counted the money again. Five thousand, all in hundreds, just like the first time. Hot damn! He opened all the desk drawers but didn't find anything that held his interest. Mostly just paper—invoices, statements, receipts—the type of stuff that any businessman might have in his home office. He was tempted to go through all the filing cabinets, but he resisted. The house was large and there were lots more interesting places to explore. He could always come back and look at them later.

He walked back through to the kitchen waving the money. "Lookey here, Ray, you was right again! I knowed you was smart for a Mexican! I checked that back office, just like you said, and found this wad of cash. Five grand, all in hundreds. Not a bad way to start, and I'll tell ya what, I ain't even hit the honey hole yet. You wait and see."

Ray had not moved. Not at all. Skooley got closer. There was still bloody snot oozing from Ray's nose, and pink spittle had puddled on the table by his mouth. He was breathing shallow, rapid breaths, like a bird. The gurgling sound had all but stopped.

"Geez, Ray, I guess I walloped you pretty good, huh? I used to play ball when I was a kid. I bet you didn't know that, though you might have guessed being on the wrong end of that fry pan. I wasn't too good a fielder, but, man, I could hit a baseball a mile. The other kids used to back way up in the outfield every time I got up to bat. And that wasn't just sandlot ball, either; I played one year in the Little League. You probably didn't notice my swing as you was busy checking out your Spam lunchmeat, but it was a beauty. If your head was a baseball, you could say I knocked the cover right off. Speaking of which, you're making kind of a mess of the table there. Who do you think is gonna have to clean up that snot you're leaving all over the table? People eat here for Christ's sake. Let me go see what we can do about all this. Don't bother getting up, you stay right there and don't move a muscle."

He walked into the kitchen and rummaged around in some of the cabinet drawers. He came back to the breakfast room with a yellow plastic Shop-Rite grocery bag and a roll of gray duct tape.

"I found just we need, Ray. Now you hold still and let me get you all fixed up."

Skooley gently slipped the bag over Ray's head, tugging it down, then cinched it tight and began winding the duct tape around Ray's neck. "This'll keep all the snot and spit off the table, Ray. It's always good to keep a place just as neat and tidy as when you found it, don't ya think?"

He felt Ray's body tense, then shudder as the air was cut off, but he held firm and kept winding the duct tape over the plastic bag, working his way up Ray's neck and over his chin, then his mouth and nose and eyes. In a few minutes, Ray was still. Skooley couldn't hear any breath, and Ray's chest wasn't moving in out. He eased Ray's head back onto the table and let it lay as it had before, then patted it gently.

"Adios, amigo."

SEVEN

It was a clear, crisp early fall afternoon. The sun was shining brightly and the temperature was comfortably settled somewhere in the high sixties or low seventies. Skooley walked the perimeter of the house once just to get a better feel for the place. He saw a tool shed about twenty-five yards or so from the house. Parked next to it was the small backhoe he had noticed earlier. He strolled over for a closer look. There was a mound of construction debris in a small pile next to the backhoe. He could see broken pieces of concrete, some with small bits of rebar poking through, piled haphazardly around. He scanned the house but didn't see any signs of recent construction or demolition and couldn't figure out where the debris had come from.

He walked back toward the house, then continued walking clear around it and into the backyard. There was a short fence surrounding the pool area, which he figured was to keep critters from entering. Not really good for much else. Even kids would have no trouble hopping over. Back behind the pool was a small pool house. The door was unlocked and Skooley went in. There was a flat-screen TV set up on the wall behind a small wet bar with three bar stools in front of it. There was also a small couch, two wicker chairs, and a coffee table. A door off in the right-hand side of the back led to a small bathroom with a stall shower. Skooley went in and took the opportunity to pee in the toilet. He flushed, then looked at his reflection in the bathroom mirror. He gave himself a big "great-guy" smile. And part of it was genuine too. Five thousand bucks in his pocket, and things hadn't really gotten started yet.

On the other side of the room was another door that opened into a small back room containing a large pump and heating unit for the pool and hot tub. On the wall were bare wood shelves with boxes, bags, and plastic jugs of various pool chemicals. Skooley thought about it and realized that someone must be stopping by every few days to check on the pool, probably cut the lawn as well. Though the pool and hot tub were covered, it was just to keep leaves and debris out of the water. It didn't seem like the pool was yet closed for the season. Maybe they kept it open and heated all winter long.

He left the pool house, walked through the gate of the pool fence, and hiked back to the woods in the rear of the house. He didn't know how much property these people owned, but the woods seemed to go straight back for quite a ways. He couldn't see any other houses or even clearings on either side. The woods were thick in all directions. The front of the house was relatively clear for about a hundred yards or so to the main street. The house could probably be seen through the trees and bushes that lined the edge of the property near the street, but if so, only in certain spots and then just barely. The foliage was still thick, though some leaves were just starting to turn color. But the back was like a forest. He hiked into the woods and explored for a little while.

About seventy-five yards in, he found a small, muddy clearing that contained a patch of skunk cabbage. The ground was soft and marshy with a mild odor of rot. He walked back to the house and went to the tool shed he had seen earlier on the far side of the house opposite the garages. The door was locked with a padlock. He picked up a piece of broken concrete and banged at the padlock. Though the lock held tight, the hasp broke easily from the old wooden door, and he pulled it open and went inside. Another lawn tractor, more spreaders and a thatching machine, a push lawn mower, gas-powered edger, and a small generator lay scattered about. On the walls hung rakes and shovels and picks and garden sheers. A fat green hose, rolled up and fastened with a fluorescent orange strap was also hanging from a hook in the ceiling. In the back was a small wooden bench upon which sat a fairly new Stihl chainsaw. There were also three well-used five-gallon gas cans lined up one next to the other along one wall. Right next to them sat a wheelbarrow with two front wheels, loaded with three forty-pound bags of lawn fertilizer. Skooley grabbed a shovel and a pick and headed back toward the house. He laid the hand tools by the back door, entered, and walked through a small family room which led to the breakfast room, past Ray who looked like a Halloween dummy with his head wrapped in plastic and gray duct tape, and then back into the kitchen. He grabbed another Stella. There were only two more on the shelf. He'd have to check around that food closet and see if he couldn't rustle up a few more. He had some thirsty work ahead.

He found the bottle opener, opened his beer, and decided to explore the downstairs portion of the house before he got started in on the dirty work. He walked down a hall leading out from the kitchen and entered a formal dining room. There was a large, dark, highly polished wood table with eight high-backed chairs: three along the sides and one on each end. There was no tablecloth. A heavy, crystal candelabra holding five tall candles sat directly in the center of the table under a crystal chandelier. Everything sparkled in the soft sunlight that leaked into the room from a window in the adjoining living room.

There were dark wooden china cabinets along one wall. Skooley opened one of the cabinet doors and saw fine china plates and bowls with delicate gold plating around the rims, neatly stacked. He opened one of the drawers and pulled out a handful of dull forks and examined them. Sterling silver. He put the forks back.

He opened other drawers, and each seemed filled with dinner place accessories—more cutlery, assorted crystal salt and pepper shakers, doilies, fine cloth napkins. He moved on into the adjoining room. It was a formal living room with stiff uncomfortable-looking furniture that appeared to have never been used. Oil paintings hung all around the room, and Skooley remembered what Ray had told him about the woman being a famous artist. He looked closely at the paintings. Skooley knew nothing about art, but he liked each of the paintings he saw. Each was different: a portrait of a young girl, a seascape, a vase of colorful flowers. They were different sizes and the frames were inlaid wood and looked expensive. Skooley wondered how much these paintings would be worth and how he could go about selling them. He was pretty sure selling stolen art, particularly stolen from the artist herself, was a good way to get caught, but he let the thought roam around the back edges of his brain. He knew he could get rid of a lot of stuff quickly. He actually had the name and number of a guy in New York City, who bought all manner of goods, that he had gotten from a friend before he left Florida. That was where he planned on taking whatever he decided to lift from this house. But he had to play things smart, particularly with the unexpected problem of Raymundo in the next room. He was playing a whole new ballgame now that he had ripped the cover off his late amigo's head with a fry pan and he knew it. Not just B&E any longer, but something a tad more serious. It was a game he had played before, but still, he knew he had to be careful.

He took another sip of his beer and decided to head outside. He had a hole to dig, and he figured he better get to it while he still had the light. If anyone was to happen along, he didn't want them to find any trace of what had happened to Ray in the house. That was his first priority. He already had the five grand in his pocket and he knew there was more to be had.

Probably a lot more.

EIGHT

He got the hole dug pretty quickly. The earth was moist and loose for the first two feet or so, and then turned to thick reddish clay as he dug deeper. He didn't even need the pick, just forced his way down with the shovel. He stopped every so often to listen but didn't hear anything or anyone in the woods. He thought about the construction debris and the cans of gasoline in the shed and decided he'd douse the body with gas once he got it in the hole, then pile some of that concrete on top before covering up the hole with mud and dirt. Maybe the smell of gas would discourage any critters from digging. With all the skunk cabbage around, even if the smell of gas leaked up from underground, it would be hard for anyone walking about to detect. He didn't think anyone wandered back in these woods too often. He was back far enough that landscapers wouldn't travel this far to dump leaves or grass, plus, he hadn't seen any sign of anything resembling a hiking trail. No beer bottles or candy wrappers either. No place that looked like it might be a good spot for kids to sneak back to drink beer or screw.

When he was satisfied that the hole was wide enough and deep enough, he stuck the shovel hard into the ground and headed back to the house. This was really the only part that made him a bit nervous. He'd have to carry Ray over his shoulder into the woods. He didn't want to use the wheelbarrow through the woods because it would leave a trail right to the hole. Chances were slim that anyone would see him, even if someone happened to come strolling up the long driveway that looked like a road. But if someone did see him, there would be no mistaking what Skooley was carrying and that would lead to a whole world of problems. Once he got past the backyard and into the woods, he figured he'd be home free. He was going to take a different path to the hole so as not to leave any more signs of trespass.

When he got to the back door, he took his muddy shoes off and left them on the mat in the back. Then he went inside, dragged Ray's body from the breakfast room through the small family room out the back door, and laid him down next to his shoes. He put his shoes back on, then walked to the side of the house by the garages and took a long, lazy look down the driveway. Nothing. He walked back to where he had left Ray, picked up the body, and threw the little Mexican over his shoulder. He guessed it was part adrenaline and partly that Ray was a little fella to start with, but he picked up the body easily and then hustled past the fenced-in pool area, found a different entrance into the woods and bushwhacked his way back to the hole.

He dropped Ray's body down into it where it settled a bit awkwardly, one leg sort of sticking up and out, both arms spread wide. He jumped into the hole with the body and arranged it so that Ray fit better. Then he reached around into Ray's pockets and pulled out a wallet, a set of keys, a faded blue bandana that was probably used as a snot rag, and some loose change. He checked the wallet. About forty or fifty dollars in assorted bills, driver's license, a few business cards, some folded pieces of scrap paper with handwritten names and phone numbers, some official-looking papers written in Spanish that he had no idea about. He put the wallet into his own pocket, not sure if there was any reason he might need it later but figured if he did, he didn't want to have to come back out here looking for it. Once he was satisfied that the body was laying in the hole just right, he stepped up and out and grabbed the shovel. "See ya around, Ray-mun-do." He raised the shovel up over his head intending to slam it down with all his might onto Ray's skull. Then he saw the pickaxe on the ground, dropped the shovel, and grabbed the pick. One side of the pick was a metal spike; the other had a curved blade intended for digging. Better to make sure the little fucker was dead. Not that he had much doubt, but Skooley had learned in his life that when it came to things like this, it just couldn't hurt to be sure. And at this point, old Ray wouldn't feel anything one way or the other.

He raised the pickaxe and swung the spike end down as hard as he could into the center of the yellow Shop Rite bag. It struck home with a muffled thud. *One to make sure*, he thought to himself. He struggled a little to pull the pickaxe out again. It came out all bloody with what might have been pieces of brain tissue speckled about the business end. Blood was oozing out of the hole he had just punched in the yellow bag, turning it into a bloody red mess. He then raised the pickaxe once again and drove it with all his might into the bag once more, *And one for good measure.*

When that work was done, he cleaned off the pick as best he could by taking a few whacks into fresh earth. He rubbed it good in whatever muck was around, making sure that no blood or tissue or yellow plastic was stuck on anywhere. He then carried the pickaxe with him as he worked his way back to the shed, replaced the tool where he had first found it, and grabbed the lightest of the gas containers. He went back to the hole, doused the body with gasoline making sure that it was soaked entirely paying particular attention to the bloody head area, then poured the remainder of the gas around the body, mixing it into the mud with the shovel.

Back to the shed with the empty can, taking a different route again, he emptied the fertilizer bags from the wheelbarrow and then filled it with concrete chunks and pushed the barrow skirting the outside of the lawn up to the edge of the woods. Then he made several trips back and forth carrying the debris by hand and arranged the various chunks to cover the body. When he was satisfied, he grabbed the shovel and began filling in the hole with the damp dirt and clay. When that was done, he walked over the area, tamping everything down with his feet, thought better of that, and then tamped the earth down by repeatedly whacking the ground with the back end of the shovel, removing any footprints that could be seen. Lastly, he carefully camouflaged the area with leaves and twigs so that it was indistinguishable from the area around it.

He kneeled down, shook a Marlboro Light out of the pack in his pocket, thought for a second, then got up and walked away from where he had buried the body.

He could smell traces of gas, though he wasn't sure if it was just residue from some that might have spilled on his hands. But still, a couple of gallons of gasoline in a hole, no telling what could happen if he lit a match. He began walking back toward the house. After he had walked about twenty or so yards, he turned around for a last look. Satisfied, he lit his cigarette and continued toward the house. Shit, he thought, anyone finds old Ray after all that digging and rock laying I done, then I guess they'll have earned the pleasure of watching me take the needle.

NINE

When he got back to the house, he sat on one of the lounge chairs that were arrayed around the pool. He was filthy. His shoes, socks, and pants were covered in mud. His T-shirt was soiled with leaves and dirt and sweat. He took the money out of one pocket and Ray's wallet out of the other, then stripped down naked. He left his clothes in a pile next to the chair with the wallet, picked up the cash, and went into the pool house bathroom where he took a long, hot shower after placing the pile of hundred-dollar bills that were stuffed into an envelope on the closed lid of the toilet seat. When he was done, he dried off as best he could with the small hand towel that had been left on the towel rack and headed back outside. He grabbed his shoes and rinsed them off with a hose that was lying next to the pool house, then gathered the rest of his clothes along with the wallet and headed back to the house.

He found a washer and dryer, that looked like they belonged in the space shuttle, set in a closet off the hall near the office where he had found the cash. He put all his clothes into the washer along with a cup of cheap laundry detergent that was sitting on a shelf over the washer. Damn, he thought, the fucking washing machine is so high-tech you need an owner's manual just to figure out how to turn the damn thing on and these people use cheap-ass laundry detergent. Not Tide or Wisk or some other such name brand, but Shop Rite detergent. What the fuck? They probably got three thousand dollars' worth of washing machine here and they cheap out on laundry soap? Fucking rich people.

He didn't want to let the money out of his sight, so he carried the envelope with the cash in it, grabbed the wallet, and headed up to the master bedroom naked as a blue jay. The bedroom was large with a king-sized bed, a huge master bath that was bigger than his rented room back in Bernardsville, and two large walk-in closets, a his and hers. He went to the man's closet and rummaged around for something to put on. The owner was shorter than Skooley, and definitely rounder, but Skooley found a sweatshirt and sweatpants that had a cord around the waist that allowed him to cinch the pants up tight so they wouldn't fall. The best part was the pants had two back pockets, so Skooley folded up the envelope and tucked it into the right-hand pocket and put the wallet in the other pocket. The pockets bulged, but instead of being uncomfortable, it was a comfort to know all that money was sitting there stuffed into the pocket on his hip. The sweatshirt's arms and the pant legs were too short, but he figured it was just for a while, so what the hell. Besides, it wasn't like he had much choice in the matter.

He was eager to explore the house, but he headed back downstairs to the kitchen and found some cleaning supplies in a cabinet under one of the sinks. He grabbed a roll of paper towels from the pantry and walked into the breakfast room to clean up after Raymundo. He carefully wiped the blood and snot off the table with a paper towel, then sprayed a goodly amount of Windex and scrubbed the area clean. Then he sprayed and wiped again. He checked the chair and the floor around where Ray had sat. He picked up the overturned beer bottle and put the gun back on the table. There was beer still spilled on the floor and he wiped that up and then went through the spray and wipe exercise several more times. He brought a plastic garbage container from the kitchen into the breakfast room. He checked to make sure that the bag inside was empty, then gathered up the beer bottles and threw them in along with the corn chips and Ritz crackers that were left on the plates. He pulled the bag out of the plastic container and left it next to the table. He was going to carry all of his garbage out with him when he left. Just like camping in the Everglades, he thought. Then he grabbed the plates and went into the kitchen to wash them and the cast iron fry pan. Washing dishes was something he often did for a living, and he was going to make sure that he did a very good job on that fry pan. He didn't want any traces of blood or hair or burnt skin on that thing. When he was done, he dried the pan and slipped it way in the back of the cabinet where he had first found it, and then cleaned out the sink with bleach. He smiled to himself because he knew he was being a bit paranoid, but he figured that sometimes it just didn't hurt any to be paranoid. Then he went back to the garbage bag, pulled out the bloody paper towels, and walked them back to the half bath by the garage door and flushed them down the toilet.

Paranoid my ass; let's see those CSI fuckers get that evidence out of the sewer hole.

The washing machine had finished by the time he was done cleaning up, so he took his clothes out of the washer and put them into the dryer. He found some cheap-ass dryer sheets, shook his head, and then threw one in with his clothes. He puzzled for a while on how to get the dryer started, finally figured it out, and hit the start button.

He didn't want to keep Ray's wallet with him, but he didn't want to get rid of it just yet either. He went into the kitchen, grabbed the dishtowel, and wiped all of the surfaces of the wallet including the laminated driver's license. Just a precaution. Then he carried the wallet into the garage, found a spot behind some lawn chemicals on a low shelf, and pushed the wallet behind that. No one would find it there, and he would think about what to do with it later. Might not be a bad idea to leave a clue as to who robbed this place later, like a driver's license or maybe the whole damn wallet. Most criminals he knew were dumber than shit. Cops knew it too. He was sure they wouldn't think twice if they found a wallet, maybe by a window or a door or right in the middle of the goddamn driveway. Hell, some of the cops Skooley had come across were dumber than shit too. If he was going to plant the wallet, better to leave it where even a numbnut would find it. No one was ever going to find Ray, and it might be a good idea to set them looking for the little Mexican if something should go wrong and he needed time.

He headed back inside and decided it was time to explore the rest of the house.

He walked back through the formal dining room and the formal living room where he had been before and stopped in a hallway. To his left was the front door. He peeked out into the yard looking through the small glass window he had earlier used to look into the house. To his right was a wide staircase that led up to the second floor. He crossed a hallway and entered a large, dark room. It was as wide as the house, about the same size as the three-car garage on the opposite side. This was the room that Ray's girlfriend must have been talking about. There were paintings lined up along each wall like you might see in an art gallery. Several small shelves hung on the walls held little statues and sculptures. Track lighting lined the ceiling with small bulbs aimed at where the paintings hung. He threw a switch on the wall and soft light came on. He walked slowly, examining each and every painting. They were all different, yet similar on some level. Again, the subject matter of each painting varied, each radically different from the next. He saw a painting of a clown that was both amusing and somehow unsettling. A portrait of a woman in a wedding dress with a soft smile and the saddest eyes Skooley had ever seen. He stopped and stared at the woman for a long while. He got close and looked at the detail, the brush strokes that could only be seen when he got up real close. Then watched amazed as the strokes coalesced into a bouquet of flowers or the crease of a wedding dress. It was like a photograph coming into focus as he backed his face away centimeter by centimeter. There was a painting of a train traveling across a barren landscape on a foggy night. He wondered if the painter had actually seen each of these images at one time, or if she had just imagined them and drawn them from her thoughts. He walked through the room, staring at every painting, then he walked through again and then once again.

There were no more rooms on the main floor. There was just a doorway that led to the family room in the back of the house, which then could take him outside or into the breakfast room. He looked out the window toward the backyard and noticed the light fading. He headed into the kitchen and saw from the microwave clock that it was after six o'clock. He went and retrieved his clothes from the dryer. They smelled clean and fresh, and all signs of his work in the woods were gone except for some light brown, washed-out mud stains on the bottoms of his sweat socks.

He changed right there in the laundry room, then carried the sweatsuit up to the walk-in closet and put it back where he had found it. He was going to search the closet, but it just didn't feel like a good place. Maybe he'd find some old photos or nudie shots of the guy's wife or something, but he was sure there wasn't going to be any big score in here. There might be a gun, probably surely a gun hidden somewhere in one of the drawers or on a top shelf, but he had Ray's snub nose downstairs and he just wasn't in the mood to look. He was in a mood to celebrate. He had cash in his pocket, and he could sure use some new clothes and maybe a fine steak dinner and a few beers.

He decided to go out. He remembered seeing car keys hanging on a hook next to the garage. He was sure one of them would be for the Range Rover. He'd take that, travel a few towns away, and do some shopping. He was sure no one was coming back soon. He could search the rest of the house tomorrow. He'd keep a close eye out for anyone checking the pool or cutting the lawn. He'd also have to be mindful of one of their kids maybe stopping by to check on the house. He didn't know where their kids lived, but he couldn't believe anyone would just up and leave for a month without having someone check in every once in a while. He wouldn't stay long. Just long enough to clean a few things out. For now, though, he figured he might as well just move in and make himself comfortable.

TEN

He usually bought his clothes at Walmart, but he wanted to splurge a little. He drove the Range Rover across Mendham and headed back the way he had ridden on the bikes with Ray to Old 24, then onto Tempe Wick Road, which crossed over to Harding. Once there, he knew his way to Route 287 and headed north to Route 10. He got on Route 10 West and found a Kohl's department store just up the road. He liked driving the Range Rover. He liked the feel of the car, the smooth, quiet ride, the power under the hood and the soft, comfortable leather seats. The inside still had that new car smell. The guy kept the inside immaculate. There was no dust on the dash, no mud or dirt on the floor mats. The parking lot was pretty crowded, but he guessed that Friday was a big night for shopping being payday for most. A big night for eating out too as he remembered that he was supposed to be at work washing dishes at the Lion's Head Inn, the restaurant in Bernardsville where he had just started last week. He smiled at the thought. He was almost tempted to go there for dinner tonight and order the most expensive thing on the menu— then send it back. He smiled again and patted the wad of cash in his pocket. Hot damn!

He walked around the men's department, saw a mannequin that looked pretty good, and bought the matching set of clothes in his sizes. Then he figured what the hell, and picked out two additional mannequins and bought those clothes as well. He also bought socks, new boxers, and a new pair of casual shoes.

He drove out the parking lot to an Atlanta Bread restaurant on the corner, walked in a side door that led right into the bathroom, and quickly changed into a set of new duds.

He drove down Route 10 looking for someplace to eat. In the parking lot of the Tabor Road Tavern, he pulled out his wad of cash and quickly thumbed through it. He had dropped a little over four hundred dollars at Kohl's. He took five one-hundred-dollar bills and all the smaller bills he had gotten as change, and then reached behind the passenger seat and stuffed the envelope with the remaining stack of hundred-dollar bills under the floor mat in front of the back passenger seat. He didn't like to leave the money behind, but he also didn't want to carry that thick a wad of cash in his pocket. Flash too much cash and you became a target. He knew because he had himself lightened the pocket of several people, both men and women, over the years who had made the mistake of trying to impress with how much money they had and left them crying and bloody in the parking lot. Looking around, he saw mostly newer, high-end autos and felt reasonably sure no one would be breaking into his Range Rover. Even so, he made a mental note to come outside and smoke a few cigarettes and check on the car every once in a while.

He clicked the remote lock button on his key, then tried the door to make sure it locked and headed inside.

The Tabor Road Tavern was a large, new building that was made to look old. A lot of stone and thick, timber beams and dark, polished wood. It was crowded, but not yet packed. Skooley was met in the lobby by a pretty young girl, the hostess, who asked if he had reservations. He gave her his best "great-guy" smile and said that he was just planning to grab a seat at the bar if he could find a spot to have a beer. She smiled back and pointed him toward the bar.

He found an empty stool near the end of the large bar and sat down. There were two male bartenders behind the bar and one of them came right over.

"You got any of them Stella beers here?" he asked the young man.

"Stella Artois? Sure, we have it on tap. Is that alright?"

"Right as rain, amigo."

The bartender drew his beer into a chalice-type glass with the Stella Artois label on it and put it in front of Skooley.

Skooley reached into his pocket and put down a hundred-dollar bill.

"Okay if I start a tab with this? Also, you got a bar menu? Don't look like there's gonna be a table for one opening up any too soon."

The bartender came back with his receipt in a small leather holder and placed it on top of the hundred. Then walked back near the cash register and came back with a leather-bound menu.

"The monkfish tacos are amazing here and the Prince Edward mussels are great too, if you like mussels." It was a dark-haired woman sitting next to him on his right. She was about forty or so, reasonably attractive and not too overweight, which seemed to be a rarity with women nowadays. She was wearing a white, silky blouse and had just a hint of cleavage showing. There was a half-finished glass of white wine in front of her.

He brought out his great-guy smile again.

"Monkfish tacos, huh? Well, I can't say as I ever even seen me a monkfish before, not swimmin' in the ocean nor sitting on a taco. Amazing, you say?"

She smiled. "That's a strange accent. Are you from the South?"

"Yes, ma'am, I most surely am." He reached out his hand to shake. "My name is Ray. Ray Mundy. Not to be mistaken with Ray Mundo which I got a lot of as a kid, you know, the other kids kinda teasing me and all."

"Loretta," she said, shaking his hand lightly. He noticed that she didn't provide a last name.

56

"Well, Loretta, I'm not really a mussels-type guy, more steak and potatoes, you know, but I'm gonna order me some of them amazing monkfish tacos, just to try 'em. I like regular tacos just fine, and even though I just met ya, you seem like a good judge of tacos to me, so what the hell. But I'm gonna count on you to help me eat 'em, seeing as I ain't never had 'em before."

Before she could answer, he called to the bartender.

"Excuse me, can we get an order of them amazing monkfish tacos to start, and maybe another glass of wine for Miss Loretta here."

The bartender came over.

"And would you like to order anything for dinner, sir?"

"Loretta, would you care to join me for dinner?" He smiled at Loretta.

"No, that's very kind of you, Ray, but I'm not staying long."

"Okay then, just a glass of wine for the lady here, and I'll have me the NY strip steak, done more rare than medium and one of them loaded baked potatoes." He handed the menu back to the bartender and watched him walk to the other end of the bar to place his order.

"Thank you for the wine, Ray, that was very sweet but totally unnecessary. So, what part of the South are you from?"

"Well, originally I'm from the Fort Myers area of Florida. But I been moving around a lot, with my business and all."

"Fort Myers, isn't that near Sanibel Island? I love Sanibel. When I was married, we used to vacation there often. I think we flew into Fort Myers. Have you ever been there?"

"Where, the Fort Myers airport? Oh, I'm just kidding. Well, I been to Sanibel once, but to be honest, I don't really remember much. I done a few jobs in the Naples area, you know, renovating some of them big homes and such, and me and one of the other contractors drove over to Sanibel one night, just to have a few drinks, you know, but that was the only time."

"Are you a builder?"

"Well, yes, ma'am, I am."

"What's the name of your company?"

Skooley took a sip of his beer as his mind started working.

"We call it Par D Construction. Now I know it sounds like 'party,' but it ain't. It's Par and the letter D. You see, we used to do demolition, you know, dynamite big buildings and take down old homes and such. So, the name started out as Partial Demolition Company on account of we just knocked the shit down but didn't haul out all the debris. But one day, I started thinking, hell, I knock 'em down, why not put 'em up as well. Gotta be more money on that side, you know. I can make it both coming and going. But I figured ain't nobody gonna hire a builder with the name of Partial Demolition Builders, so I shortened the whole damn thing to Par D. Now I'm making money hand over fist, and after I finish each and every project, well, I throw a big bash for all my guys. Party, not Par D."

Skooley smiled. He liked lying. It came easy to him. He could talk, sometimes for hours, and just go round and round in circles.

"Are you working on a project around here? Is that why you're in town?"

"Well, yes and no. I'm not actually *working on* a job—I'm *looking at* a job. You ever hear of a town called Mendham?"

"Of course. It's not very far from here."

"No, it ain't. Well, there's this guy in Mendham owns this big old house on a huge lot of property, maybe ten or twelve acres. He also owns a lotta other houses in Florida and Arizona and California. The house he got here in Mendham is getting kinda run-down, you know, and he was familiar with me and my company from some work we done for him down south and he flew me up here in his private plane to look at knocking his old house down and putting up a brand-new mansion. I believe he intends to sell this new home and all the property and make himself another boatload of money. See, he done the same thing with the project I worked on for him back home."

"Really, where in Mendham is his property? I don't know if I mentioned it, but I'm in real estate. Do you have a card, Ray?" She reached into her pocketbook and pulled out her wallet, then slipped a card out with her picture on it.

Ray took the card, looked at it for a second, and then put it down on the bar.

"Loretta, I'd love to trade cards with you, I really would, but I'm afraid I'm swore to secrecy on this one, leastwise till we make ourselves a deal." He smiled at her. "Me and the owner, that is. Look at that, I think I'm going to be saved from revealing anything more by an amazing monkfish taco."

He left her condo early the next morning, before she was even awake. Hell, it would have taken a stick of dynamite to wake her. She was lying on her back, snoring with her mouth open. They had shared the monkfish taco, he ate his steak, had a few more beers, and bought her a few more glasses of wine. She worked him hard for the name of his client and he told her a few more stories, hinting at other big jobs and big-time connections. When she told him she was ready to leave, he insisted on walking her to her car, then offered to follow her home in his Range Rover, just to make sure she got home safe, and he ended up in her condo which was right up the road from the restaurant. She opened a bottle of wine, and after a few glasses each he made a big show of giving her the name of his client and made her swear not to tell him where she got it, and she tried to write it down on a piece of paper but Skooley couldn't make out a word on account of how drunk she was, and she ended up passing out after a spell.

He took her into the bedroom, undressed her, and then fucked her every way he could think of. She was unresponsive to most of it, but he didn't care. It wasn't like he was planning on seeing her again, ever. He thought about going through her wallet and actually checked to see if there was anything worth stealing in her place, but then thought about it and decided it just wasn't worth the risk. She'd wake up hungover as all hell and sore in a few places she probably wouldn't want to tell anyone about, which made him smile, but he knew that would be the end of it. She wouldn't want to go around telling anybody about getting herself all drunk and then getting the snot fucked out of her by some stranger she picked up in a bar. He was sure of it. Of course, if she found some stuff missing, then she might start thinking about it some more, maybe make up some bullshit story and call the cops. He just didn't need the attention and besides, she didn't really have anything worth taking a risk for. So, he just left everything as it was, found the drunken scribbled note she had tried to write with the fake name of the client that he had given to her and shoved that into his pocket. Leave her with nothing but a fond memory. Maybe not so fond, he thought. Hell, she was so damn drunk he'd be surprised if she remembered anything at all. He laughed as he got into his Range Rover and skedaddled out of Dodge before old Loretta even knew what hit her.

ELEVEN

Saturday

It was a beautiful Saturday afternoon. The sun was shining, and the weather was warm. It was no longer summer, but wasn't quite autumn yet either, and the temperature seemed to fluctuate between the two seasons, day to day. Esmeralda had a car today; her boss at Smiley Maids where she worked days sometimes let her keep the car on weekends. Esmeralda had worked at Smiley Maids for just over five years and was now supervisor of one of the cleaning crews. On Mondays, she had an early day and the boss let her keep the car so she could pick up the other girls and get an early start. Her boss said it was okay to drive the car for errands and such on the weekend, but she had to be extra careful and always had to replace the gas she used.

"Mom, I'm going out!" she yelled to her mother as she gathered up a spring jacket she was sure she wouldn't need.

"Hija, a donde vas?" It was hard to hear her mother in the kitchen over the noise of the TV and the younger children all playing and talking in the living room.

"Trabajo," she yelled and headed out the door. She wasn't really going to work, but it was easier to lie than to have to explain anything to her mother. She walked down the long flight of stairs and out into the sunshine. She got to the sidewalk and pulled out her smartphone. Still no message from her friend Raymundo.

She was nervous. He had told her that he and a friend of his named Stoolie or Tooley or something like that might head over to the Russells' home to check things out. She wished she had never said anything to Raymundo about the house. The Russells were nice people. Mrs. Russell in particular. She always had kind words for her and her crew. Most days she put out sodas or iced tea and sometimes she even prepared lunch for the girls—sandwiches or snacks—one time, she ordered them a pizza. And the husband was nice too, though more reserved. He smiled a lot but didn't say much. Still, he seemed nice.

She didn't know how or why she started talking about the Russells, but she did. Raymundo worked as a busboy and dishwasher at the same restaurant that she did. He was a handsome Guatemalan boy with a ready smile and he was very easy to talk to. He told her stories about when he lived in Newark and some of the mischief he got into—nothing violent, but he made himself sound like a bit of a criminal. He was nice, fairly good-looking, charming, and not too smart. And she liked him. It was late, after the restaurant and bar had closed and they had finished cleaning up the place. The owners sometimes allowed the staff to sit at the bar and have a few drinks after work, and they had sat together and talked over a few rum and cokes. They talked about their jobs and their lives and somehow they got going about all the rich people in this area. She told him about some of the houses she cleaned and then about the beautiful house in Mendham and the pool and how much money these people must have to live as they did. She told him about how they went on vacation at the end of every summer for almost an entire month leaving the house empty, and he got quiet and more serious as she explained about the beautiful paintings and nice cars and his eyes got slightly wider and began to sparkle and shine.

It was her idea. She couldn't deny it. She never actually told him to go rob the house. But she knew what things were leading up to. She was a bit drunk, true, but what she had to admit to herself was that more than drunk, she was tired. Tired of working three and four jobs. Tired of supporting her mother and her three siblings. Tired of the cramped apartment that always smelled of fried food and sleeping on a pullout couch with a metal support bar across her aching back and tired of stepping over toys and listening to the voice of SpongeBob Squarepants nonstop blaring from the old TV. She wanted out. She wanted to go to school. She wanted to make a life for herself. She wanted money.

And the Russells had money—plenty of it.

Raymundo said he would check it out. He had this friend who he said had just moved up from Florida and was living in the same rooming house as him. A guy who apparently had some connections in New York and who could sell things without leaving any trace of where they came from. Raymundo said they would split whatever they got three ways. Esmeralda was nervous. She didn't want to be found out. Not just because she would go to jail, but also because if it came right down to it, she just couldn't face that nice lady, Mrs. Russell.

Raymundo said they were going to check out the house on Friday. That was yesterday. He was going to text her after they were back, and they would meet up and talk things through. She hadn't heard anything from him. She wasn't sure if maybe they hadn't gone, or if they had gone and decided to just cut her out. She was afraid to call. What if they had been arrested? What if the police had his phone and then she called and they found out that she worked for the housecleaning service? She was sweating. She walked up the street to the Morristown Diner where there was still a payphone by the door and dialed his cell number. The phone went to voicemail and she hung up without saying anything.

She had told him not to go in. Just check things out and make sure the family was gone. She was debating telling him where in the house to look for things. After all, she had cleaned the place every week for about four years. In that time, she had come across some interesting things. And not entirely by accident, either. It started about two years ago when she found about a thousand dollars in cash in a shoebox in Mr. Russell's office closet. She hadn't been snooping then, just vacuuming and straightening things a little. She came across the box while hanging up a coat that Mr. Russell had left on his office chair. The box was on the floor in the back of the closet, which seemed odd to her since there were no shoes in the closet. So, when no one was looking, she took a peek inside it.

She didn't take anything, not ever, but after that, she began poking around to see what else they had hidden. And she found plenty. There seemed to be cash hidden somewhere in just about every room of the house. The amount of money in these hiding spots varied week to week. She wasn't sure what to make of that. But there was a lot of it. Sometimes hundreds, sometimes thousands. Perhaps they used the money to pay bills or for shopping or for drugs. Who knew? She also peeked into Mrs. Russell's jewelry box in the master bedroom and, in another room, she found another box—not a jewelry box—with what looked to be very expensive jewelry. She decided not to tell Raymundo where to look, thinking that if robbers found all the hiding places where the Russells hid things, then suspicion would fall on people who had access to the house. Like maybe family members—and probably the cleaning crew. If Raymundo and his friend didn't know where to look, then it might just be perceived as a simple robbery or maybe even just local kids in the neighborhood up to no good who may have broken in as a prank.

She walked around the Green and then east on South Street looking in shop windows without really registering anything. She felt nervous and uneasy and like she had to do something. If only she could talk to Raymundo, even if she didn't get any of what they stole, just to know that they hadn't been caught.

She decided to drive over to the rooming house where Raymundo was staying in Bernardsville. Maybe he partied last night and was still in bed. Maybe he was all talk and hadn't even gone to Mendham. That was what she hoped anyway.

TWELVE

He slept like a log and woke up around two in the afternoon. He hadn't planned on sleeping that late, but then again, he wasn't really in a hurry to get anywhere. The king-sized bed in the master bedroom had one of those foam mattresses like you see on TV. The one where the lady jumps up and down and doesn't spill a drop of wine from the wine glass sitting there on the mattress. The sheets still smelled freshly washed which made him think that the owners had not been gone too long which meant he probably had a goodly amount of time before they would return. He knew he still had to be careful, but he worried less about them coming home and surprising him. It had been quite a while since he'd had a night like last night. A wad of cash in his pocket, a nice dinner, and a couple of cold ones to go with it—hell, he even got his dipstick wet to round out the evening. He wondered how old Loretta was feeling and smiled as he walked into the master bathroom. He was planning to take a leisurely crap and then have himself a nice, long hot shower. There was a lot more house to explore, and he was eager to see what new treasures he would unearth. As he sat on the toilet, he tried to remember if there was a coffee maker set up in the kitchen and what brand of coffee he had seen on the shelf in the food closet.

THIRTEEN

He spent two hours searching the bedroom. He searched slowly and methodically. First, he went through all the dresser drawers. He didn't find much in the drawers, mostly clothes, bras and panties, pajamas, socks, T-shirts, scarves, belts, and some costume jewelry. Skooley was no expert, but his experience had taught him to distinguish between what was junk and what were gems. The bed had matching two-drawer nightstands on either side, and in the bottom drawer of the left side stand he found a beat-up old tin box. Inside was a heavy men's Rolex watch, some assorted cufflinks, three tarnished silver dollars that dated to the 1800s, two silver money clips, an antique pocket watch, and an eighteen-karat solid gold ring with a shiny green emerald set right in the middle. He slid the gold ring onto his finger and put the other items on the bed.

He put his arm under the foam mattress and felt around, then pulled out a worn leather billfold with two thousand dollars in cash and a small Beretta Model 21A .25 ACP automatic pistol. He put the cash and the gun on the bed with the jewelry. In the woman's walk-in closet, he found a jewelry box. There was an assortment of gold chains and bracelets, a few watches, one a Piaget that looked to be real and should be worth a few grand at least, pendants and brooch pins, also some nice earrings, and a few diamond studs that he was sure would bring a nice chunk of change as well. He crawled to each corner of the closet and tried to pull up the carpet. He found nothing there. He searched inside all of the shoes, he checked the pockets of all coats and pants, looked inside old hat boxes and several small plastic storage containers that held mostly old family photos—photos that appeared to date back to the early fifties and sixties, maybe even earlier. Must be her parents and aunts and uncles, a few shots of her and her siblings and cousins. He put all the photos back in the boxes. He wasn't interested in stealing this lady's memories.

When he was through with her closet, he moved on to her husband's. He went through the same routine but didn't find anything of value beyond a beautifully crafted Perazzi shotgun broken down and stored in a wooden presentation case lined inside with green velvet that was stashed up high on a shelf. He never heard of Perazzi shotguns, but the gun just reeked of big money. There were beautifully detailed engravings of hunting scenes on the ornate break action, and the stock was high-quality wood grain. He put the shotgun case on the bed with the rest of his finds and sat down next to everything to take stock. Not bad for a few hours of exploring. But he knew that he had not found the real honey hole yet. He had been sure he would find it here in the bedroom. It was just as he had explained to his ex-partner, Ray: finding some valuables was going to be easy, but the real treasure would take time to unearth. He smiled. Time he had. And now he had some more pocket money to add to his stash of cash. Seven thousand dollars in just two days, plus this pile of jewelry and assorted knickknacks that he could unload for a few grand more. He lay back down on the bed and smiled at the ceiling.

What should he do next? Well, searching through someone's house was thirsty work. He decided he'd better go find some more of those Stella Artois beers that he was quickly acquiring a taste for.

FOURTEEN

She drove the 2005 Toyota Matrix with the Smiley Maids magnetic signs stuck to the doors out of Morristown and down Route 202/206 toward Bernardsville. The car smelled of Windex and Clorox and Pledge furniture polish, which were carried in abundance in the back of the car along with two vacuum cleaners, brooms, mops, brushes, rags, buckets, and assorted other cleaning implements.

Esmeralda rolled down the window to get some fresh air. She drove past a sign for Jockey Hollow State Park and briefly considered turning in and taking a walk in the woods for a while, just to clear her head. Then thought that if she didn't continue on to Raymundo's, she might lose her nerve or maybe just miss him if he went out somewhere. She passed the Grain House Restaurant and the Old Mill Inn where she worked one summer when she was still in high school cleaning rooms. The start of her "career," she thought with no humor whatsoever. She continued into the town of Bernardsville, turning off of 202, then crossing the railroad tracks and into a parking lot next to an old house that rented rooms by the week to many of the waiters, busboys, dishwashers, and other hourly laborers who worked serving and cleaning up after their wealthier neighbors. She parked the car, turned off the ignition, and looked the house over. She had never been here in the daytime before. She had come back after work once or twice with her girlfriend, Diana, a Colombian girl like herself whose boyfriend rented a room here. But that was usually late at night or very early in the morning before the sun came up. Diana worked at the same restaurant that Esmeralda did and owned a car, so she was usually Esmeralda's ride to and from work. The rooming house looked a lot more dingy and run-down in daylight.

There were several boys sitting on the stoop in front of the house smoking cigarettes. She knew a few of them from the restaurant and began talking to them casually in Spanish before asking where Raymundo stayed. One of the boys told her his room number and walked her to his door. She knocked lightly to no response. The boy then banged on the door with his fist and yelled for Raymundo to get up. When nothing happened, the boy simply opened the door and they both peeked in. The room was small. There was a dresser with a large, flat-screen, high-definition TV with wires from a game console leading to an unmade bed. The TV sat upon a beat-up dresser with one drawer partially open. Next to the TV sat a hot plate with pot on top of it. Dirty clothes littered almost every square inch of the floor. She knew the clothes were dirty because the room reeked powerfully of body odor. She didn't go in. She told the boy to close the door and they both headed back outside. She waved goodbye and headed back to her car. Over in the corner of the large parking lot, she saw a dirty white Toyota Camry with Florida license plates edged up close the fence.

FIFTEEN

She cruised past the long driveway slowly and continued up the road peering between the shrubs and bushes trying to get a look at the Russells' house. It was hard to see anything. The shrubs and bushes were thick and still mostly green with leaves. She could only manage a brief, sporadic glimpse of the house and couldn't tell if anyone was home. She continued up the road looking at the beautiful homes, a few of which she routinely cleaned, and wondered what it would be like to own one of them. She would have to marry rich or work like a dog to ever have a chance of affording one. She would rather work, she decided, and yearned more than ever to get the money to start beauty school. It wouldn't be easy, but nothing was— ever. She just had to start down the path. And she had to start soon because she knew that even once she got her cosmetology license, she would still need to start at the bottom as a shampoo girl, maybe handling walk-ins until she could develop a clientele, and then she'd need to work at a quality hair studio and learn not only how to cut and style hair but also how to run a business before she could even begin to think about opening a place of her own. Esmeralda's Hair Studio. No, something glitzier, maybe Starlight Hair Studio or Starlight Salon & Spa.

She decided to make another pass of the house and made a U-turn. As she approached the house, she saw Mr. Russell's Range Rover coming down the driveway and turn left onto the road in front of her. Her heart started racing and she slowed down not wanting Mr. Russell to see her or recognize the car she was driving with the company's name and logo on the side. The Range Rover sped up and she stayed back, following from a distance as he made his way down side streets all the way to Main Street in Mendham. There, he turned toward the center of town and went into the parking lot of the King's Supermarket. Esmeralda followed him in, pulled into the first spot she found, and got out of the car. She could see the Range Rover drive slowly around the small shopping plaza until it pulled into a parking spot on the far side. She pretended to fuss in her pocketbook as she watched a young, skinny, blond-haired man emerge from the truck. He definitely wasn't Mr. Russell. Nor was he either of Mr. Russell's sons, both of whom Esmeralda had met, or at least seen, at the Russells' home over the last several years.

The blond-haired man went into a liquor store. Esmeralda walked quickly toward Kings, grabbed a shopping cart and, keeping an eye on the door of the liquor store, slowly made her way back to the car pushing the cart in front of her. The young man emerged a minute later carrying two white cartons, obviously beer, back to the Range Rover. It looked like he also had a pack of cigarettes clamped in his mouth. Esmeralda left the shopping cart next to her car and unlocked the door, all the while keeping the young man and the Range Rover in the periphery of her vision.

It could be a relative or maybe just a friend house sitting. Maybe even someone who works for Mr. Russell checking on his property.

No, it was him. Stoolie or Tooley or whatever his name was. She was sure of it. And if he was out here buying beer in Mr. Russell's Range Rover, then the house must be empty except for Raymundo, who was probably stuffing his pockets with Mr. Russell's money and Mrs. Russell's jewels.

SIXTEEN

Skooley drove back to the house, put the Range Rover in the garage, and shut the door with the wireless remote. Then he loaded up the fridge with the case of Stella that he had just bought. He wondered if he should have bought some food too, maybe lunchmeat or some frozen dinners in case he got hungry later. But then he thought, hell, he had plenty of money, why bother cooking? He could just go out and eat anywhere he felt like. Shit, maybe even pick himself up another woman should the opportunity arise. Besides, there was tons of canned goods and pasta in the food closet downstairs. He wouldn't starve even if he decided to stay in, though he told himself that he was definitely going to stay away from eating any more of that damn Spam.

He opened a beer and went back upstairs to the bedroom to look again at what he had found so far. He had a nice little pile of valuables, and he was going to need to turn that pile into cash. He didn't have a cell phone and realized that he should have taken Raymundo's phone before he dropped him in the hole. Like most kids, Ray had one of those smartphones and he was on it constantly, checking email and texting and doing whatever the hell everyone did on those damn things. Skooley tried to remember when he had seen the phone last. Ray usually kept it in his shirt pocket, but Skooley couldn't remember if Ray's shirt had a pocket or if the kid had carried his phone in his pants pocket. Shit, he should have grabbed that damn phone. It could have helped solve a few problems.

Skooley didn't have a cell phone because he knew that people—law enforcement—could trace a person's location by his phone or listen in on conversations and read emails and such that he just never felt comfortable having one. Besides, he usually had nobody to call. But now he did have to call someone. He had the number for a guy in New York. He got it from a guy he knew in Tampa named Big Bill who used to buy things from him. A fence who could move stolen property easily and who usually paid pretty well, particularly for nice items like the ones sitting here on this bed. Skooley had told Big Bill that he was heading north for a few months to get away from the heat. Bill smiled because he knew that by "heat" he didn't mean the temperature and told him to call the guy in New York should he need to sell something, said to mention his name. He just had to find a phone so he could call. He didn't want to use the house phone because the number could be traced, and if something happened and it came back to Skooley, he knew that would cause a world of problems for his guy in Tampa. And if the guy in Tampa felt any heat, then Skooley knew that he would probably call someone in Miami and that would mean a whole nuther world of trouble. The kind of trouble that could land him in the same kind of a hole that his buddy Ray was laying in right now.

He decided that he'd go out later, find himself a Walmart or some such store and buy himself one of those disposable phones. It didn't make any sense trying to steal one from somebody as who knew what the hell type of app they might have installed. With all this new tracking technology, these Goddamn phones were getting a whole lot smarter than the people that used them. That was also why Skooley always stole relatively old cars—though he was growing awfully affectionate to that Range Rover in the garage. The newer, more expensive cars usually had satellite navigation or some sort of tracking device installed, and unless you could unload the car fast to someone who knew what they were doing, it was just as good as driving up to the police station wearing a sign around your neck that read "I stole this car!"

He would buy a disposable phone, make his calls, maybe hold onto the phone for a day or two, and then smash the damn thing with a hammer before he dumped it someplace far from this house.

Skooley had at least peeked into every room in the house except one. He headed over to that one room that he hadn't been in yet, not even for a quick look-see: the painting studio over the garage. He wasn't sure why he had saved this room for last, but he had. He thought that maybe it had something to do with the way the paintings that were displayed in the room downstairs had made him feel. He wanted to see where they were created. He wanted to see what she used to paint with: the easels and paint tubes and brushes and canvases, the actual tools she used. He opened the door and entered the studio. It was a large room with big bay windows on each wall. The panes of glass were coated with some type of UV protection as the light coming in was dulled, almost as if you were looking at the daylight outside through tinted sunglasses. There were also several skylights with horizontal shades covering them, which lit the room in soft natural light. Canvasses were stacked against almost every wall, some clean and bright and some with partially finished paintings or sketches. Two unfinished paintings stood on easels, one of a naked girl that wasn't at all like a dirty picture, but just a curvy young woman holding a sheet or blanket with eyes that were tired and sad and not at all sexy. She had a pretty face that looked, how could he explain it, not older than her years, but maybe wiser somehow. Like she'd lived some. The other painting was of two young children playing with a dog in a garden. There was also a painting on its easel that was covered with a paint-spattered tarp. He walked up to the painting intending to lift the tarp and look at what was unfinished under it, but for some reason as he reached for the tarp, he simply decided not to.

There were brushes of varying sizes lying about on a wooden drafting table, some used brushes that had apparently been washed lay side-by-side on paper towels, others brand-new still in plastic sleeves lay right next to them. As he had imagined, tubes and jars of paint littered the table. There were several wooden trays loaded with more paint tubes stacked on the floor next to the table. He saw a cardboard box on the floor containing several bricks of what looked like modeling clay, each wrapped tightly in plastic. Also, against two of the room's walls were what Skooley could only think of as artists' toolboxes. These were wooden cabinets on wheels with multiple drawers, some half open containing brushes and pallet knives and assorted other tools that Skooley didn't recognize.

The room smelled of paint and turpentine and mineral spirits and fresh canvas. Something in the back of Skooley's mind recognized some of the odors, perhaps from art class in kindergarten or grade school. It was just a fuzzy recollection, not even a memory but just a warm feeling of recognition. The room itself seemed messy—but it wasn't a mess. There was a sort of sense to how everything was strewn about. Not like someone just went in there to work and dirtied the place up; it wasn't clean and neat, but it was an ordered mess. It reminded Skooley of the shop of a carpenter he had once worked for back in Florida. He remembered the guy was working on some custom doors and there were tools and wood scraps and sawdust all over the place, but it wasn't dirty. The carpenter knew what he was doing and where every power tool and hand tool and screw and hinge was. It was a workspace, just like this artist's studio, and he understood and respected that. He decided right then and there that he would not take anything from this studio. It wasn't just that he didn't see a whole lot worth stealing, but it was something more. This lady, she created things that had meaning, even to a shit-heel like him, and it just wouldn't be right to mess with that. He would make do with whatever other treasures he could tease out of the house. Sure, she would be upset when she came home and found that her belongings had been violated and her house ransacked, but maybe in his own small way Skooley would be contributing to her artistic muse. Maybe a wonderful painting would result from her anger and emotional turmoil. Skooley smiled; it was a nice feeling knowing that he was contributing to the arts. He turned and left the studio, closing the door gently behind him.

SEVENTEEN

He was sitting on one of the lounge chairs outside next to the pool wearing nothing but a pair of aviator sunglasses he had found in the Range Rover and some new undershorts that he had bought at Kohl's the day before. He had not thought to buy swim trunks at the time, and the only trunks he could find in the man's closet were for a short, fat guy. He had already pulled the cover off the hot tub and had figured out how to turn the thing on, and he was just waiting for it to heat up to his satisfaction. He had placed a few bottles of chemicals, a skimming net, and some tools from the pool house in a small pile just to the side of the tub.

There was a fresh Stella on the little side table next to his chair and a fresh cigarette in the ashtray, and he was reading an old issue of *NJ Monthly* magazine that he had found on a coffee table in the family room. A towel sat on the floor next to him and underneath that was Ray's little Saturday night special revolver. He had placed the Beretta that he'd found under the mattress in the glove box of the Range Rover. He would take that with him when he went out of the house and leave the revolver here. He figured even if he got pulled over, at least he could say he had no idea the gun was in the glove box and since both the car and the gun—he assumed—were registered to the guy who lived here, it would be hard to dispute that fact. The worst they could get him for was B&E and maybe stealing the car, but then again, maybe he could just talk his way out of any trouble. After all, the car would not be reported as stolen, and Skooley knew he had the talent to spin a yarn as tight and snug as a birthday sweater, and so he was happy to take his chances. But an unregistered gun was something that he couldn't talk his way out of. He didn't expect any trouble here at the house and if someone did happen upon him, well, he had already thought up a story or two that he could use. The gun was there to aid his escape as a last resort if he needed it. He wasn't planning on shooting anyone, no matter what happened. But he figured that a guy in his underwear waving a gun around would be a whole lot scarier than just a guy in his underwear waving his pecker, and it should buy him enough time to gather some of his loot and make an escape.

Well, that was his thinking anyway.

He heard the gate slowly swing open but kept his eyes down on the magazine he was reading. The article was about an airport in Monmouth County here in Jersey that was being sold. It was a family-owned airport that had been in business since the 1940s and was now being bought by a conglomerate of some sort. The current owner—the son or grandson of the guy who founded the place—seemed like a pretty cool guy. He was a Vietnam vet who never went to college and had worked at the airport since he was a teenager. He liked owning the place and dealing with the town and the people who flew in and out. He ran the place, doing everything from fixing runways to tidying up around the small terminal to all the paperwork. A one-man airport maintenance crew. Skooley wondered what it would be like to work at an airport. Probably lots of bullshit to deal with. After 9/11, the feds would be watching everything and everybody, even in a crappy little airport like this one. He had never flown in an airliner before, but he had gone for a ride in an old biplane once. There was an air show a few years back at Page Field, a small airport just outside of Fort Myers, and he had paid fifty bucks to go for a fifteen-minute ride. It was okay, though he had found himself holding on pretty tightly to the seat handles even though he was strapped in securely with a seat belt. Of course, the plane was old and beat up and the engine was right there in front of him, loud and belching exhaust in his face the whole time, and besides, he wasn't sure that heights were his thing anyway. But he was willing to give an airliner a shot if he had reason to travel and needed to get somewhere in a hurry.

"Are you Tooley?"

It was a girl's voice, young, and with just the slightest hint of a Hispanic accent. Skooley slowly turned the page of his magazine before glancing up at the young girl. She was pretty, dark, but not too dark with black, shoulder-length hair that hung straight down framing her pretty, round face. Her hands were in the pockets of her jeans and she looked nervous, but not really scared.

He gave her a warm smile but didn't say anything.

"Where's Raymundo?" she asked. "He inside?"

Skooley grabbed his beer and took a long, slow pull. She didn't say anything else, just stood there looking at him and not smiling. Skooley put the beer back on the table, grabbed the cigarette daintily with two fingers, and took in a lungful of smoke. Finally, he said as he breathed out a cloud of smoke, "You must be Ray's friend Esmeralda. Say, Esmeralda, you ever been in a hot tub before?" He got up from the lounge chair, took another hit of his cigarette, and then flicked it over the fence and onto the backyard lawn. He then walked over to the hot tub and delicately dipped his toe in the water.

"Yeow, that's hot." He slowly immersed his foot all the way down to the seat ledge, sat on the edge of the tub, eased his other leg into the water, and then slowly lowered his body into the hot, bubbling water.

"Damn, I feel like a wet noodle."

Esmeralda walked a few feet away to another lounge chair, dragged it over so that it was next to Skooley's, and sat down.

She reached for the pack of cigarettes on the small table, shook one out, and lit it with a disposable lighter that was also sitting on the table.

"You just help yourself," said Skooley as he slid his body lower into the water and let his neck rest against the lip of the tub. "There's cold beer in the fridge if you want. Over in the kitchen inside the house. Maybe you could grab me one too if it ain't too much bother."

She didn't move for a second. Then, as if she had just made up her mind, she quickly got up and headed out the gate toward the house. She returned with two beers, handed him one and then went back and sat on the end of the lounge chair she had dragged over earlier.

"Where's Raymundo?" She asked again.

"Thanks for fetching the beers, girl." He tipped his beer to her and then took a sip. "Man, that tastes goo-ood! You know, I never had me one of these Stella beers until just recently. Gotta say, I believe I have acquired a taste for this brew. Was a Bud man most of my life. Well, for a short while started drinkin' Coors Light on account of this girl I was dating, but found I couldn't stomach the beer or the girl for too long and went back to Buds. But I believe I'm turning into a Stella man now. As for your buddy Raymundo, he lit out for parts unknown. Left yesterday, just shortly after he and I arrived at this beautiful resort."

"Why did he leave?" She took a light puff of the cigarette and then a short pull on her beer.

"Well, I guess he found what he come here looking for."

"What did he find?" she asked.

He didn't answer right away. Then he looked at her and said, "Cash."

"He found money?"

"From what I could see, a nice wad of hundreds. Musta been a few grand as the stack was about, oh, so thick to my eyes." He held his thumb and forefinger about a half inch apart from each other.

"He just left? Why did he do that? You just let him go?"

"Well, Esmeralda, I didn't really have much say in the matter. You see, this weren't my deal. Ray was the one that brung me in on it making him the jefe, so to speak. We started out partners, but I guess after I got us inside with no bother, Ray got other ideas in his head."

"We were supposed to be partners, me and him. And you too," she added quickly.

"How about that. Anyways, we got into that little room, you know, the office right there next to the kitchen, and he started just tearing the place apart, pulling out drawers and dumping stuff on the floor. I told him there weren't no need to make a mess, but he's a stubborn son of a bitch. Anyways, he found that stash of cash and decided to light it out of here."

"Where did he find the money? In the desk drawer?"

Skooley heard something in her voice that set a caution alarm going off inside his head. He sometimes got a feeling from people and he got one now. He was an expert at telling lies, and so maybe that was why his antenna was pinging. He took a long pull on his beer thinking. Finally, he said, "No, not in the drawer. He crawled into the closet and pulled out an old shoebox if you can believe that. Had a rubber band tied around it, you know, for security I guess." He noticed Esmeralda nodding her head just, following his story. "Anyway, he takes a peek inside without showing me anything and then pulls out this wad of cash. He was grinning like the Joker in that old *Batman* movie. Ever seen it? The one with Jack Nicholson where he plays the Joker and he's got that grin painted on? He pulls out that stack of cash and starts counting the hundreds. I just got a quick look, but it was a pretty big stack. I had to guess, I'd say about four or five thousand, easy. Well, I'm grinning too because we was partners and I'm thinking, damn, this is just the first place we looked. Well, that was when he shoved the stack of money into one pocket and pulled out this little revolver from the other. And that, my dear, was all she wrote."

"So, he left with the money?"

"That he did."

"And you didn't try to stop him?"

"Nope."

"Why not? You afraid he was going to shoot you?"

Skooley didn't say anything for a minute. Just sipped his beer, smiling and enjoying the hot water working away the tension in his muscles. His antenna was humming softly again and he was thinking about what to say and waited to see if she would say anything first, and to her credit, she didn't say a word.

Finally, he downed the last of his beer and put the bottle down on the ground next to the lip of the hot tub.

"Man, that Stella was especially good being as it was so cold and I'm just settin' here like a parboiled potato in this hot tub. But to answer your question, I guess there was a chance that little fucker might shoot me, but I wasn't scared of it. I do believe if I had a mind to, I could of snatched that gun right out of his hand and shoved it so far up his ass he could of pissed bullets. But I think deep down that your boyfriend, Ray-Mondo, is just a little no account, motherfucking pissant Mexicali beaner and I was happy to be done with him. Besides, I'm a fair person and I figured if he was happy leaving with what he come for, then hell, I should be just as happy to help myself to what's left."

He lifted the sunglasses, which were beginning to fog in the steam, up to his head and looked over at the young girl sitting on the end of the lounge chair drinking his beer and smoking his cigarette. He smiled at her, curious to see how she'd handle it, his remarks about her boyfriend and all.

She put her cigarette out in the ashtray and set her empty beer bottle on the table.

She looked at Skooley and said, "Guatemalan."

He wasn't sure what she had said. "How's that again?"

"Guatemalan," she said. "He's a no account motherfucking pissant Guatemalan and he's not my boyfriend. Hey, you want another beer?"

EIGHTEEN

He gathered up the towel, keeping the gun concealed in it, and told her he was going to take a shower in the pool house, wash some of the chlorine from his skin. He went inside and ran a hot shower, letting the water run over his head and body and tried to think what to do about Esmeralda. She couldn't say anything to the cops, not now, because if he thought about it, it was her that really had set the whole thing up. She was smart, he could see that right away, and she was pretty too, and he wondered if maybe after a few more beers he couldn't tease her out of them tight jeans and into the hot tub, maybe even into that big old king-sized bed upstairs. He wouldn't push it though, had to keep things nice and friendly and see how this played out.

He didn't know if Ray really had offered her a share, but if he did, then Ray should have said something to Skooley. Not a problem yet though. But he had to see what she knew, probably have to cut her in on something just to keep her quiet after this was over. But he thought he might play it hard, at least to start, see what she was made of. He had the five, no, more like six grand still left and that was his. She didn't know about that and he wouldn't need to share it, not any of it. And there was still more to come. Maybe lots more. Had to get rid of the jewelry and maybe some of the electronics and silverware. That transaction wouldn't concern her either. He could always throw her a few bucks if he needed to. Just see how things played out, that was going to be the plan.

When he came out of the pool house, Esmeralda was gone. He carried his wet undershorts in a ball around the gun and wrapped the towel around his waist as he made his way back to the house. He slid on his pants and shirt, which he had left on the arm of an easy chair in the family room. He heard a toilet flush upstairs and then her footfalls as she came down the stairs. He slid the gun under the cushions of the couch in the family room and then went over to the fridge to get another beer.

"There's a toilet right down the hall here," he said as she walked into the kitchen, "but I expect you knowed that since you probably spent a good deal of time with your head in there, you know, scrubbing her out." He gave her a friendly smile, but his voice had just the slightest edge to it.

She walked into the breakfast room and he noticed that she sat in the seat where he had sat, not in the chair that her late amigo Ray had occupied. He was glad that he had cleaned up good after getting rid of Ray's body. He also wondered if there was maybe some kind of scent that lingered, you know, like something so slight as to be almost subconscious that caused her to choose another chair.

"I spent lots of time with my head in all of these toilets, Tooley. I cleaned this house, every week, for years. I see you found some of Mrs. Russell's jewelry. Got yourself a nice pile up there in her bedroom."

He hesitated for just a second, and then grabbed another beer out of the fridge, carried them both to the kitchen counter and used the opener to pop the tops. He walked around the counter and into the breakfast room, put one beer in front of Esmeralda, and then settled himself into a chair on the other side of the table, not Ray's seat.

"It's Skooley," he said to her, "like where kids go to learn their ABCs only with a SK at the front and a EY at the end. Not Tooley with a T. Not that I'm sensitive about it or nuthin'."

"Yes, I can see that. Sorry. I thought Raymundo told me your name was Tooley."

"Yeah, well, your buddy Ray is not the brightest bulb, if you know what I mean, or maybe it was just his Mexicali accent that got you confused." He took a sip of beer. "Look, Esmeralda, I don't want us to get off on the wrong foot here. I must admit that I am a bit vexed by the actions of your amigo, leaving here with all that cash and all, not to mention bringing a gun on a job like this. And I am also a bit perplexed by finding you settin' here at this table right now. But it's a situation we both got to deal with, so I guess we better get straight, right up front, what is it that you're doing here? What do you want? You really want to be involved in the robbery of these nice folks?"

"Can I have another one of your cigarettes?"

He slid the pack and the lighter over to her. She got up, went into the kitchen, opened a cabinet, and pulled out an ashtray. He noticed that she knew exactly where to look for the ashtray.

"Neither one of the Russells smoke, but they're very nice. If they have company and those people smoke, they give them ashtrays. Let them smoke right in the house. Mrs. Russell told me that her husband's father smoked. He was a nice old guy and she just thought it rude to ask him to take his habit outside. Even though he's long dead, died of lung cancer, she still thinks it's rude to ask someone to smoke outside. Kind of old-fashioned, but I think that's nice, don't you?"

"It is," Skooley agreed, "you just don't see people with sensibilities like that no more." And he meant it, too, liking the artist, Mrs. Russell, all the more for hearing the story.

She shook out a cigarette and lit it. Skooley waited her out, knowing that she was stalling for time, thinking about what she was going to say.

"I am involved in this robbery already. I got involved the minute I opened my mouth to Raymundo. I knew he was coming here, I knew he was going to bring you with him. He said you were experienced in these types of things. A petty criminal, I guess." Here she smiled at Skooley and he gave her points for that. "I came here today looking for Ray," she said. "He was supposed to call me, let me know how things went. He said that you and he were going to come here to the house yesterday, just to check things out, and then he was going to call me. But he didn't call or text and he didn't answer his phone, so I got worried."

"Weren't you afraid coming here all by your lonesome like this? What if the Russells was still home, or maybe one of their kids, or a neighbor. What were you going to do?"

"I wasn't planning on coming inside. I was just going to drive by, check things out, see what I could see from the road. Then I saw Mr. Russell's truck leaving with you driving, and I figured that you and Ray were still here."

"How'd you know it was me driving?"

She took a drag on the cigarette and said, "Educated guess. I saw you behind the wheel and I knew you weren't one of the Russells, so who could you be? I followed you to the beer store. Besides, you don't look like you're from around here. I can't explain it, I just knew that you were you. It's that simple. That's why I drove my car right up and walked around back."

Skooley nodded his head. He understood. She was real smart or real stupid, maybe too smart for her own good, like her buddy Ray. But at least she had balls. Certainly bigger *cojones* than her beaner buddy had.

"So, what is it you want?"

"I want my share, just like I talked about with Raymundo."

"Yeah, well, unfortunately you had that talk with Raymundo. Me and Ray never had that talk. He never mentioned anything about a three-way split, of course he never mentioned anything about his own one-way split either, but that's not really part of this here equation. You want your share, maybe you should go find your buddy Ray-Mundo and get it from him."

They looked at each other and sipped their beers and smoked their cigarettes, neither one speaking for a short while.

Finally, Esmeralda got up and went into the kitchen. She leaned on the counter looking back to where Skooley sat at the table.

"They may talk to me after the Russells come home, the cops I mean. I'm sure they'll talk to all the girls and probably the landscapers and pool people and who knows who else. And I'd never say anything because it could get me in trouble too, I know that. But then, I'm just a poor cleaning girl, and if they heard from somewhere that I happened to talk about my job at say one of my other jobs, the ones I need just to keep food on the table for my family, my poor mother and my little brothers and sister, and someone just may have happened to overhear and took that information and acted on it, well, maybe I'd get in trouble and then again, maybe I wouldn't, you know."

Skooley just sipped his beer and didn't say anything. She was working her angle and he let her talk. He liked the way she looked, the way she was handling herself. He found himself listening, but thinking about the hot tub and the big bed upstairs.

"And if I never actually stole anything, then, what could they do to me? Arrest me for talking about my job? Poor little cleaning girl always with her head in other people's toilets looking at big houses every day, daydreaming, just like anybody would. People understand that, Skooley. I bet you're not so different. Raymundo said you sometimes work at the same restaurant as him, washing dishes. I bet that's a fun job." She took another sip of beer. Her cigarette was just about burned down to the filter, and she walked over to the sink and ran tap water over the end and then slid open one of the cabinets and threw the butt into the trash bin.

"Of course, if I actually took something, well then, that would be a different story. Then I'd really be an accomplice, you know. I'd have to be careful and not say anything that could jeopardize my situation and that of my cohorts. Or cohort, whatever the case may be."

She went back into the breakfast room and sat back down at the table.

"Plus, I could help, Skooley. I'm sure you found more than what's on that bed upstairs, but I bet you didn't find it all. How are we going to get rid of that jewelry?"

She said it just like that, "we," like it was already a done deal and he hadn't yet said anything, not even a word. It made him smile and then laugh out loud. She smiled too.

"Well," he said, "I got a guy knows a guy will buy that stuff upstairs. So that's what I'm bringing. What you got?"

Esmeralda got up from the table and walked back into the kitchen. She reached up on top of the refrigerator and moved aside several glass and ceramic jars. She took down a rather large grey jar that had "MOM'S COOKIES" written across it and brought it back to the table. She popped the lid and put her hand inside. She came out with a large cookie, which she placed in front of Skooley. She then reached inside again, working her hand down to the very bottom of the jar, and came out with a folded cellophane envelope. She put the cookie jar down, then wiping her hands on her jeans, she opened the envelope and counted out seven one-hundred-dollar bills and assorted fives and singles.

"This is called pin money," she said, sliding three of the hundred-dollar bills in front of Skooley and three in front of herself. "Good for last-minute grocery shopping or tipping the paper boy or maybe even for paying the delivery guy who brought the pizza you ordered for your cleaning girls."

She counted out the smaller bills putting equal amounts in each of their piles.

"I know where they hide some of their goodies. They have little stashes like this all around the house. I worked here for years cleaning every inch of this house. After I found one or two of these piles of money, I started looking for more, you know, like a game. Not to steal anything, understand? I never stole anything."

He gave her his great-guy smile. "Until now, that is."

She looked down at the table for just an instant, and he almost regretted saying anything.

"Yes, until now." When she looked up, her eyes were sad and he had the feeling that he had seen those eyes before.

"You seem like you're pretty smart, Skooley, and you may have found a few of their hiding spots already. Actually, I'm sure you have and you may find more without me, or you may not." She held the last bill up in her hand as if contemplating it. Then gently put the hundred dollars down onto Skooley's pile. "I'm not greedy, Skooley. I don't know how to get rid of stolen stuff and get paid for it. You do, so you deserve to get paid for your knowledge. But understand that I'm not just some stupid girl either. We're going to be partners, it's gotta be fair."

He liked her style, head on and smart, but not bossy. And he wouldn't have thought of looking in the cookie jar, even though it was so goddamn obvious that he almost laughed out loud again. Another four hundred and change to add to his growing kitty and he didn't have to do anything for it either, plus a pretty girl to hang out with, maybe more than just hang out.

"So, Skooley, what do you think?"

"Let me ask you something," he said, draining the last of his Stella Artois. "You happen to know about any more houses get left empty by dumbass rich people?"

NINETEEN

She went from room to room, opening drawers and cabinets, reaching into vases and behind cabinets, pulling out assorted stacks of cash. He had never seen anything like it. She went to the silverware cabinet in the dining room, opened a drawer and removed a tray of forks, then pulled out a vinyl-covered box that was sitting underneath it. When they opened the box, it turned out to be a coin collection of some kind.

"I always wondered what was in this damn box," she said as she bent down to examine the gold and silver coins, "I found it in this drawer, but I never got the opportunity to pull it out and open it. There was always someone around, either Mrs. Russell in the kitchen or one of the other girls vacuuming or Mr. Russell just walking around. I was too scared."

He followed close behind her with a large plastic garbage bag. She dumped whatever she found into it, and she carefully closed the lid of the box and slid the case with the coins into the bag. Mostly what she found was cash; sometimes she pulled out a ring or other piece of jewelry—usually it was in its own velour-covered box like they just brought it home from the store and threw it in a drawer. He'd have to look at those later. He assumed they were some of their cheaper jewelry. He knew that these pieces were mostly what they intended to be found should they ever be robbed.

As she worked, he watched her hands and fingers closely, making sure she didn't try to slide anything into her pockets or panties, keeping her honest. If she managed to take a little something, she would have to be pretty good and he wouldn't hold it against her, but he was keeping a good eye out just the same.

"They got a safe or anything like that? A lockbox maybe?" he asked her.

"If they do, I never found it. They just have all these little hiding places all around the house; in almost every room there's something. I guess they must figure if they get robbed, the thieves will find some things, but not everything."

See, she was pretty smart.

She stopped her searching for a minute and looked at him. "You ever see anything like this before? You broke into other homes; where do most people keep their stuff? I mean their good stuff: money and valuables? If I were rich, I wouldn't hide things all over the house. I think I would keep my things at the bank. Get a safe deposit box. Maybe I would buy a big, iron safe and keep it in the basement. What about you, Skooley?"

"You sure there's no safe? You ever look behind any of them paintings they got hung up all over the walls in their museum room over there? Or what about in his closet upstairs? That's where ya find most of the smaller safes and lockboxes, hidden away in the man's walk-in closet. Usually in the corner where you can peel up the rug or maybe they got a false bottom in a shoe or sweater bin."

"Well, I never found a safe. But he has some guns. He has a gun in a box upstairs in his closet. It's a rifle, all taken apart. I peeked in the box. But maybe he has more guns. Maybe there's a safe, a gun safe, downstairs in the basement. I was only down there once. Mrs. Russell asked me to help her carry some boxes down. It's unfinished, kind of dirty and full of junk, like the garage. I didn't see any safe though."

"It ain't a rifle, it's a shotgun he has in that box. And by the looks of it, it cost a pretty penny too. If he got a gun safe, I'd be puzzled why he didn't put the shotgun in there unless he only just got it or he wants to keep it looking pretty in that presentation box. But no matter, we'll check the basement out later."

"Why do you suppose they do it, hide this stuff, I mean. Why not just put their money in the bank? Have you seen this before? Do people hide money like this?"

"Yeah," he said, "all the time. Lots of people do."

"Really? Why?"

"Well, where I come from down in Florida, folks like to keep an emergency stash of cash, you know, in case the banks close down."

"Why would the banks close down?"

"Hurricane can shut down a whole county. Hell, sometimes the whole damn state. Good to have some cash on hand."

That's right, she thought. She remembered superstorm Sandy that had hit just a year or two earlier. There were still trees down and all sorts of devastation, statewide. And just a few short years before that, Irene had tore through causing flooding and assorted other damage. After Sandy, the power had been out in her apartment for almost two weeks, perhaps the coldest two weeks she'd ever spent in her life. Luckily, her uncle from Pennsylvania had driven over right after the storm to check on his sister and her family. Esmeralda had sent her mother and the children home with him, but she stayed in case the power came back on and she had to work. She remembered packing the family into his work van. It stunk of gasoline. Her uncle had brought two five-gallon gas cans all the way from Pennsylvania. He'd heard that it was hard to find gas stations open in New Jersey. He poured the gas into the gas tank before they left. She learned later that they had to drive with the windows open almost the whole two and a half hours back to his home. Before he left, he had handed her just over two hundred dollars in cash. She almost choked up remembering. As it turned out, she ended up working almost every day with her housecleaning crew. There was plenty of cleaning to do for a long time after Sandy hit town. She used the money her uncle had given her but paid it all back about a month later.

"We had a hurricane not too long ago. Hurricane Sandy. We lost power for about two weeks."

"Yeah, I heard. Stopped at a few towns along the beach on my way up here, tried to get work doing construction. But nobody would give me the time of day. Said they only hired local boys. Can't say as I blame them."

"Maybe that's why they hide money."

"Maybe. Hurricane can really put a scare into some people. He's got a brand-new generator there in the garage. Looks like it's hooked right into the electric panel. But I think this here is a bit different. Could be they both squirrel money away, think they're hiding it from each other, and forget where the hell they put it. More likely, it's business. Construction can sometimes offer opportunities to make money on the side. I knew a guy who worked for a paving company once building roads. His company was working on an old section of highway outside of Baltimore. They were ripping up the highway and right alongside ran miles of what was an old-time cobblestone road. So they ripped that up too and sold them cobblestones for cash. Then they billed the city for hauling and dumping what they said was debris. But every night big trucks would come in and haul the blocks away. Guy told me he was in the trailer one night when the project manager was handed a bag filled with money. He heard later that it was over eighty thousand in cash, went right to the company owner—I guess after that project guy took his cut."

"So, they have to hide the money?"

"You ever hear of anybody walking into the bank with eighty thousand dollars cash in a paper bag and making a deposit?"

"No, but I did hear about a twelve-year-old boy who walked into a Mercedes-Benz dealership and tried to buy a car, cash. He made the money dealing drugs on a street corner in Newark."

"Well, ain't it nice that the young man wanted to buy the car instead of going out and try to steal one."

Esmeralda looked over at Skooley. "I guess he was just brought up right."

"Yeah," he agreed, "anyway, don't really matter to me any why they hide it. We find it, we keep it. Just like hide 'n seek. I'm sure there's a suitcase full of money here somewhere. If he's got this kind of cash lying around for us to find, then he's got a lot more that we ain't supposed to find. These people, they just ain't too smart. They hid a key in a fake rock outside. You can't believe how many houses I got into with the old key-in-the-fake-rock trick. I'm gonna check inside their fridge, see if maybe they got some fake bottles of mustard or those plastic vegetables with the hidey-hole in the bottom. I think I'll pull out all of the electric sockets and look behind them too. I seen a lotta that before. Found all kinds of stuff in them fake sockets, mostly money or drugs—usually both."

She looked at him and smiled, probably the first true smile he'd seen from her and it gave him an unexpected warm feeling behind his ears. "You're pretty smart for a petty criminal, you know that, Skooley?"

He felt himself smiling back, and not one of his practiced smiles either, but the genuine article. "Yeah," he said, "I guess. I'm just hoping your Mr. Russell turns out to be a road contractor with a side business selling drugs on a street corner in Newark."

TWENTY

Esmeralda led the way from room to room throughout the main floor of the house. She pulled small caches of cash from almost every one. To his credit, Skooley looked into every hiding spot there was, pulling up corners of rugs and looking behind paintings and mirrors and checking for envelopes taped to the bottoms of drawers. He overturned furniture and checked the seat cushions and looked under tabletops and pulled out couch cushions running his hand along the seams and checked for false bottoms in drawers and bins and boxes. He moved all electronics and checked behind them, looked in the plastic sleeves of CDs and DVDs and even pulled out most of the books he found on the odd bookshelf and leafed through the pages. He removed the covers of all of the electric outlets with a small screwdriver he found in one of the kitchen drawers but didn't find any that appeared to be hiding places. Toward late afternoon, they carried their plunder back up to the master bedroom and added what they'd found to the pile on the bed. The additional cash came out to just over three thousand dollars. They also found several store credit cards, a fifty-dollar gift card for Outback Steakhouse, three American Express Gift Cards of unknown amounts, and two Visa credit cards—one that was expired—and the assorted small jewelry items.

"I thought we'd find more." Esmeralda seemed dispirited.

"Well now, it ain't really a bad haul so far. We don't know what the jewelry is worth, and we ain't done looking yet either. We got the whole upstairs to look forward to. I went through this here bedroom pretty good, but you ain't had your crack at it yet. It's usually the bedroom where you find the honey hole, though I must admit I come up dry my first go 'round. And we got all them other rooms up here. These people, and even this house, they got secrets hiding. We just got to find them, that's all. You can't always rush this sort of thing. We ain't had time to 'walk in their shoes' so to speak."

Skooley was hoping her mood would improve. He knew there was a big stash somewhere in the house. He could feel it. And he knew that he would find it too. It would help to have her looking with him, at least in the short term. She was thorough, and she had a feel for these people, a connection. That would help him get a feel for them as well, and that's probably just what he needed. Ideally, he'd like to have her look some more, maybe find a few more things. Then he would call New York, sell some of this stuff, and pay her a little something, tell her they had found everything that was to be found and send her on her way. Tell her it was time to bug out before someone came and checked on the place and called the cops. Then he would come back and really tear the house apart. But for right now, what he really wanted was to see her smiling again. Mainly because that warm feeling behind his ears had made its way down to his balls.

He suggested that they take a break, go out and have dinner somewhere. Not in Mendham, or Bernardsville, but maybe Morristown where there were a lot of restaurants and a lot of young people. She said she wanted to keep searching and so they compromised, and she spent another hour and a half going through the bedroom and both his and her walk-in closets. He laid on the bed mostly, watching her as she methodically went through drawers and dressers, doing as she had seen him do downstairs and looking under the drawers and even pulling them out and off of their tracks and reaching her hand in behind to feel around. There was a minute or two of excitement when she thought she had found something stashed behind one of the bottom dresser drawers, but it turned out to be just a package of nylon stockings that must have fallen out of the drawer at some point and gotten stuck. When she was done, she sat on the bed looking dejected again.

"We missed something here, Skooley, I just know it. Something important."

"Well, I don't disagree. I spent a goodly amount of time going through this room earlier. I'm pretty sure I got most of the obvious stuff. Still, I am embarrassed to admit that I did miss them pantyhose and that ain't no joke. That's why it's good having another set of eyes looking. Them stockings could've been more cash and I might have left it sitting right there in the bottom of that drawer."

"Did you check the electrical sockets in here?"

"No," he said, "I did not. I had intended to come back in here and look some more, but that was before I decided to run down to the liquor store and then have me a hot tub bath."

"I guess I sort of interrupted your plans."

"That you did, girlie, yes indeedy."

He got up off the bed and started unscrewing the electrical outlets. Esmeralda took his spot on the bed and watched him work.

"I can't imagine that you can hide very much in an electrical outlet. You said you found drugs and sometimes money. How much did you find? How can they hide anything in such a small space?"

He gently pulled off the outlet cover that he was working on and then tugged at the actual socket itself.

"Well, I done this very same thing one time in a condo in Miami, took the cover off and saw an outlet just like this one here. It looked a little loose and so I pulled. And when I pulled, the damn socket slid out easy as you please and right behind it came this little tin box about the size of one of them boxes like you get your bank checks sent to you in, you know what I mean? Had a lid and everything. And it wasn't like the guy that owned the house made this thing in his basement. It was manufactured. It was manufactured to fool people, people like us. You can fit a nice bundle of cash in a box like that, weed, coke, diamonds, hell, good things come in small packages. One time in another house, a guy dropped a little bag with his stash inside and tied it to the real electrical outlet and let the bag hang down behind the plasterboard. Shit, I seen some amazing things."

"Did you find a lot of money in the box?"

"Yeah," he said, "I did."

"So, what are you doing here in Jersey washing dishes?"

He turned and looked at her lying on the bed, "Well now, girlie, that's a whole 'nother story." And even though he beamed his best "great-guy" smile at her, he could see suspicion in her eyes and knew that the wheels were turning. She was a smart girl, this one. Unfortunately, she was too young or too naive to realize that being too smart was not always good for one's health. Best to watch his step. And she would be wise to do the same, he thought.

They sat in silence not really looking at each other, he on the floor twiddling with the screwdriver in his hand and she half lying on the bed staring at the ceiling.

Finally, he said, "Let's go get us some dinner. I ain't ate nothing yet today and it's almost tonight already. You been to anyplace good in Morristown? I drove through, but I didn't stop in anyplace. Looks like they got a nice little strip right there off that park, you know where I'm talking about?"

"It's called The Green, The Morristown Green."

"Well, I drove through that town, once in daylight and once at night. Was packed both times, but a bit of a different crowd at night if you know what I mean. You know a spot where we can get us a few beers, maybe a decent burger or burrito? I'll even buy, use the money from my half of the cookie jar."

"You got more than half."

"Well, if I buy dinner I guess that makes it just about an even split then don't it."

She didn't say anything for about a minute or so.

He got up. He had decided to go get something to eat. If she didn't want to go out then he'd pack up all the loot from the bed into a bag and bring it downstairs with him into the kitchen. He didn't trust her alone with the money or the jewelry, too easy to take something and too tempting. It was better for him and certainly much better for her if he just kept everything within sight. He could bring it all downstairs and rustle himself up some dinner. There was plenty there to eat, he just didn't feel like cooking. Maybe he could get her to do the cooking. Or maybe he'd just have chips and salsa, something like that.

"What about smoke alarms?" she asked.

"Huh?" He wasn't thinking clearly. Between the beers he'd had already and the lack of food, he was starting to feel a little fuzzy around the edges.

"I've been looking at that smoke alarm, right up there." She pointed to the round plastic disc on the ceiling with a small, steady green light. "I remember what you said about good things coming in small packages and how people usually keep their real valuables in their bedroom. We already checked the light switches and the electric sockets; I think that's the only place we haven't checked yet. I can't think of where else to look."

He sat back down slowly and looked up at the alarm. She was right. And he would have gotten to it eventually. Probably would have done it already if it wasn't for them Stellas earlier and the surprise guest he had gotten that was sitting right there on the bed pointing out the obvious to him. Problem was he was tired and hungry. Starting to get hangry he thought and smiled. Then he remembered old Ray sitting at the table with that yellow Shop Rite bag duct taped around his head and the smile faded. He looked up. The ceilings were high.

Not your standard eight feet. Looked more like a twelve-foot ceiling, so he was going to need a ladder and he didn't feel like going down to the garage or out to the shed to find one.

Esmeralda hopped off the bed and walked over to one of the tall dressers. She took everything off the top of it and laid it all on the floor, then started trying to muscle it away from the wall and under the smoke alarm.

"Skooley?"

"Yeah?" He was watching her slow progress as she moved the dresser a few inches from the wall.

"Want to get up off your ass and help with this?"

When they got the dresser under the alarm, Esmeralda removed her shoes and Skooley boosted her up onto it. First, she sat, then slowly she worked herself onto her hands and knees, and finally, carefully, she stood up. She reached up and placed the fingers of her left hand on the ceiling to steady herself, and then slowly twisted the disk with her right. It came off easily, but there were wires attached to it leading back into the ceiling.

"What do I do?" she asked, looking down at Skooley.

"Can you see up into that hole?"

"Not really. I mean I can see a little, but it just looks like wires."

"Reach your fingers up in there and wiggle 'em around some, see if you feel anything that don't seem like it belongs there."

She did, reaching her fingers in as far as she could and moving them around in all directions. "I don't feel anything. Just the wires and some sort of bracket."

"I'm gonna grab hold of your ankles, just to steady you. Then you hold the alarm with one hand and try and pull them wires out with the other. Now, you're gonna find that they're snapped in there pretty tight and sometimes they're not so easy to pull out, so feel around for a little plastic tab right where the wires go in and try pressing down on it and pulling apart at the same time."

It took several tries, and she had to let go of it and drop her hands down to her sides and shake them to get the blood flowing back into her fingers again, but she finally got the wires out and threw the smoke alarm onto the bed, and slowly and carefully got back down on her hands and knees and then back to a sitting position and Skooley helped her down off the dresser. She slipped her shoes back on and they both walked back to the bed.

"I thought that was it, Skooley, I thought that was where we'd find their treasure."

He picked up the alarm and started working on it with the screwdriver. He popped the cap where the battery was stored and peered in. There was no 9V battery inside. He pulled out a small metal cylinder.

"What's that?" she asked.

Skooley looked at her, then back at the cylinder. He unscrewed the cap, opened his hand and poured the contents into it.

A small metal object that looked a lot like an old roller skate key rolled out.

"Well," he said, "if we was pirates, I'd say we just found us the key to a sizable treasure chest."

She started jumping up and down and clapping her hands like a little girl. Skooley watched her and could actually feel the muscles forming a wide grin on his face.

"We did it, Skooley! You were right, it was here in their bedroom just like you said."

"Take her easy there, girlie. We just found the key, but we still ain't found the treasure chest."

TWENTY-ONE

Early Saturday morning, Loretta awoke with a start and knew that something bad had happened to her. Her head hurt, a splitting headache that ratcheted up every time she tried to move, and she was thirsty as could be. She was in her bed in her own condo, she knew that much, but she was naked and had a very bad feeling, and this caused her heart to start beating faster. She could feel the cold sweat which usually singled the beginnings of a panic attack forming all over her body and decided not to open her eyes hoping maybe that sleep would take her back down so she wouldn't have to face what was coming for a while longer. She concentrated on remembering what had happened last night. She had gone to The Tabor Road Tavern and met a guy. Blond, skinny, southern. What was his name? Raymundo! No, no, not Raymundo. Ray Mundy, that was it! Kids teased him by calling him Raymundo when he was growing up. The night was coming back to her slowly, and she became more and more apprehensive the more she recalled.

He was a builder from Florida. He had some kind of deal going in Mendham. She had ridden the evening out, trying to get the client's name from him figuring the more he drank the looser his tongue would be. What the fuck was she thinking? The scumbag had been feeding *her* drinks and *she* drank them. Shit! She started berating herself in her mind. *How fucking stupid could I possibly be! He played me all along, but I kept after him like some simpleton. It was the wine. And that joint I smoked in the car in the parking lot before I even went into that damn place.* She knew it wasn't a good idea to smoke a joint before drinking, but it was always hard for her to go to a bar by herself, even just for a happy-hour drink. The joint made it easier for her to relax, and she was able to talk to people without feeling like they thought she was on the make. God damn it! Maybe he had slipped her something. What was that rape drug? Roofers or roofies? She had read about them on the internet. Maybe not. She knew that she had drunk way more wine than she was used to.

He was a talker. Part charm, but mostly just bullshit. She knew that even last night when he had started in, before she got totally plastered. But there was always a kernel of truth in what he said, something that made the lie seem plausible, like maybe, just maybe, it wasn't all bullshit. And he had money, which he wasn't shy about spending. Cash, as she never saw a credit card come out. No, of course not. A credit card would leave a trail. But then, what could he have spent, a couple of hundred, tops? Not really that much. He was working on a deal. Some guy was subdividing or selling his place in Mendham. Big money there, that's for sure. Probably another reason why she acted so stupidly. She could really use a nice deal. Needed one, in fact. She remembered him following her home. How the hell did she drive? Jesus, she must have been so shit-faced she could hardly walk. Thank God she didn't have an accident or get pulled over! He had a nice car, a Range Rover. She remembered that. She had let him in, even opened another fucking bottle of wine! What the fuck had gotten into her? And then she must have passed out. She felt sore and forced herself up and into the bathroom. She checked herself carefully. Her labia were red and swollen, and she could feel the friction burn when she touched herself, but there was no discharge that she could see. Her rectum hurt as well, and a new round of cold sweats started as she made her way to the full-length mirror that was her bedroom closet door, and she bent over to see what she could see.

As she was bent over looking at her reflection, her eye caught the shine of something on the floor next to the bed, and she walked over. Three torn and empty Trojan condom wrappers, Ribbed for her Pleasure, were lying there. Thank God that motherfucking rapist scumbag found the rubbers that she kept in the drawer next to her bed, she thought. *How could I be so stupid*, she thought to herself, *how could I possibly be so fucking stupid?* She began to shudder uncontrollably and then she started tearing a bit and then she began crying in earnest with deep, heaving sobs. She felt queasy, getting closer and closer to vomiting as she sat on the bed hugging herself, fighting to control her emotions which some rational part of her brain told her were equal parts hatred for him and shame for herself.

TWENTY-TWO

She wanted to keep on looking. "We're on a roll now, Skooley, think about it. This is what we were searching for. We just have to find the lock that this key fits into."

His initial pleasure at finding the key did not last long. He started thinking in terms of "if only." If only he hadn't decided to go to town and buy beer today, then she wouldn't be here right now; if only he had checked the damn smoke alarm when he went through the bedroom the first time; if only he had slipped the damn cylinder right into his pocket or told her it was part of the wiring system and waited to come back for it when she decided she had to go pee.

"This is a good find," he said. "It tells us what we both know: that there's more to be found. But it's getting late. We'll need light to keep searching, and I don't want to open every damn light in an empty house. You can't really see the house from the road in the daytime, but at night it will be a different story. You'll be able to see the lights through them bushes. Some of these lights are on timers, but not many. These people ain't too smart, but I bet if they go away every year, they must tell the local cops to drive by and keep an eye on the place every once in a while. All we need is for one of them cops, or even a neighbor, to drive by tonight and see lights or movement or anything that they ain't used to seeing, and we're done for."

She didn't say anything, thinking it over. "We could use flashlights, be real careful."

"That's worse still. Think about it, what would you think you see even a glimpse of a flashlight through a window of an empty house at night? That maybe the people that live there are just saving electricity?"

"What if someone sees us driving out of the driveway?"

"Well, that ain't really going to look so suspicious if we're driving their car. Also, you can't see the driveway from them other houses, and there ain't many cars on this road anyway. We see someone, we act like there ain't nothing wrong. This guy's cars, they ain't reported stolen. We got to be careful, that's for sure, but people don't notice much if it don't look suspicious. They'll think maybe these folks come home early or that it's just a relative or someone who works for the guy checking on the house. See what I mean? Besides, we got time and I'm starved. My head ain't too clear right now, and I suspect we'll miss something and have to search everything twice anyways if we keep at it. Took us a while just to find that key. How long you think it'll take for us to find the lockbox? Shit, could be anywhere. We got to get away from here and look at things fresh tomorrow."

As he talked, he slipped the cylinder into his hip pocket. "Let's get the rest of this stuff in a bag. We got to find someplace safe to hide it. No telling what kind of lowlifes might be prowling the neighborhood."

They agreed to take separate cars. He wanted to just take the Range Rover, but she didn't want to leave her car there, and he knew that leaving a car outside in the driveway wasn't a good idea. Even putting it in the garage meant having to move cars later and that wasn't good either. So they agreed to take two cars and maybe leave the Toyota wagon in town somewhere.

She didn't tell Skooley that she wasn't going to come back to the house tonight. There was no way she was sleeping there alone with him. She saw him slip that cylinder with the key into his pocket, but didn't say anything. He was smooth and sleazy, and she didn't trust him. And she wasn't stupid. There was something scary about him, maybe even dangerous. He was a serious and experienced criminal, that was for sure. He knew where and how to search a house, and she could see that he didn't fluster very easily. Actually, he didn't seem to get nervous or scared about anything at all. It made her wonder again what he was doing in New Jersey washing dishes. Something wasn't right. She knew she had a made a mistake asking him that, but only realized it after she had already opened her mouth. He had to be hiding out, but from who or what she didn't know. And she wasn't about to ask. She had to be even more careful from here on in. She knew he wasn't going to go anywhere until they found whatever there was to find. Or he found it. And when that happened, there certainly wasn't going to be an even split no matter what she did or how much she helped. She had to think about that. She wished that Raymundo hadn't run off and was still involved. It would have been much easier to handle him, get him on her side. Then it would have been two against one. But now that she was in as deep as she was, she had to figure out how to get through this and not come out with nothing, or next to nothing. Or end up in jail. She had to think about what to do. She would call Raymundo again. Maybe he'd answer his damn phone and she could meet him and talk things out. Tell him about the key. Maybe he would come back, bring his gun with him.

For now, she decided she would go out to eat with Skooley, have a few drinks, then go home, make sure he didn't follow her. She didn't want him to know where she lived. Then she would go back to the house in Mendham early in the morning and find that lockbox or whatever. If there was enough in it, maybe she could work something out with Skooley, settle for less than what she felt was her full share. She was keeping a mental note in her head of what they had found so far. She knew he'd take some of it, probably tonight after he found out that she wasn't coming back to the house. He wanted to sleep with her and probably figured that he could too, she being a little Hispanic cleaning girl and him a big-time criminal. Like most guys who didn't get what they wanted, he'd probably get angry, and then try and get even.

That would be when he would think about swiping some of the loot out of the bag, take what he figured was rightfully his. She wondered how much he would decide to grab. Might be a lot, to teach her a lesson and show her who is boss. Maybe even all of it.

Then she wondered what she could do about it.

TWENTY-THREE

They met at The Morristown Green, on the corner right across from Starbucks. Esmeralda had told him that parking would be hard to find, and they had agreed to meet at the Green. Sure enough, the town streets and parking lots were full. Skooley followed her most of the way into and around town, and when she happened upon somebody pulling out of a spot on South Street, she waved him into it, then continued around the block and across town to the Burger King parking lot near her home where she had a parking sticker allowing her to park overnight. She crossed Morris Street and entered the municipal parking lot, then continued on to Pine Street turning right on South Street toward the Green so she would arrive from a different direction than where she had actually left her car.

He was sitting on a bench, leaning back with his legs sticking straight out toward the sidewalk, crossed at the ankles, smoking a cigarette.

He looked up at her as she approached the bench. "For the life of me, I can't figure out what makes people buy their coffee at a Starbucks. You ever had one?"

"Of course. The coffee there is good, don't you think?"

"Well, I guess. I mean, it oughta be for the goddamn prices they charge. You really think the coffee is a whole lot better than say, a regular old donut shop or a McDonald's?"

"Sure, I've been to lots of places where the coffee was just awful. Besides, I like my coffee strong. Didn't you like your Starbucks coffee?"

"It tasted okay. I just didn't like all the bullshit that went with it, you know, like them kids that work there, the counter help, calling themselves bar-eestas. Can you believe that? Christ. You can't even ask for a large cup of coffee, gotta ask for a vinty or venty or some such crap."

"That's just marketing. And look how good it worked. There's a Starbucks in just about every city in America—across the world, actually."

"Yeah, I guess," he said, looking over at her and smiling. "They're making plenty of money and there's nothing wrong with that—they just ain't getting any more of my money."

"That's very diplomatic of you, Skooley," she said, smiling back at him.

He took one last deep drag of his cigarette and flicked it into the street. "Well, to be honest, what I could really use right now instead of an overpriced cup of coffee is a buffalo-sized cheeseburger or a beef and bean burrito with lots and lots of that hot sauce. Maybe one of each and a couple of cold beers to wash it all down with. You know anyplace around here we could get something like that?"

She sat down next to him on the bench. "Let's see, there's the Urban Table, right there across the street. Food's good, they have burgers and sandwiches and such. There's also Tito's, a little burrito shop just up the street, but they don't serve beer. How about the Famished Frog? It's a bar/restaurant. We can get burgers, they have some Tex/Mex stuff, that's probably our best bet. It's right up the street, too. And they used to have a cigar bar where you can smoke and drink beer right in the bar. I'm not sure if it's still open, but we can check. It's going to get packed later, but we should have no problems getting a table now. Or we can just sit and eat at the bar if you want."

He got up. "Let's do the Frog. I'm 'bout ready to pass out from hunger, and burgers and Tex/Mex and beer and cigarettes sound damn near perfect to me."

They sat at a table that looked out on Washington Street. Skooley ordered a pile of appetizers and his buffalo cheeseburger while Esmeralda ordered a chicken quesadilla of which Skooley ended up eating half. She was amazed at the quantity of food that his slim frame could put away. But he just kept on eating and talking and drinking beer until all the food was gone.

Skooley did most of the talking during dinner, telling her about the different places he had been, mostly in Florida. He seemed to have traveled all over the state and worked at a lot of different jobs, mostly in construction. She noticed that in his stories, he was always a crew boss or some kind of manager, not just a worker. Sometimes he even partnered with this contractor or that contractor on a particular job. She knew he was just bullshitting her, making himself sound important, and so she mostly kept quiet and let him tell his stories. He didn't mention anything about how he had learned to break into houses or where he had gotten the name of the guy in New York who bought stolen property.

When he had run out of food and seemed to be slowing down on construction stories, she decided to test the waters on her own.

"Skooley, do you mind if I ask you something?"

"Ask away," he said, looking her in the eye.

"When I walked up to you today, there at the pool, you didn't even flinch. Now I realize that once you saw me, you guessed who I was. But it could have been anybody walking through that gate into the yard: landscapers or neighbors or even one of his kids. What if I was someone else? Aren't you scared someone might surprise you?"

He smiled at her. "If I sit around scared of what might happen, then ain't nothing *ever* gonna happen. You just got to be ready to act is all. You remember when you walked back there, I was sitting by that hot tub ready to jump in and get cooked?"

She nodded.

111

"You remember seeing those bottles of chemicals? Them tools right by the tub?"

She thought, and then nodded slowly remembering the scene.

"I put that stuff there before I set down. If you was someone else, then I'd a been someone else. If you was a neighbor, I would'a said I was fixin' the hot tub. Work for Mr. Russell, got sent over by the company to fix 'er up. Thems my tools right there. My partner, he just left to pick up a part we was missing. I was just waiting by the pool, taken a little break, getting some sun. If you was the landscapers, I would'a walked over and said I heard you was coming today, thought you'd a been here earlier. Mr. Russell, he asked me to stop by and tell you he needs an estimate, wants to plant a bunch of hedges right over there; let me walk you over, show you exactly where. He said to leave the estimate in the mailbox next time you come to cut the grass."

"What if it was one of his kids?"

"Probably same hot tub story as before, see how it goes. But I gotta expect that won't work for long. Kids will probably call the old man on the cell phone. Whoever shows up, just gotta get 'em talking, keep 'em off guard and get ready to boogie first chance I get. But I ain't too worried. Grass looks freshly mowed, pool's clean. Unless his kids live right close by, I don't expect they'll be stopping by all too often. Probably been by once already, won't come again for a week or two. Besides, I ain't really planning on spending a whole lot of time in the hot tub. Only real worry I got is the Russells themselves, maybe cut their vacation short and come home unexpected like. You say they go away for a month, same time every year. Own a house somewheres, so they probably got clothes and such stored there already. Both cars are in the garage, so they musta flown somewhere. I checked the mailbox, didn't see no letters, no junk mail, no newspaper on the stoop or in the driveway. If they was just leaving for a few days, coulda had someone stop by and pick all that stuff up. But no,

I expect they stopped delivery. Hell, even the phone ain't rung once since I been here. Still, anything could happen. If we're inside, we'll hear a car pull up or the front door open, then we just gotta play it by ear. If that happens, we grab what we can and try to sneak out nice and quiet, then hightail it to them woods and get gone! But we sit around all worried and scared, hell, we may as well just go home now and call it quits."

They both sat quiet for a minute, sipping their beer.

"Skooley, how'd you learn about all this stuff we're doing? You know, where to look for things and how to get into places? If you don't want to talk about it, I understand. I'm not trying to pry into your personal business, I'm just curious."

He had drunk about four beers during dinner and they seemed to not have had any effect on him whatsoever. His speech had not changed, no slurring of words nor any change in his speech pattern. His eyes were shining a bit more than when they had first sat down perhaps, but that could also have just been a trick of the light. She had nursed her one Miller Lite throughout dinner.

He didn't answer right away. It was like he was thinking about whether or not he was going to respond.

"I met some guys when I was just a kid. They did these kinds of things, along with some other kinds of things, and I learned from them mostly. Once I got the hang of things, I done some on my own."

"How'd you meet them?"

"Well, I guess you could say they sorta came and found me."

Esmeralda didn't say anything. She decided to let him talk if he wanted, or not talk. She started thinking of how she could slip out of the bar and sneak home without getting him mad.

After a minute or two of silence, he said, "I was about fourteen, washing dishes when I could get the work, crash at people's houses or sleep in shelters, hang out with runaways sometimes. It weren't easy, but it weren't terrible either. I mean, I was getting by; eating pretty regular and I had some friends sort of watched out for each other. There was this guy used to cruise around, you know, talk to the kids, try and take 'em home and fuck 'em in the ass or try to get them to give him a blow job. Sometimes it was him giving them a blow job. He'd feed 'em or give 'em a few beers and a few bucks. I knowed some kids went along. I got in his car one night and he drove me to his house, a nice place, not real big or anything. I was little for my age then, I guess I didn't look like much. He sits me on the couch of his living room, pulls out a bong and a bottle of wine. I tell him to go ahead and fire up the bong and as soon as he starts to take a toke, I grabbed me that bottle of wine then wham, I hit him as hard as I could, right here." He pointed to his own temple. "He went down like a rag doll. I found me some packing tape and trussed him up good, then searched that house, top to bottom. Took everything I could carry and loaded it up in his car. Came back in and told him if I ever seen him again, any-where, I was going to kill him. I think I meant it too. Then I kicked him in his head and his stomach and his balls till my leg was so tired I couldn't kick no more and then I left in his car. I went around to pawn shops and second-hand stores and sold what I could. Then I just left his car by the side of a road with the keys right there in the ignition. I ate good for the next few days, got a motel room too. A few days after that, these two guys track me down and throw me in the back of their car." He started smiling. "I thought I was dead, you know. I mean really, I thought they was going to kill me. I knowed lots of people, mostly kids, that got killed. Sometimes you see them one day and then never again. Word gets out, sometimes you learn what happened, sometimes not. But these guys, they didn't kill me. They had this old building, like a clubhouse, where them and a bunch more hung out. Said they heard about what I did to that queer. Knew about the car too. I started cleaning up for them, sleeping there on a cot they had in the back. They'd pay me, feed me sometimes too. Then

I started doing little jobs, learning what I could. I was small, could fit through windows and crawl spaces. Looked younger than fourteen too, so I was less obvious. Lasted about a year and half, then the cops busted up the place. I wasn't there when they got raided, but most of 'em got locked up. I had some money saved up by then, left and started working landscaping and construction jobs. Kept my hand in, though, you know, when the opportunity arose. Came across some nice homes working those construction jobs. Was careful and didn't have much trouble. Sometimes I ate good, and sometimes things didn't go as planned."

She almost said "Like that condo in Miami" but caught the words just as they were about to come out her mouth and coughed instead.

"Why'd you get in the car?" she asked.

"What car?"

"You know, with that child molester. You knew what he was, what he did to those other children. Weren't you afraid?"

"No," he said, "not really. He was just a pervert is all."

She looked at his eyes and could tell that he wasn't lying.

"But you knew what he wanted. He was a predator who went after kids."

"Yeah," he said, looking around absently for the waitress, "but what he wanted didn't really matter to me. It's what I wanted what mattered. He tried something funny like that, I had already decided I was just gonna kill him. Hey, you want another one of them Miller Lites?"

He paid the bill just as he had promised and left the young waitress a nice tip. They decided not to stay at the Famished Frog, and they both smoked a cigarette as they walked leisurely down Washington Street back toward the Green to South Street, then past Starbucks. There were several bars, one right after the other, and they walked until they had both finished their smokes and then turned into one of the bars at random.

The place was packed with young people, mostly white professional types, some trendy, some not so much so. There was music playing loud, but not so loud that you couldn't talk. They found one empty stool at the bar and Esmeralda sat and Skooley stood next to her and ordered them both beers.

"So, where do you think we should look first?" she asked him, leaning into him so that no one else could hear.

"Well, that key looks like it fits some type of lockbox. I seen keys like that before. It's not a safe key or for a suitcase or anything, looks like a small lockbox, for sure. If it was you, where would you hide a lockbox?"

She thought about it. "I'm not sure how big a lockbox is. Probably steel, let's say it's the size of a small suitcase, is that about right?"

He shrugged, then nodded his head without saying anything.

"It's got to be put away, out of sight. We already checked most of the rooms. We didn't go through all of the rooms upstairs, but I can't believe the box is just lying in one of the closets or under a bed. I also can't believe they would leave it outside the house, like say the garage or the pool house, even though the pool house wouldn't be a bad spot in my opinion. So I'd say we need to check the basement, see if we can find the attic and check it, and also look for a false wall, maybe behind one of the closet walls, but not in the master bedroom. That would just be too obvious. What do you think, Skooley?"

He smiled at her and nodded his head again. "Not bad, girlie, thems all good hiding spots." He went to take a sip of beer just as someone behind bumped into him. She heard his tooth hit the bottle and then felt the bottom of the bottle tap her on the side of the head as she was still leaning close in to talk. She saw that some of his beer had spilled down the front of his shirt, and she saw his eyes go just a little wide. He slowly lowered the beer bottle and with two fingers of the other hand felt the tooth that got struck by the bottle. He seemed satisfied and put his beer bottle down on the bar, turned and tapped the offending man on the back.

"Excuse me," he said. The offending back turned around to face him. He was a large young man, obviously drunk, with a blotchy red face and beard stubble on his cheeks and chin like he hadn't shaved in a day or two. He was talking to another large man right next to them at the bar.

"Yeah?"

"I feel like I got you sitting right here in my back pocket," said Skooley, putting on his best "great-guy" smile. "Would you mind moving over just a scooch and I'll do the same and maybe that way I can finish my beer here without chipping another tooth." He continued smiling at the young man who was about a foot taller.

"Fuck off, asshole." The bigger man turned his back on Skooley and began talking to his friend again.

"Skooley," Esmeralda grabbed his arm lightly, "let's get out of here."

"Take it easy there, girlie, we're okay right here. Maybe you could just move your chair a bit that way and we'll give this big fella here a bit more room. Like I was saying, those are all good hiding spots. We get up tomorrow, we can split up and start checking all them places. Maybe you could start in the basement, I'll check the higher elevations. Sometimes an old house like that has got a pull-down attic and small crawl spaces. You know, all the rebuilding over the years probably left a lot of hidey-holes. I'll also check in some of the air ducts and vents. If the box ain't too big, could be they hid it right there just inside a vent. Easy to get to, but hard to see because of the grate in front."

The big guy laughed out loud and leaned back as he did so and bumped into Skooley again. Skooley didn't react at all this time.

"Let's go, Skooley, please. I don't like it here. I'm going to go home. I left my house this morning and my mom must be worried." She reached into her pocket and pulled out a twenty-dollar bill and left it on the bar as she pulled him along and out onto South Street.

"I'll meet you at the house tomorrow morning around nine. I'll leave my car up the road. There's a little lot there where you can park and then walk to Patriot's Path. Lots of people leave their cars there and go hiking. I can leave the car there all day and no one will notice. You like chili? I'll bring everything we need and I'll cook and we can eat right there at the house and not worry about going out."

He didn't seem angry, not at all. That was good.

"Yeah, I like chili," he said absently, "with beans and meat and lots of cheddar cheese on top. You make it hot? With them hot Mexican peppers? I like it so hot I can't feel my tongue after. You make it like that?"

"Sure," she said, "any way you like. Maybe I'll make some real Colombian rice too."

They had begun walking away from the bar on South Street toward where Skooley had parked the Range Rover.

"You need a ride to your car?" he asked.

"No, I'm parked right around the corner. I'll see you to-morrow. Around nine. We'll find that strong box and eat chili to celebrate."

He patted his pockets. "Damn," he said, "I think I left my cigarettes on the bar."

She stopped walking and looked up at him. "Go back to your own place tonight, Skooley, at the rooming house. Sleep in your own bed. Or go back to the Russells' house and sleep there if that makes you feel better. I'll meet you tomorrow morning. Don't go back for your cigarettes. That guy is just a big fat drunk. He didn't mean anything. Don't get into trouble. We don't need any trouble."

She leaned in again and gave him a quick peck on the cheek and then she turned and left him standing there on South Street, patting his pockets and looking a little bewildered.

She walked further down South Street and then turned left

down Pine Street. She walked one block to the roller rink and turned left on Dumont, then cut across the municipal lot and headed toward the Dunkin' Donuts. She decided to buy donuts and bagels to take back home with her for the kids' breakfast in the morning. Just as she opened the door to the donut shop, she heard the first police sirens approaching from somewhere in the distance.

TWENTY-FOUR

Sunday

On Sunday mornings, Loretta liked to get up early and walk. She lived in a condo development on a hill, and she would walk from her unit all the way down Foxwood Drive to Route 53 and then turn around and walk back up to the very top. She did this several times, power-walking the whole way, working up a sweat. She did this to keep in shape and also to burn off some of the stress that was a big part of her daily life. Her reward for all this exercise was a big breakfast at the Whippany Diner right up the road from her condo on Route 10. She usually ate alone at the counter. Because she went there almost every Sunday, she knew most of the staff and they knew her. There were always one or two other regulars and she didn't feel ill at ease eating alone. The waitress behind the counter or one of the owners or managers would sometimes sit and talk for a few minutes, and then she would read *The Daily Record*, the local Morristown newspaper, and enjoy a delicious and leisurely breakfast, then perhaps tackle part of the *NY Times* or the *Star-Ledger* to get the regional and national news.

She usually enjoyed her Sunday mornings, but this Sunday was not usual. She still suffered the aftereffects of her hangover from Friday night. The exercise helped, but she still wasn't fully recovered. Her stomach wasn't quite right yet and a slight headache still lingered at her temples. Worse still, the feeling of shame and the humiliation from allowing herself to be raped by that animal burned hot in her breast. Allowing it to happen because she let herself get so goddamn drunk. She still had not totally given up on the roofie theory, but deep down she knew that she had just let herself go. She hadn't done anything like that in a long time. But she had done it before, in college, more than once and with similar results. She was also still foggy on what had happened for most of the time in the Tabor Road Tavern and hoped against hope that she hadn't run into anyone she knew at the bar. She feared learning that one of her clients or prospects had spotted her stumbling around or leaving with that Mr. Mundy or whatever the hell his real name was. One thing was sure, she wasn't going out for happy hour again for a few weeks, and she wouldn't be setting foot in that Tabor Road Tavern again for months.

She had not gone to work on Saturday. Had called in sick, in fact. Luckily, Robin had been able to cover for her. She had told her office that she must have caught some type of stomach bug and would do her best to work from home, but she had spent most of the morning just lying in bed trying not to throw up. By mid-afternoon she was on her computer doing multiple searches on anything she could remember that her rapist had said. She searched for Ray Mundy and Par D Construction in Naples and Fort Myers. Then she expanded to all of Florida and then to New Jersey. There was a lot of information to go through, but it led her nowhere. The more she searched, the more she realized that everything he told her had been a story, a big fat lie. She couldn't believe she had even hung around to listen to it. She was smarter than that. She wondered, not for the first time, if perhaps she had a drinking problem. She wasn't an alcoholic, at least not in the traditional sense. She didn't drink every day, or even every week. And even when she did, she didn't usually drink to excess. But every once in a while, she went on a bender. Like she did on Friday night. Not often, but when she did, it was full tilt, no holds barred, sloppy drunk leading to blackouts and often to consequences that she just wasn't equipped to deal with, particularly at her age. Like being raped by some redneck sleazebag. What if he hadn't found those Trojans? Then she'd have to go and get herself tested for AIDS. Probably still a good idea. She shuddered again at the thought of him in her home, of him on top of her and inside of her, breathing cigarette breath in her face.

She finished her walk and returned to her condo, showered, put on a fresh, dark red velour sweatsuit, fixed her hair and makeup, and headed over to the diner.

The parking lot was about half full, and she managed to get a spot right near the front door. It was just about 9:00 a.m. and she knew that in about an hour or so, the line to get in would be out the door. Many families stopped in after Sunday morning religious services, most dressed in their Sunday best, and the diner got loud and busy. She tried to time it so that she got in and out before the big rush. She bought copies of the *Star-Ledger* and *The Daily Record* from dispensers by the front door, then went inside and stopped at the cashier's counter to say hello to Helen, one of the owners. Helen was a lovely woman, a grandmother of four who was always friendly and pleasant and had a smile for every customer. She then waved to Sarah and Antonio, two of the waitstaff who were both busy carrying plates of eggs and fried potatoes and pancakes and waffles to hungry patrons, and headed to her usual spot on the right-side end of the long dining counter.

Colleen, another waitress, magically appeared with a cup of hot coffee and placed it in front of her.

"Good morning, Loretta. How are you today, doll?"

"Okay, I guess. How about yourself?"

"About the same. Do you need a menu today?"

"No, Colleen, just give me a mushroom and American cheese omelet with well-done home fries and whole wheat toast, no butter. And, Col, keep the coffee coming, would you?"

"You got it."

Though the diner was just starting to get busy, there were only a few customers seated at the counter. Loretta was seated in the second seat from the end, and three empty seats separated her from the next customer: a large construction worker type with a big square head and a crew cut, wearing dirty blue jeans, a navy sweatshirt, and soiled work boots. He was working his way through a huge stack of pancakes while leaning to his left away from Loretta, his head hovering just inches over his newspaper that he had placed on the counter, chewing thoughtfully.

Loretta took a sip of coffee and decided to read the regional news first. She placed the *Star-Ledger* on the counter and started leafing through it. Her breakfast came, and she ate as she read, folding the paper into quarters to take up less room on the counter. She read through the main section, then the op-ed and business sections, arts and leisure. She put the sports section to the side along with all the store supplements which she never looked at, then read the regional New Jersey news and finally, *Parade Magazine*, and then the funnies. More and more people were entering the diner and even the counter seats were beginning to fill up.

When Colleen had taken away her plates and refilled her coffee, Loretta took out the local paper, *The Daily Record*. She was thinking about just taking it home to read, but decided to have another cup of coffee and enjoy the noise and bustle of the diner. She liked her condo, but sometimes on a Sunday morning, it could just get a bit too quiet. So she read the front page and then opened it up and started skimming until a photo stopped her dead.

The headline of the story directly below the photo read "Barroom brawl in Morristown leaves two hospitalized."

The photo showed a blond-haired man apparently heading toward the exit of a crowded bar. A young employee of the newspaper who just happened to be out with some friends at the time of the fight took it with her cell phone. She saw the commotion and snapped this picture just as the assailant was walking away. She used her iPhone, and the photo was sharp and clear. The photo and a short description of what had just happened were then emailed back to the paper, literally within minutes of the occurrence.

Loretta put the paper down for a second and picked up her coffee cup. Her hand started shaking and coffee spilled onto the counter and her red tracksuit. She grabbed the cup with both hands, but the cup and the hands holding it kept shaking, and so she put the cup down with a loud clatter that made the man sitting two seats away from her look over. She picked up the paper again. Son of a bitch, she couldn't fucking believe it. The guy in the photo was a smiling Ray Mundy.

TWENTY-FIVE

Esmeralda awoke around seven on Sunday morning. The TV was already on and all three kids were sitting on the floor in front of it quietly eating donuts and watching cartoons in their pajamas. She had not bothered opening up the sofa bed when she got home last evening. She hadn't gotten home late, but the kids were already asleep in their room. Her mom was awake and watching something on the Hispanic TV channel on cable. They chatted for few minutes, Esmeralda making up a story about working all day at the beauty salon and then hanging out after work with some of the girls. She gave her mother a do-nut from the bag she had carried in and handed her one of the hundred-dollar bills she had gotten from the Russells' house, telling her it was what she had made from the salon that day. Her mother took it and told her she'd go food shopping with it that afternoon. They chatted for a few minutes more, then her mother went into her bedroom and closed the door.

Esmeralda changed out of her jeans and put on the sweats that she normally slept in, closed the lights, grabbed her pillow out of the hall closet, and lay down on the couch in the dark. She lay awake for what seemed like a long time, staring at the ceiling and thinking about what she had gotten herself into. She was in trouble, she knew that much for sure. She had a bad feeling about the sirens she had heard earlier. But Morris-town could be a rowdy town on a Saturday night. She could hear loud conversations coming through the closed living-room window from the young people who gathered outside of The

Grasshopper smoking cigarettes. The noise was almost a constant, even on weeknights, but from Thursday through Sunday nights, it was even louder than usual. Maybe the cops had been called because some kids were getting too loud at a party, or maybe there was a fender bender in town. Those sirens could mean anything on a Saturday night. Still, she had a bad feeling, and when she finally fell asleep, it was a restless, fitful sleep.

She got up off the couch, the children totally ignoring her, and made her way to the apartment's only bathroom. She relieved herself, flushed, then turned on the hot water in the shower and stripped naked. When the water was coming out sufficiently hot, she took a long shower, taking her time washing and conditioning her hair, luxuriating in the hot water and steam that enveloped her body. When she was done, she wrapped a towel around herself and, as quietly as she could, let herself into her mother's bedroom and got some underwear from the dresser that they shared and some fresh clothes that were hanging from a rack they had set up in one corner of the room for Esmeralda's things. The closet in the bedroom was small and so Esmeralda had let her mother use it while she used the improvised clothes rack. She gathered her things and crept out of her mother's room, closing the door silently, then went into the children's room to get dressed.

As she finished drying herself and putting on her clothes, she started a mental list of what she had to remember that day. She would need to call the restaurant where she worked and call in sick again. She had called them yesterday afternoon using her cell phone from the upstairs bathroom of the Russells' home after Skooley had gone into the pool house to shower. She had told them that she was sick with some type of stomach illness. She needed to call them again this afternoon. She also remembered telling Skooley that she would cook them chili.

That had been a good idea, get his mind off going back to that bar and also easing into the fact that she was going to go home instead of letting him think that she was going to go to bed with him. He seemed to take that news pretty well, and she thought that maybe she had misjudged him somewhat. Then again, maybe he was just drunk and not thinking straight. She hoped that he hadn't gone back to the Russells' to drink more beer and brood, or worse yet, that he hadn't gone back and found their treasure chest. Then again, a very small part of her hoped that maybe he had found that chest and just left town. Then she could be done with this business. She had mixed emotions about the whole matter. On the one hand, it was sort of fun poking around someone else's home when they weren't there and finding their hidden treasures instead of having to clean up their mess after them. And it was also exciting just taking what she wanted. She already thought of the money she had taken out of the cookie jar as hers, not theirs, and found herself daydreaming about paying for cosmetology school and maybe getting a new pullout couch that didn't leave her back aching every morning. She found it was easy to spend that money, too. It felt good going out with a few hundred dollars in her pocket instead of just a few dollars. She did the math in her head. She took about three hundred and forty dollars from the cookie jar for herself. A hundred to her mother, twenty at the bar and maybe about another twelve bucks for donuts. So she still had over two hundred in her pocket. Then her thoughts started changing direction. If she got arrested for robbing a house, even of just the three hundred and forty dollars she took, what would happen? Would she go to jail? What would she tell her mother? Or her brothers and sister? Or that nice Mrs. Russell?

She tried to stop her mind from going in that direction. It was too late. She was in this thing, and if she was going to go to jail, it wasn't going to be for three hundred and forty dollars. It was going to be for a treasure chest.

She started thinking again about what she had to do: call work, get ingredients for chili—beans, ground beef, tomatoes, bell pepper, onion, some type of chili mix, plenty of hot peppers, a few jalapeños, and maybe even a habanero pepper—and start thinking about where the hell that Mr. Russell would hide his treasure-laden lockbox.

TWENTY-SIX

Loretta sat in her car outside of the Whippany Diner for a good half hour, thinking about what she should do. She kept picking up the paper and reading the story, looking at the photo, then putting it down again. The story was brief. The man in the photo had gotten into an altercation with two other bar patrons. Nobody had really noticed anything until the fight broke out. The guy she knew as Ray Mundy had apparently grabbed a bottle off the bar and struck one man in the head with it while his back was turned, then grabbed another bottle off a nearby table and struck the second man as he went to the aid his friend. He then proceeded to kick and stomp both men while they were down and dazed, sending each to the hospital. Eyewitnesses said the fight lasted less than a minute, but everyone that was interviewed who had a good view of what happened was struck by the savagery of the attack. No one seemed to know what precipitated the incident. One bartender said that the attacker may have been in earlier, but he wasn't sure. When the fight was over, the attacker grabbed what appeared to be a pack of cigarettes off the bar and calmly exited. Police arrived a short time later and called an ambulance. Both men suffered lacerations, possible concussions, and other unspecified injuries and were admitted to Morristown Medical Center for observation. Police are asking anyone who may have information about the incident or who may know the man in the photo to contact the department. A phone number was listed at the end of the article to reach police.

She knew him all right. But did she really want to go down to the police department? Most certainly not! They would file a report. She would have to tell them about getting drunk and inviting that scum bag into her home and opening another bottle of wine, and they would ask her how could she claim rape if there was no evidence and why did she wait so long to call the police and how many rapists used a rubber? Three rubbers, actually. Maybe she would get her name in the paper, and how would a story of rape and sodomy go over with prospective clients, or her friends and coworkers and parents, or even her ex-husband? Drunk, divorced woman alone at a bar at happy hour goes off with a stranger and invites him home. Everyone, including her stuffy parents, would think she was a slut who got what was coming to her. No, going to the police with her story was certainly not an option. She had suffered enough over this. But she had to do something. She had to get that fucker back somehow, get him caught or get him killed, she thought with absolutely no remorse.

She started thinking about calling her information in anonymously. But how? She couldn't use her home phone or cell phone. She needed to find a payphone. But where the hell could you find a payphone these days? Did they still make payphones? Maybe embellish the story a little. Like he had a knife or a gun. She had to think about that. She didn't want anything coming back at her later. Shit, the cops probably record all calls. They'd have her voice on record. Maybe best to just stick to the truth. She could always deny making the call, but hell, with all the technology they had these days maybe they could get a voiceprint or something to tell them exactly who called. They probably have an app for that she thought almost automatically. She picked up the paper and read the story again and looked at the cocky, smiling face of that asshole and could hear his smooth, southern accent in her head saying "Par D, not party" and it made her skin crawl.

Revenge. Retribution. She wanted to see him burn but not

get close to the fire. She pulled out of the diner and got onto Route 10 heading east. She slowed as she passed gas stations, checking both sides of the road and looked quickly to see if she could detect any payphones. It was hard to look and also keep one eye on the road and so she decided if she didn't see any, she would stop in every gas station on the way back to her condo and see what she could find. As she arrived at the traffic light on the corner of Ridgedale Avenue and Route 10, right next to the large Novartis Pharmaceutical plant, she remembered that there was a Ramada Inn up ahead next to the Target store on the other side of the highway. The hotel had a sports bar attached to it as well. She had never entered either the hotel or the bar, but had passed them both many times when shopping along this busy part or Route 10. There were always signs in front of the bar announcing parties for all the big games for every season. Maybe they would have a payphone in the hotel lobby. She remembered when she had traveled years ago, before everybody had a smartphone, that most hotels and motels and inns had banks of payphones, usually right off their lobbies next to the restrooms. She had used them often when she had worked as an outside sales rep right out of college. If they had done away with the lobby phones, maybe there would be one in the bar. She drove through the light, passed the plant entrance and then past the bowling alley, and veered into the U-turn jug handle next to the movie theater. She thought she might try the Target store too if she struck out at the hotel. There had to be a payphone left somewhere.

She parked in the lot and walked through the front door of the lobby. She felt a little self-conscious and didn't want to attract any attention to herself. There was a waiting area just to the right of the lobby, and she sat down on one of the chairs and looked at her watch several times like she was waiting for someone and re-read the article again. Each time she looked at the photo, her stomach ached and her face flushed, and she could feel a slight sheen of sweat form on her forehead. That fucker had to burn.

She looked at the story again and read the name of the reporter right under the headline: Pamela Reese. She thumbed back to the inside front page and found the phone number of the paper, then took out her cell phone and dialed. A recorded voice answered, and she went through a series of commands, pushing various numbers until she finally got a live operator and asked to speak with the reporter. She was patched through, and the phone was picked up on the second ring.

"Hello, this is Pam Reese. Can I help you?"

"Hi, Ms. Reese. I'm calling about the story you wrote in the paper, about the bar fight in Morristown?"

"Sure, of course. Can we start by you giving me your name, please?"

"I'd rather not give you my name if that's all right. I just wanted to tell you that I know that man, the one in the picture. I mean, I met him."

"Were you with him at the time of the altercation? Were you in the bar?"

"No, I met him two nights ago. In another bar. He said his name is Ray, Ray Mundy, at least that's what he called himself, but I don't think that's his real name."

"Why do you say that?"

"Well, I think he was just trying to pick me up. He was telling stories; you know how some guys will start talking and you just know they're lying? Anyway, he was driving a Range Rover, a dark green Range Rover. He said he's from Florida, and I believe that part because he had this southern accent, and I don't think he was faking that. It wasn't very flattering. He sounded like a real hillbilly, but he did say that he's staying in Mendham. He's some type of construction guy, and he said he's looking at a job, a construction project for a wealthy homeowner in Mendham. I don't know if he was lying about that. Probably, but I thought you'd like to know. Maybe being a reporter, you can find out more about him."

"Where in Mendham is he staying?"

"I don't know. He didn't say exactly. Just that he was staying in Mendham."

"Did you call the police? I put a number at the end of the article."

"Umm, well, I was planning to call them right after I get off the phone with you. I thought, well, I thought maybe since it was your story, you might be able to take the information I gave you and use the paper's resources to find him. You know, help the police."

"Is there anything else you can tell me about him? Did he do anything to you or to anyone you know? Did he give you his cell number or did you give him yours?

"No. That man is a pig. I wouldn't have given him my number."

"Okay, I've written down what you've told me so far, and I will see what else I can find out about him. I have had a few other calls. It seems he was spotted in town earlier. Someone even told me that he might work in a town nearby."

"Really, where?"

"I can't say any more until I've substantiated everything. I can tell you that you're right about him not really being named Ray Mundy. This guy is unstable. He hurt those boys last night. He hit them both with beer bottles right in the head. He didn't seem to be drunk when he did it. He was trying to take their heads off. Then he stomped them when they were down on the floor. Kicked them viciously. From what I gather, it was a totally unprovoked attack. He didn't say a word. I think this man is dangerous."

"He is. He's very dangerous."

"It sounds like you know more—" but the sound of the reporter's voice was cut off as Loretta ended the call.

She sat there staring at the picture of Ray Mundy in the paper. She was seething inside. After a few minutes, she got up and with her newspaper in hand asked the young clerk at the front desk where the restrooms were located. He directed her down the hall with a smile, and she walked around the corner the way he had pointed and found both the men's and women's restroom separated by a bank of three payphones stuck on the wall.

She picked up one of the phones, then hung it up and went into the ladies' room and into a stall where she closed the door, sat down on the toilet without even pulling down her sweats, and thought about what she would tell the police. She wouldn't say anything about her call to the reporter. Better not to mention the Tabor Road Tavern either. They might go and talk to the bartenders, and what if one of them remembered her. She had been in there before. All she wanted was for them to get the guy. She would just tell them what she knew, what she had just told that reporter, and then hang up. It was really up to the cops to find him.

She went to the sink and looked at herself in the mirror. She didn't know why she was so nervous about making the call, but she was. She waved her hand in front of the paper towel dispenser and took the sheet of towel with her out to the phone. She peeked up and down the hallway. No one was visible. She grabbed the phone she had picked up earlier, wiped it down with the paper towel, and then used the towel to hold onto the receiver. No fingerprints, she thought. She knew she was going a bit overboard, but whatever.

She dialed the number of the police that was listed at the end of the article.

"Morristown police," said a male voice on the phone. "Can I help you?"

"I just read that article in the local newspaper, about that fight in the bar."

"Could you hold on for just a second, ma'am, I'm going to transfer you to the Detective Bureau." Before she could answer, she was put on hold. A few clicks and beeps sounded in the receiver, and another male voice got on the line.

"This is Detective Thomas Aletta. Can I help you?"

"I'm calling about that fight last night. The one I read about in the paper. I think I know the man in the photo. I mean, I met him. A few nights ago."

"Can I have your name, ma'am?"

"No, I don't want to give you my name. That man, he's dangerous. He told me his name was Ray Mundy, but I know that's not his real name. He told me he owns a construction company named Par-D Construction, two words, one is the letter D, and that he's from Florida, but that's not true either. I mean about the construction company."

"If he was lying to you, ma'am, how do you know he's from Florida?"

"He had a southern accent, like a shit-kicker. He sounds like redneck trailer trash." The words started coming out faster, and she could feel the hysteria in her voice, but she couldn't seem to calm down. "And he drives a late-model Range Rover, dark green, very dark, and he said he's doing an estimate for some construction work for a guy who owns several acres in Mendham." Her breath was coming in gasps now, and she realized that she had begun to cry, and the tears were streaming down her face. "And I think that's where he's staying, in Mendham, and he followed me home to my condo and I was drunk and didn't know what I was doing and I let him in and opened another bottle of wine and then I must have passed out or maybe he spiked my drink and then he raped me. Officer, he raped me." She was crying now, and her mouth was open and she used her other hand to wipe her face and a string of saliva stuck to her hand as she pulled it away from her mouth.

"Take it easy, ma'am. If you tell me your name or where you're calling from, I'll send someone from our crisis center right over, someone you can talk to. She'll be able to help you."

"Just catch him. He's a monster," she was whispering into

the phone now. "Look what he did to those poor kids in the bar. And...and...I think I saw a gun. I'm not sure, but I think he has a gun."

"Did you say he has a gun?"

"Yes. He has a gun. And he's driving a dark green Range Rover, a new one. He said his name is Ray Mundy, he's from Florida, look in Mendham, those are clues, right? Just catch him." She hung up the phone, went back into the ladies' room, stumbled into one of the stalls, and threw up her breakfast into the toilet.

TWENTY-SEVEN

There was a brand-new Shop Rite that just opened up over on Hanover Avenue, and she decided she'd go pick up her supplies there. She sat at the table just off the kitchen and began writing a list of things she'd need to buy: the ingredients for making chili, a large bottle of Diet Pepsi for herself, a flashlight—no, make that two flashlights and batteries for them. She thought for a minute more, then wrote down a note to pick up a pack of Marlboro Lights for Skooley. He'd probably be going nuts without cigarettes. She didn't want to give him any reason to be more agitated. She knew that today was going to be a pivotal day for her, maybe even life-changing. Best to try and keep everyone on an even keel. She'd go to Shop Rite first, then head up Hanover Avenue just past the Acme and turn right on Speedwell. There was a Dunkin' Donuts just up the road in a small strip mall. She'd pick up two coffees and some donuts to bring over to the house. She couldn't really think of anything else, so she got up, grabbed her purse and keys, went over to the children, and said goodbye. They said goodbye back, their eyes never leaving the TV screen.

The Shop Rite was massive, more like one of those warehouse stores than a local supermarket. She picked up everything on her list, though it took some time to find it all. Her mother did most of the food shopping for the family, and it was she that had said how wonderful this new store was. It seemed just too big to Esmeralda, too many choices and too many departments. Though she had to admit, there seemed to be more people working the check-out registers than there were shoppers. But that might just have been the early hour. She loaded her shopping bags into the car and drove down to the Dunkin' Donuts that was just down the road.

It was just past eight o'clock. She had told Skooley that she would meet him at the house around nine. There was a line at the counter of the donut shop when she went in, but it moved quickly, and it seemed like most patrons were taking their coffee and donuts to go. This particular store was set up with not only regular tables but also with larger chairs that looked like they could be in someone's living room. Esmeralda waited her turn, ordered a medium coffee and jelly donut, and then grabbed a few napkins and took her breakfast over to one of the large easy chairs. A small coffee table was situated right next to her chair with someone's discarded newspaper and a used napkin. She set her coffee and donut down, grabbed the used napkin by one corner, and walked it over to the trash bin. Then she returned to her chair, took a sip of hot coffee and a bite of her jelly donut, and decided to scan the paper. It was today's paper, *The Daily Record*, Morristown's local news. She quickly scanned the top stories, then started flipping through the other pages.

She stopped dead when she saw the headline about the fight in the bar. Shit. She looked at the photo and at Skooley's smiling face and couldn't believe it. Her very first thought was what if someone had seen her with him. Her heart started racing as she read the story quickly, looking for any mention of a girl seen with the assailant. Nothing. The bartender had seen them, but the bar had been packed. He would have seen hundreds of people over the course of the night. And they hadn't drawn any attention to themselves when they were there. Thank God she left when she did. She knew last night that if she didn't drag him out, he would have started something with that drunken guy. She thought about the people she had seen at the bar. She couldn't remember seeing anyone she knew. She lived in town, but with three jobs, she really didn't go out much. Why the hell did he go back into that bar? For a pack of cigarettes? She read the article again. Witnesses said he hit the guy from behind with a bottle. No words traded back and forth, no talking or yelling or punches thrown. It wasn't a fight. It was an assault. He didn't go back there for his cigarettes. He went back in there to clobber that guy. And for what? For bumping into him? He hit the guy with a beer bottle, his friend too. He hit both of them over the head with a fucking beer bottle. It's crazy. She knew that hitting someone with a beer bottle wasn't like in the movies where the bottle just shattered and the guy made a funny face and fell down. A hard blow to the head with a bottle could do serious damage, even kill someone.

She read the article again, more slowly this time. The bartender wasn't sure if he'd seen Skooley earlier. That was good. And he didn't mention seeing him with a girl. They took both victims to the hospital. Lacerations, concussion. Shit, she hoped they were all right. She looked at the photo again. She looked at Skooley, smiling, his eyes shining, like a little kid who just got off a merry-go-round without a care in the world. Must be a psycho. This was going to get around, probably be all over the internet by later this morning. Look at how happy he looks in the picture. Crazy. Someone would report him to the cops. Shit, he works at the restaurant where Raymundo works, washing dishes. They don't pay people off the books there. His coworkers will know him, his boss will know him, he'll have his name, his social security number, his address. By tonight, or by tomorrow at the latest, the cops will be looking for him.

Shit!

Why didn't he just go back to his place last night? Or to the Russells' house? Why did he have to go back into the bar? She didn't understand. He didn't seem all that upset when she

left him on South Street. Why did he go back? She remembered hearing the sirens last night and having a bad feeling.

Shit.

She looked at the photo again, his smiling face. What a
fucking idiot.

Shit, shit, shit!

TWENTY-EIGHT

She parked the car in the lot near the entrance to the Patriot's Path hiking trail. The path meandered through several towns in the area. This one was just about a quarter mile from the Russells' house. She took the Smiley Maids magnetic signs off of the doors, threw them onto the back seat, locked the doors, and started walking toward the house. She carried the Shop Rite and Dunkin' Donuts bags with her as she walked along the side of the road. No cars passed her as she approached the house. When she got to the long driveway, she stopped and looked around again. Satisfied, she turned into the driveway and then walked off into the tree line that bordered the right side of the driveway and into the woods so that if someone should drive by, they wouldn't see her walking toward the house. She walked a short distance into the woods to be sure that she couldn't be seen, then started making her way toward the house. When she was about halfway to the house, she came upon two bicycles lying in the dirt. There were a few empty beer bottles and crushed cigarette butts there as well. She put the plastic Shop Rite bag down for a minute and looked around. She walked over to a tree where there were four beer bottles in a small pile. She kneeled down and noticed that she had a clear sight line to the house, if say she had happened to be sitting in that spot, drinking beer, smoking a cigarette, and looking to see if anyone was home. Two bikes. Skooley and Raymundo. She thought about it for a few minutes. They must have ridden the bikes from Bernardsville.

How else could they have gotten here? There was no car in the driveway. She remembered seeing the car with Florida plates in the parking lot near the rooming house in Bernardsville where Raymundo and Skooley had rooms. That would be Skooley's. Raymundo doesn't have a car. No way they would have walked all that way. And they wouldn't have taken a cab either. So it made sense to ride bikes. But why were both bikes still here? How did Raymundo get to wherever he went off to if he didn't take one of the bikes? Maybe he called someone to pick him up. Maybe he decided to walk into the town of Mendham, which wasn't really all that far. Call someone or take a cab from there and go—where?

She picked up the Shop Rite bag again and started walking toward the house. She needed to try and call Raymundo again. Things were going to start to get dicey with Skooley. She knew he'd know nothing about the newspaper, but she had to tell him, let him know the cops would be looking for him. No telling how he'd react. But if she didn't, he'd probably do something stupid and get himself caught.

Do something stupid, what a joke. Probably hit someone else with a beer bottle.

And then she thought, if he did, who would he probably hit?

Shit.

TWENTY-NINE

The back door leading into the garage was unlocked so she went in that way, then in past the mudroom and into the kitchen. She put the Shop Rite bag down on the island counter. She could hear noise coming from a TV in the family room in the back of the house. She found him lying on the couch, watching a movie on the big-screen TV wearing just his underwear. He had a cigarette burning in an ashtray that was sitting on his chest.

"You ever seen this movie, *Butch Cassidy and the Sundance Kid*? One with Paul Newman and Robert Redford? Great movie. I seen it a bunch of times," he said without taking his eyes off the screen.

"I see you got your cigarettes."

He turned and looked over at her, smiling. "You brung me a coffee? Man, that's just what I need. Was going make me a pot, but I settled down here after I got out of bed and found Butch and Sundance just starting on the TV, and I haven't moved since."

Esmeralda opened the Dunkin' Donuts bag, took out two large coffees, and handed him one. Then she pulled out another smaller bag from inside and handed that to him too.

"I didn't know how you like your coffee, so I got yours like I like mine, just a little cream and three sugars. There's a couple of donuts in there too."

He put the coffee and donuts on the floor, grabbed the ashtray off his chest, and swung his legs off the couch so that he was sitting. He put the ashtray on the end table next to the couch, picked up his coffee, and took a delicate sip.

"I normally take mine light and sweet, but, hey, this is fine. Thanks for the donuts too. That was nice of you." He opened the bag, grabbed a greasy donut, and took a large bite.

"Skooley, why did you do it?"

He looked at her as he chewed, then took another sip of coffee.

"Do what?"

"Go back into the bar last night. Why didn't you just go back to your room or come straight here? I thought you were leaving."

He looked at her some more, then took another bite of donut and chewed thoughtfully.

"I told you last night. I left my cigarettes in the bar."

"You could have bought another pack on your way back here. I bought you another pack. They're right there on the counter in the kitchen. Why'd you have to go back into that fucking bar?"

"What'd you do, follow me? I thought you went back home to your momma, sleep in your own bed with your snuggle bear."

"I heard the sirens," she said. "My first thought was that it was you, that the cops were coming for you. You got in a fight with that drunk. Then I thought, no, Skooley's too smart for that. He wouldn't do something to stir up trouble, not when things were going so good. Not when we found all that money and jewelry and then that key. Why would he go back into the bar? For a few lousy cigarettes? No way. Or maybe because he wanted to get even with some drunken kid that bumped into him? That didn't make sense either. No, I said, Skooley's too smart for all that. Must be someone called the cops on some kids at a house party getting loud or maybe a car accident, you know, a fender bender."

"Well," he said, swiveling his head to take in the room,

"you don't see no cops in here. I didn't sleep in no lock-up last night; I slept snug as a bug in that nice big bed right upstairs. So tell me, girl, who peed in your oatmeal this morning? Why exactly are you giving me a bag of shit to go along with this nice bag of donuts you brung? What do you know that I don't know?"

"Wait here," she said. "I'll show you."

She got up, walked back into the kitchen, reached into the Shop Rite bag, and pulled out the newspaper. She flipped through the pages as she walked back to the family room until she found the page with the article detailing the assault and that nice picture of Skooley smiling happily right after he left the two young men dazed and bloody on the floor.

She handed Skooley the paper, then walked over to an easy chair on the other side of the room and peeled back the small tab on the plastic lid of her Styrofoam coffee cup and took a sip.

"See that? You're a celebrity now, Skooley. Got your picture in the paper and everything."

Skooley read the article slowly. She could see from the look on his face that even he understood that this was not good news.

"I never saw no one with a camera. How'd they get this photo? Security camera?"

"No, iPhone. I'd be very surprised if someone didn't film the whole episode on their phone. If they did, you'll probably end up a celebrity by later today."

"What do you mean?"

"A video, Skooley. People shoot videos with their phones all the time. Then they send them to their friends, or to the papers just like this girl did, or post them to YouTube so that everybody in the whole fucking world can see them."

Skooley didn't say anything for a minute. He just kept looking down at the paper. Finally, he looked up at her and said, "They don't mention my name here, and besides, ain't nobody in this town knows who I am. Them boys ain't hurt bad. Geez, town like that with all them drunk kids, they must

have fights every night. I can't believe it even made the paper."
He closed the paper and dropped it on the floor next to the
bag of donuts.

"Did you see that last line? The one where the cops are
asking for anyone who knows who that smiling guy in the
photo is to call."

He looked at her and smiled. "You ain't fixin' to dime me,
are you?"

"Of course not. It's not me you need to worry about. I
don't really know you. I just met you yesterday. But I do
know that you worked with Raymundo washing dishes at the
restaurant. So he knows you. And if he knows you, I'm sure
some of the other dishwashers know you too. And maybe
some of the waiters and bartenders. I bet you already hit on
most of the waitresses, too. And your boss, he sure knows
who you are. Has your name and address and social security
number. They don't pay off the books there, so you had to
give him something. Maybe you have a fake ID, I don't know.
Maybe your name isn't even Skooley. But someone is going to
call the cops and tell them whatever they know about you.
You can count on it."

"I think you got to take it easy there, Esmeralda. This ain't
nuthin'. This will blow over in a day or so. Who's gonna
care? Them two big boys that got beat up by one lone skinny
guy? Hell, I was them, I'd be ashamed of myself. And there
weren't no damage done to the bar. Nothing got broke or
busted up, 'cept maybe a beer bottle or two. Hell, this just
means free publicity for them. Gets the name of their place in
the paper. They're probably happy as hell."

Esmeralda took a sip of coffee. Then shook her head slowly.
"This isn't good, Skooley. I know you think it's no big deal,
but this isn't Florida. If this happened in some other town
around here, someplace a bit more blue-collar, then maybe it
would be okay. But not Morristown. You've seen all the restaurants and bars and banks and stores. People with money

go there, and they spend plenty too. Those places, they don't like shit like this in the paper. You read the story. It wasn't written up as just a bar fight. It was an assault. It said that you walked up to that guy and hit him with a bottle from behind when he wasn't looking. Never said a word. You could have really hurt him, maybe even killed him. That's not a fight. People are going to be mad about this. The bars, they don't want stories like this getting out. They have enough problems with all the noise those drunken kids make going home at night. And what about that other guy? You didn't have any reason to hit him. He just bent down to help his friend. I'm sure he had no idea what was happening, and you hit him with a bottle too. Why'd you do that? Why'd you hit the second guy?"

"You ever been in a fight, Esmeralda? I bet you ain't. You see some boys go at it in the hallway when you was in high school or maybe seen something on the TV or in the movies and you think that's what it's like. Fair fight, may the best man win. That's one reason I like this here movie so much. You ever seen this movie? Remember the part where Butch and Sundance go back to the gang, and that big guy, he was in one of them old James Bond movies, had these metal teeth, I just love that guy; anyway, he challenges Butch to a fight, see if he can take over the gang? Well, Butch starts talking to him, you know, just to distract him, then, wham, he kicks old Metal Teeth right in the balls. That's more like what a real fight is."

"Skooley, what are you talking about?"

"What I mean is, there ain't no such thing as a fair fight. You either win or you don't. You hurt someone good or they put the hurt on you, them's your two choices. Kick 'em in the balls or hit 'em with a bottle, same thing. I hit that first guy from behind and didn't give him a chance to hit me first. Same with the second guy. I'd a given either one a minute to think, they would'a come after me. You saw the size of them two. What do you think they would'a done to a little guy like me? But who walked out of that bar? Who was smiling at the end of it all?"

"That's great, Skooley. You won. You really showed those two drunks who's boss. But why did you go back? Why even bother? It meant nothing. I don't get it."

Skooley reached into the bag of donuts on the floor and pulled out the last one and held it up in front of him.

"You mind if eat this last donut? You bought 'em, so it's your call. You can have it if you want it."

She shook her head.

"I guess it's just how I'm wired. I don't take shit from nobody. Never have. Even as a little kid. Didn't take shit from other kids, didn't take shit from teachers, didn't take shit from my old man. Got whupped on plenty too. That guy in the bar last night, he kept shoving into me, even after I asked him nice and polite to lay off, maybe move over some and I'd do the same. I weren't looking to start nothing. Then he done it again and told me to fuck off. I don't usually let people talk to me like that. You drug me out of there and I let you and that was good. But I left my smokes inside, and after I went in there to get 'em and seen that big guy and his buddy and I remembered how polite I was and what he said to me in return, well, it just happened is all. I shouldn't a done what I did, but it's done and I can't undo it. Maybe now he learned to keep his big mouth shut and not bother other people when they're having a quiet drink at the bar. You really think the cops are gonna bother about all this?"

"Yes, Skooley, I really do. And someone is going to call them. You can't go back to your room in Bernardsville. Where's your car? Is it registered in your name?"

"I ain't worried about the car. What you said about word spreading on the computer, was that bullshit? Is anyone outside of this here area gonna hear about this little incident?"

"What, you mean about the video on YouTube? No, I

wasn't lying. I don't know if anyone shot the whole thing on their phone, but if they did, it might end up on the internet. I think if someone sees you hit those guys and then they see you walking out with a big happy smile on your face, that's going to spread. It might go viral, you never know. Why are you asking?"

"I don't watch a lot of YouTube stuff. Or that Facebook."

"I'm not following you. Even if no one got video of the fight, word is still going to get out about who you are. Once the cops know, they'll probably tell the paper or the paper will just find out. Then that will probably be in a follow-up story."

"Will that be on the computer too? I mean the internet."

"Sure. I think every paper is on the internet now. Besides, you can find out anything on the computer. What's this all about?"

"Suppose someone else was looking for me. Suppose they was trying hard to find out where I was. Would it be easy for them to find this here story on the internet, get my name, find out what town this happened in?"

Esmeralda looked at Skooley. She took a sip of coffee. Skooley looked back at her, then took another bite of his donut.

"Are you talking about someone in, let's say, Miami?"

Skooley swallowed, then popped the remainder of the donut into his mouth.

"Maybe Miami," he said with his mouth full. "Does it matter where? I mean, does it make a difference where the computer is that they're using to look from?" He finished his donut, and she watched him upend his coffee cup and finish that in two long swallows.

She shook her head from side to side, getting a little frustrated. She wasn't tracking this. Then it hit her. He didn't own a smartphone. Probably hadn't used a computer since he was in grade school.

"It doesn't matter where the computer is that they're searching from, Skooley. I think what really matters is why they're searching. Because if they're really pissed off and searching hard, it won't take them very long at all to find this story."

"How long do you figure?"

"I couldn't say. Maybe no more than a day or two, again, depending on how hard they're looking. Maybe just a couple of hours. I'm no computer genius, but I used computers in high school. I had to look stuff up all the time. I still have an old laptop at home. Even my little brothers and sister look stuff up. If someone is good with a computer, shouldn't be too hard to find that story. I bet there are people or even companies you could hire to keep an eye out for stories about something or someone. What did you do, Skooley? Who's looking for you?"

Skooley grabbed the empty bag of donuts and stood up.

"I gotta use the toilet, then I'm going to take me a nice hot shower. We gotta wrap things up here at the house a bit more quickly than I thought. You was right about last night, going back to that bar was a mistake. I should of just left it be. But like I said before, what's done is done. You was right about Miami too. I'll tell you that little story when I get done getting cleaned up. And we gotta get that stuff we found yesterday to that fella in New York City soon, see how much money we can get out of him. I think we got some good merchandise. Maybe take care of it later today if I can get a hold of the guy. Means I gotta get one of them pay-as-you-go phones too, leave no trace. And we gotta find this guy's lockbox. Busy day ahead, girl."

She watched him put his empty coffee cup into the donut bag, then watched as he walked back toward the kitchen in his underwear, absently scratching the left cheek of his backside. On the TV, Butch and Sundance blew up a train car with too much dynamite, splinters of wood and burnt dollar bills blowing in the wind.

THIRTY

"You ever hear the name Fernando Rincone? They also call him El Marano."

"The Pig?"

"Is that what it means? Well, yeah, I can see that makes sense. Man's got his appetites, that's for sure. Well, he's the fella that's looking for me."

"Why is he looking for you?"

"On account of Diggs."

"Diggs?"

"Yeah, he's a guy I knew growing up. We used to pal around together, even played baseball in the little league. Diggs got himself all tattooed up and bought a beat-up old Harley, had dreams of being one of them badass biker dudes, then he robbed a liquor store a few towns over from where we lived and cut out for the big city."

"Miami?"

"Or thereabouts. Understand, Miami ain't just a city, it's more like a bunch of towns. People hear Miami and they think hi-rise apartments and hotels and restaurants and South Beach. Well, all that is there, sure, but most of Miami is a great big shithole. Diggs rents this little house, more like a shack really, surrounded by Mexicans and niggers." He looked over at Esmeralda and smiled his great-guy smile. "No offense. I never seen such a dump as this place he got, and I've seen some dumps. Say, you want some more coffee? They got a Mr. Coffee. I used it yesterday. Maybe you could brew us up a pot?"

They were seated in the breakfast room. Esmeralda went into the kitchen and pushed the button that turned on the Keurig sitting on the counter.

"That's a coffee maker? I thought so, but I couldn't figure out how the damn thing works. Found the Mr. Coffee in that food closet."

Esmeralda walked to the pantry and found a full box of Green Mountain Dark Magic K-cups and brought it back out to the kitchen. She reached into one of the cabinets and took out a jar of Coffee Mate and a sugar bowl, brought them to the breakfast room, then made two cups of coffee and brought them to the table as well.

"Why did you go to Digg's place in Miami? You weren't living there, were you?"

"No, I had me a crappy little apartment in Bonita Beach. That's on the other side of the state. Was working for a contractor. I like doing construction work, was helping this carpenter, doing framing and storm repairs and such. But I got laid off. Got a call one night from Diggs, all stoned, tells me to come to Miami for a few days, he'd show me around. Maybe get me some work. So off I went."

"And he got you a job working for El Marano?"

"Well, not exactly. See, Diggs does a little dealing, so he knows this guy, or knows of this guy. Diggs ain't no kind of player. Deals a little weed, coke, probably uses more than he sells. Still likes to hit a gas station or liquor store every now and again. Thinks he's the world's greatest stick-up man. Says it's easy money. But I never seen the guy carrying more than pocket change. Got mostly mush between his ears. But we growed up together, and he knows from experience that I ain't opposed to a little breaking and entering, and he knows I'm pretty good at it too. See, we robbed a few places together when we was kids. Anyway, he tells me about this place, a condo in one of them walled-in country clubs. Tells me he knows the guy and that the guy's got money and that he'd be out of town for a few days. Simple job. All I had to do was throw him a percentage."

"And it was El Marano's house?"

"Sort of. It was a house owned by El Marano's organization."

"What organization?"

"You ever hear of the Jumbo Cartel?"

"Are you kidding? Anyone who reads a newspaper knows them. You robbed a house owned by them? You have any idea how many people they've killed? You must be crazy!"

"I didn't know it was owned by them at the time I was robbing it. Old Diggs, he neglected to mention that little fact until after. The place wasn't a big mansion or anything. It was just a nice condo in an exclusive development. I guess they use it for entertaining mid-level guys, let 'em play golf and fuck whores and such. I don't know, but I do know it wasn't anyone's main house. It had the feel like a place where they did business. Like a hotel. No personal stuff inside, just stuff to decorate the place. Even smelled like a hotel."

"How did they find out it was you?"

"I guess Diggs told them."

"Why would he do that?"

"I guess he must've let it slip whilst they was cutting off his fingers."

"They cut off his fingers?" Esmeralda was horrified.

"Yeah. I heard they cut off every one. Put 'em in a pickle jar and took 'em back and showed 'em to El Marano. Least that's what I heard."

"And now they're looking for you?"

"I tried to make it right. Remember last night I told you about the box I found behind the electric socket? This was the house where I found it. Was nothing else to steal in that place. That's why I started pulling out sockets. I figured had to be something there. That box had about forty-thousand dollars stuffed inside. I also found a little notebook with all these numbers written by hand in columns, like some kind of code I guess. Also, two of them little computer sticks, know the ones I mean?"

"Flash drives?"

"I guess. Once I learned about what Diggs had gotten me into, I put together a package and mailed that stuff right back to the address where I stole it from. Wrote a nice note apologizing, you know, explaining that I didn't know who owned the house, gave back the book and the computer sticks, told him I ain't never opened 'em up or copied 'em or nothing. Just wanted to make things right."

"What about the money? Did you give him back the money?"

"I gave back most of it. I kept a little 'cause I figured I'd have to get myself gone no matter what. And I was gonna need something to help with that."

"You didn't give him any of that money back, did you, Skooley? You kept the money. You kept all of it."

Smart girl, he thought, looking her right in the eyes. Maybe I can use a smart girl right now, help me get what I'm after. But maybe I don't need a smart girl shooting her mouth off after I'm gone. He smiled at her, his best friendly smile, and wondered to himself if she had ever tried Spam before, if maybe he could offer to cook her up a little breakfast tomorrow morning, after everything got settled.

"Yeah, you got me. I kept the money. I was hoping he'd be happy just to get back those other things. Guys like him, they wipe their asses with hundred-dollar bills. Forty-thousand dollars ain't but a drop in the bucket. I bet he spends more than that just one night in one of them fancy South Beach nightclubs, salsa dancing and drinking tequila and champagne."

"How did they find Diggs?"

"I don't know for sure, but I got a suspicion that my good buddy Diggs thought he might be able to make a few bucks off me, you know, sell some information, get himself in good with the Cartel honchos. That ain't gospel, that's just what I suspect. But like I told you already, Diggs wasn't too smart. I know for a fact that he never could have worked out in his own head that Cartel guys ain't gonna pay some lame-brained nobody for information that they could just as easy take for nothing. It was like the way he set me up in the first place, didn't say nothing about that El Marano or about the Cartel owning that place until after I went in. Then he told me like it was some kind of joke."

"What'd you do next?"

"I went home to Bonita Beach just as fast as I could get there. Got me a room at a motel right across the street from my apartment. Kept an eye out, see what I could see. Made up a travel bag, which I kept under the bed with most of the money and a few odds and ends, ready to boogie. Didn't see anything for a couple of days. Then one night I went out to the Seven-Eleven to pick up some cigarettes. Was nighttime, about nine-thirty or so, I seen some guys pull up and park in front of my old apartment building. Four guys got out, two go upstairs to my apartment. I see the lights go on inside. I'm about to sneak over to the motel, get my boogie bag and get on my horse and ride. Then I seen the other two guys who stayed outside with the car walk over to my motel. One guy goes inside and talks to the guy working the desk, that's when I know I'm toast. The two guys come down from my apartment; they all meet in the motel parking lot and head over to my motel room. I seen one guy pull out a sawed-off shotgun from under his jacket. That's the last I seen of them 'cause I was gone. I left most of their money in that bag. Probably about thirty-five of the forty thousand. I kept a few grand in my pocket. I started carrying it with me, just in case such a situation should come up. I hated to lose all that money, I surely did, but I guess I was lucky to just get out of there alive. And they say smoking is bad for your health, shit, that pack of cigarettes saved my ass."

"Well, that pack you went back to the bar for last night doesn't seem like it's doing your health prospects a whole lot of good right now, does it?"

"Boy, you got a mouth on you, girl."

"Skooley, do you think they followed you here, to New Jersey, I mean? Is there any chance they're already here, looking for you? Even before last night?"

"No, they ain't here yet. But I bet they still got an interest in my whereabouts. I don't think they'll keep at it for too much longer, though. They already killed Diggs. That was for show, you know, like anybody fucks with us, this is what's gonna happen. So they don't need another dead body. But that guy, El Marano, I bet he'd like to have a few more fingers for his collection or maybe get himself a nice blond-haired head hung up on his wall, just for his own satisfaction. But how much money you think he's going to spend to get back forty thousand? No, wait, to get back five thousand. He'll spend money for the sport of it, tracking down the guy broke into one of his houses, but he don't find me quick, he'll give it up. There's just no up-side for him to keep spending time and money on this. I just got to lay low for a few more months, not get myself caught. And then stay the hell away from Florida."

"This story, the one in the newspaper, do you think they'll have someone checking the internet, looking for something about you to pop up?"

"Well, it sure sounds easy. If it was me looking for him and it didn't cost much, I guess I'd sure do it."

"Yeah," she agreed, "I would too."

"I'm going to run down to Walmart, buy me a go phone. When I get back, let's take another look at what we found. I wanna try and come up with some kind of dollar value in my head. I gotta have some idea of what a fair price will be to get from that guy in New York. I hate to go in stupid, be totally at his mercy. Then we'll figure our next move. You start looking for that lockbox."

Esmeralda looked down at her coffee cup. Things were moving fast and getting more and more complicated.

"And, girl." Skooley smiled at her, but not his friendly smile, not even close. This one made his face look like that of a hungry reptile and it unnerved her. "You best be here when I get back, you hear? We're partners now, you and me. We got to look out for each other, ride this to the finish. You let me down, I shit you not, won't be no place you can hide from me, understand? Not your momma and the kiddies neither."

THIRTY-ONE

She had to call Raymundo. She didn't know what else to do. Skooley was a psycho, no doubt about it. And he had killers after him. The kind that cut off people's fingers and sometimes their hands and feet and arms and heads. She had read plenty about the Jumbo Cartel, and everything she remembered reading frightened her. When they killed, they killed indiscriminately—men, women, children, it didn't matter. And usually, the deaths were horrific. Like Diggs. And if those killers happened to find a little Colombian cleaning girl mixed up with Skooley, what would happen to her? She didn't want to think about it.

Maybe she should call the police. But she was sure, absolutely sure, that other people would be calling them. Just like she had told Skooley, dishwashers, waiters, definitely his boss at the restaurant, someone would pick up the phone and tell the cops who he was. The phone at police headquarters was probably ringing off the hook right now. Maybe all she had to do was wait, be careful, stay alert, and the cops would do their jobs, maybe have Skooley locked up before he even got back from Walmart.

Gotta call Raymundo. Maybe he would finally pick up his goddamn phone. She decided to call using her cell phone. He would recognize her number. She was in this deep already, so what if someone had a record of her calling him. He was a friend. They worked together.

She was nervous. No, she was scared. Skooley scared her

more than anything. He had killers after him, and it didn't really seem to faze him. And that smile in the picture. He enjoyed bashing those boys. She opened the pack of cigarettes she had bought for him and took one out. She felt claustrophobic in the kitchen, like she couldn't get enough air and decided to have her cigarette outside, maybe sit by the pool and clear her head. She shook another cigarette out of the pack and put that one in her shirt pocket. There was a plastic Bic lighter on the counter, and she put that in her pocket too. She grabbed her smartphone from out of her pocketbook and walked out the back door. She went into the pool area through the gate and sat on one of the lounge chairs there on the cement right next to the hot tub where she had sat when she first laid eyes on Skooley. She tried to light her cigarette and noticed that her hands were shaking. She wished she had never said anything to that asshole Raymundo about this house. Now here she was stealing from these nice people, stuck with a redneck psychopath who had just threatened her if she decided she wanted to call it quits and just bug out, a guy who just happened to have both the police and a drug cartel hit squad trying to catch him and cut off his fingers and head to bring back to their boss, The Pig. She would have laughed, but she couldn't bring herself even to smile.

Nothing funny about this, she thought, nothing funny at all.

She got her cigarette lit and thought about what to say to Raymundo if he picked up his phone. Tell him about the cartel hunting for Skooley? No, better just to tell him about the key they had found and the treasure chest they were looking for. Get him interested enough to come back, then warn him to be careful about Skooley. What if he didn't pick up, what then? She should leave a message but say what? What could she say that would make him call her back? She decided that if he didn't pick up, she wouldn't leave a message. Just keep calling until he answered. He'd see her number, he'd know who was calling. If he didn't want to talk to her, no message she could leave would make him call back anyway.

She smoked her cigarette almost down to the filter, then put it out by dipping the ash end into the hot tub and flicked the wet butt into some bushes near the pool house. Then she called Raymundo's number.

She held the phone to her ear, rapidly tapping her foot on the cement without even realizing that she was doing it. The phone rang in her ear. A second later, she heard what might have been a musical tone, but it wasn't coming from the phone at her ear. She heard it with her other ear. Just an undercurrent of sound that was coming from somewhere in the distance, far away. It was so faint it almost didn't register. She didn't know what it was at first, and sort of split her concentration between hoping Raymundo would pick up the call and that other sound in the distance. The phone rang again, then again, and the musical notes still resonated in the distance. Then Raymundo's voice came on and, speaking in Spanish, asked the caller to leave a message. She took the phone away from her ear and hung up. The musical tone had stopped.

She sat there looking at her phone, thinking. Then she got up, walked away from the hot tub and out of the gate and away from the pool area out onto the back lawn. She dialed Raymundo's number again, but this time let the phone dangle by her side. The musical tone was still muted, but it was clearer now, seeming to be coming from the woods. She walked slowly toward the tree line and then the tone stopped. She put her phone to her ear and heard Raymundo's voice again, telling her to leave a message.

Esmeralda walked into the woods, moving slowly and quietly, picking her way around downed branches and loose leaves. About ten or fifteen yards in, she dialed Raymundo's phone again. And there it was, clear as a bell, off the left but not very far. It was a ringtone. She walked quickly now, following the sound of the ringing phone, wanting to find it before it went to voicemail again. And there it was, lying in the dirt under some dried leaves, the lit blue screen of a Samsung Galaxy just visible.

Raymundo's smartphone.

She picked up the phone and carried it back to the lounge chair by the hot tub. She set it down on the concrete floor, took the cigarette out of her shirt pocket and tried to light it with shaking fingers.

Raymundo didn't leave with any money. He may have found it, like Skooley said, in that shoebox that she knew about, but he never left with it. How could he have left? The bike that he rode to get here was still in the woods. He didn't call a friend or a cab. His phone was sitting right here on the concrete at her feet. How could he call without a phone? He didn't have a car. Skooley's car is still in Bernardsville. The one he's not worried about the police finding, so it's probably not really his. He must have stolen it to get out of Florida. Raymundo didn't take either of the Russells' cars, so where is Raymundo? A voice inside her head answered her in clear, serious voice. He's dead, Esmeralda. Skooley killed him. Yes, she thought, Skooley is a true, dyed-in-the-wool psychopath. Look what he did to those two poor kids last night. He attacked them with beer bottles. Hit them over the head from behind. And he enjoyed it. You saw his face in that picture. He was smiling, happy as a clam. Skooley has that money that he said Raymundo took. He has that money stashed away someplace. She began a silent conversation with the voice in her head. Maybe Raymundo walked away, through the woods, and dropped his phone. Maybe he's okay. No, there's no reason for him to go up in those woods unless someone took him up there. That's how he lost his phone. He dropped it or it fell out of his pocket.

Esmeralda felt a tear roll down her face as she finally go her cigarette lit. She inhaled the acrid smoke deep into her lungs, and then coughed it out as a sob welled up from someplace deep in her chest.

He's up there someplace all right, she thought, but he's not ever coming out of those woods.

THIRTY-TWO

The first thing Skooley had to do was go back to his room in Bernardsville and pick up a few things. What he had told Esmeralda about his little escapade back in Miami a few weeks ago was mostly true. And she had guessed correctly that he had not returned the money to that fat pig, Fernando Rincone, even though those goons he had sent after him did end up with most of it back. What she hadn't guessed was that the whole story about returning the little book and those computer sticks was just that, a story. Those were what he had to retrieve from his room in Bernardsville. He knew those little items were worth a hell of a lot more than that cash that he had found in the box. He just had to be smart about how to collect on them, that's all. He was sure that nobody but he and El Marano knew that he had them. If others in the Jumbo Cartel found out that their man in Miami had been ripped off and lost not only money, but even more importantly, coded information, it would be pig's knuckles and a big fat pig's head that would end up in a pickle jar headed back to Colombia or Mexico or wherever the hell those drug cartel guys came from. He just had to put some time and distance between him and his pursuers right now, and then he could figure out how best to contact the big pig and begin negotiations. Better yet, maybe he'd jump over El Marano and contact someone else in the organization, look like a hero and get rid this piggy problem at the same time. Had to figure out how to copy all that stuff first, make himself a nice insurance policy.

He parked the Range Rover a few blocks away, then walked over to the block that ran parallel to the rooming house and cut across the property directly behind so he could enter from the back. The place was quiet, and he saw no one as he quietly made his way up the staircase to the hallway on the second floor and entered his room. He had the book and computer sticks all in different drawers of the beat-up old dresser that came with the room. He hadn't tried to hide them, figuring that if someone broke in looking for things to steal, they just wouldn't seem valuable enough to take. Then he went to his closet and reached up on the shelf and came down with a roll of bills wrapped in an old handkerchief. He had about three hundred dollars in it, and that was what he had left for any thief to find. Next, he reached under the rickety low end table near the window on which he kept a small reading lamp and pulled out an envelope he had taped to the bottom. This one had just over two thousand dollars, the money he still had left over from Miami. He had planned to wash dishes and lay low for a few weeks, use this cash as needed until things quieted down some. Then he met Ray and this whole thing in Mendham got started. Not a bad thing, really. And he was going to have a lot more cash soon. Still, he did wish now that he hadn't fucked up those two guys last night, even though it was them that started things. Well, what he really wished was that the little cunt with the phone hadn't taken his picture. That picture and the newspaper article were definitely going to bring those cartel goons here, and quickly. He didn't know how much time he had, but he knew that he had to get gone fast.

He looked around and there was really nothing else he wanted to take. So he checked the hallway and then made his way downstairs and out the back door.

He was sitting in the Range Rover, thinking. The two computer sticks had little eyelets on the ends, and he slipped each of them onto the key ring of his stolen Toyota. The book he put in his pocket. He wanted to keep these items on him at all times now. No telling if or when he'd have to run. He knew of only one Walmart that was close by, the next town over from Morristown. He wasn't sure of the name of the town or the name of the street, but he knew how to get there. It was in a mall with a Sears and a Dollar Store and some kind of supermarket. On the way over, he began thinking about what to do about Esmeralda. He was pretty sure that she had to go. There was only one person that he knew of so far that could connect them and that was Ray, and he wasn't going to be saying anything to anyone. Ever. But with the cops looking for him, should he take a chance on doing the girl? She was part of this Mendham deal now and so she couldn't really go and shoot her mouth off. Unless she lost her nerve and just decided to give them both up. Then he was probably in for it. If he went to jail anywhere, those Jumbo boys could take care of him inside, easy. He was sure of it. He opened the glove box and was reassured to see the gun he had taken from under the mattress still there. Wait until after he got his phone, then it might be a good idea to start carrying that little popgun in his pocket instead of leaving it here in the car where it wasn't doing him much good. He also had Ray's revolver still stashed under the couch cushions. He reached around and felt under the back floor mat. There was the envelope with the money he had found in the closet of the office. He also felt the leather wallet with the cash he had found under the mattress. He added his envelope with the two grand from his rooming house. He would take a full count later, when he got back from New York, and see how much cash he would walk away with total. That might be the deciding factor about what to do with the girl. If he got rid of her, maybe he could use something in Ray's wallet, tie it back to him somehow. He had to think on it.

He got to Walmart and found a cheap flip phone and bought one-hundred-twenty minutes of airtime. He wasn't planning on hanging onto the phone past tomorrow, but better safe than sorry. He also bought a car charger for it so he could start getting the thing ready right away. He was planning on calling New York as soon as he got back to the house. He was hoping Esmeralda would find that lockbox, but he was pretty certain she wouldn't. He wasn't sure if he could find it either, given that his time frame was getting shorter by the minute. He needed to get going by tomorrow morning, by afternoon at the very latest. El Marano would send his own boys after him, but he might make a few calls and have some local muscle start sniffing around, see if they could collar him before the heavy hitters got here. Plus, if the cops got any leads, he was sure it would take all of about ten seconds for that information to find its way back to Miami. Lockbox or no, he had to boogie. Could always put that key back in its hidey-hole, maybe come back same time next year for another look-see.

Right now, he thought, all I need is enough cash to stay hid for a few weeks. Soon as I find me someplace new, I'm going to just stay the hell indoors and drink me some Stellas and get caught up on some serious TV watching.

THIRTY-THREE

Esmeralda went into the kitchen and absently started unpacking the Shop Rite bag. She took out the chopped meat and vegetables and the flashlights and Diet Pepsi. She didn't know what she was going to do. She had turned Raymundo's phone off and stashed it behind some old rum bottles on the bottom shelf of the bar in the pool house. She didn't want Skooley to know about the phone. He might guess that she knew about what he had done to Raymundo, and that wouldn't be good for her. It might be best to call the police, she thought, and just get it over with. At least she'd be away from Skooley. Then she thought, if Raymundo really was lying somewhere up in those trees dead and Skooley killed him, wouldn't that make her an accessory? She didn't know. Skooley would probably lie, try and point the finger at her. At the very least he'd say she helped him or that she planned it and he'd make sure that she got screwed too. She couldn't just walk away anymore. Not after that threat he had made before he left. This guy is a killer, she thought, a real nutcase. And he knew about her family, about her mom and her little sister and brothers. She hadn't told him where she lived, but how hard could it be for him to find them? She didn't even want to think about that.

She was scared, but she was also getting angry.

She opened the two flashlight packages and put the batteries in them, then turned them on to make sure they worked. They were heavy, and she felt the heft of one of them in her hand

166

and thought, if needed, it would make a decent club. Maybe sneak up on that redneck like he did those boys last night, whack him on the head. So she put the second flashlight in a cabinet under the sink. Better that he not have a club too, she thought. She also went into one of the counter drawers and found an old paring knife. She rolled up her pant leg and slid the knife into her sock. If it comes to it, she thought, a fighting chance is better than no chance.

She made her way upstairs and started thinking about the lockbox. Where in the world would Mr. Russell hide something like that? She went back to their bedroom. Skooley said most people hid their good stuff there. She peeked into the closet. No, she had searched every inch of both closets, so had Skooley. She walked into the master bath. She hadn't really searched in there. She looked in the shower, then removed the lid from the toilet's reservoir tank and looked in there. The clothes hamper was empty. She looked in the linen closet and moved all the spare towels and checked inside a wooden box that had mostly over-the-counter medications. She even pushed at the wall behind the shelves, looking for a secret compartment. Next she looked in the medicine cabinet behind the mirror over one of the two sinks. There were all sorts of prescription pill bottles of various sizes and liniment tubes like Neosporin and Preparation-H and small items like nail clippers and emery boards and deodorants in there. She started pulling the pill bottles out one at a time—Percocet, Ambien, Valium, Sonata, Lipitor—it was like a pharmacy in there. She looked at the labels. Every bottle was prescribed for Mrs. Russell, none for her husband. Strange, she thought, Mrs. Russell always seemed so healthy and alert. Her husband was the one who seemed like he might be suffering from some sort of health problems. He was a little overweight and his face always seemed red, like he might have high blood pressure or something. She recognized most of the names, having seen just about all of them advertised on TV at one time or another.

She didn't see anything else in the cabinet and so slid the mirror closed and moved on to the drawers and cabinets under the vanity.

Nothing. There was nothing here.

She lay down on the bed like she had yesterday evening and stared at the ceiling.

Was it really only yesterday when this all had started, she thought? It felt like a lot longer than just a day.

It felt like a lifetime ago.

THIRTY-FOUR

Loretta looked at herself in the bathroom mirror. Her eyes were red, and tears had made the black mascara drip down her cheeks, reminding her of an old Alice Cooper album cover she had seen at some point in her youth and that made her smile. Her mouth tasted of coffee and stomach acid, so she cupped her hands under the faucet, then gargled with tap water and spit into the sink.

Jeez-zus, she thought to herself as she gazed at her reflection in the mirror, you look like hell. She washed her face, then reached into her purse and took out the small makeup bag that she always carried with her, and refreshed her look. That done, she ran a brush through her hair, applied lipstick, cupped her hand and breathed into it, then quickly sniffed to see if she could still detect the scent of vomit on her breath. She rummaged around her purse until she found an old packet of Orbit gum and popped one of the little white candies into her mouth.

She left the hotel bathroom and walked toward the lobby. To her left past the front desk was the hotel's sports bar. She knew she shouldn't do it, but her nerves were shot and she could really, really use a Bloody Mary. She walked past the desk clerk and entered the bar. It was deserted except for one lone bartender who appeared to be re-stocking shelves with fresh bottles of liquor from a cardboard box.

"Are you open yet?" she asked as cheerfully as she could muster.

The bartender looked over at her. "Are you a guest at the

hotel?" he asked.

"No," she said, "I'm just waiting for someone."

"Ah, what the hell," he said and smiled at her as he lifted the box with the liquor bottles off of the counter and laid it down on the floor. He then grabbed a towel from somewhere under the bar and began wiping his hands as he walked over to where she stood at the bar.

"What can I get for you, miss?"

"You are a doll! How about a Bloody Mary, and can you give it just a little kick? I need something to get me going this morning."

"Coming right up."

Loretta pulled a ten-dollar bill out of her wallet and laid it on the bar.

She took her drink over to one of the tables near the window that looked out over the parking lot. She didn't feel like making small talk with the bartender. Luckily, he was busy getting ready to open for the day, and he didn't seem to mind her moving over to the empty table. The drink felt good going down. It was spicy, just as she requested, and that, along with the alcohol, warmed her and seemed to fill an emptiness inside. She was beginning to feel a little better now. The call to the police station had been emotional for her. The shame and revulsion she had felt the morning after her assault seemed to come back at her all at once. But her head was starting to clear now, the vitamins in the tomato juice along with the vodka doing their magic.

What can I do to hurt him, she wondered? I can't do anything since I can't even find him, but the police can. I've got the cops in Morristown looking for him, but they were already looking. She pulled out her smartphone and connected to the internet. She looked up the phone number for the Mendham police department, found a pen and a small notebook in her purse, and wrote the number down. Then she looked up the number for the police department in Morris Plains and wrote it down as well.

170

Morristown, Mendham, and Morris Plains, those were the only towns that she could definitely connect him to. She would call those other two departments as well. She was sure she could control herself on the phone this time around. The gun. When she had mentioned the gun to the cop in Morristown, that was when he had really begun to take notice. That was a good idea. She would make more of it this time around. Say he was wearing a shoulder holster. No, that could make him sound like he was some kind of a detective or private eye. She'd just say she saw the butt of a gun sticking out of his waistband. A big gun. Okay, make the calls, what else? Maybe take a ride over to her real estate company's branch office in Mendham. She knew some of the folks who worked there. Maybe she could mention the conversation about the property this asshole Ray had told her about. It was a bullshit story, she knew, but still, maybe he had actually been on the property and just enhanced the story for her benefit. Maybe someone might have heard something or been on a similar property, or maybe one of the employees might even have seen this guy driving around town in his green Range Rover. It was a long shot, she knew, but she wasn't doing anything this afternoon anyway. Besides, it shouldn't take more than about an hour or so. Plus, it would feel good actually doing something, not just sitting around waiting for the police to catch him.

She finished her drink and toyed with the idea of having another. No, she really shouldn't even have had this one. She realized that alcohol could very easily become a problem for her. Hell, look at what already happened this weekend! But that one drink to calm her nerves was understandable.

But another drink, well, perhaps another really wasn't.

She brought her empty glass back up to the bar, got four quarters in change for the phone, and thanked the bartender again. Then she headed back through the lobby toward the bank of phones, this time actually looking forward to talking to the cops.

THIRTY-FIVE

Skooley headed back to Mendham, the new phone sitting on the passenger seat charging with a cord connecting it to the Range Rover's cigarette lighter. He was trying to think what else he would need to get him through until tomorrow. Next order of business was to check the loot bag, and then call New York and get that deal done. Probably be best to leave the girl at the house, keep searching for that lockbox. What good would it do to have her with him in New York? She didn't need to know nothing. He'd be nice when he got back, turn on the charm, tell her they'd make the split when he got back. He was still not sure she wouldn't just leave, call the cops, give them both up. Maybe he'd give her some money before he left, like here's just a part of your share. Make her feel good, tell her we're partners again, remind her that she'll go to jail too if it comes down to it, and if she does, what will her poor momma and them little kids do then? Then, tonight, I'll show her the money, make nice, drink a few beers, and maybe get her into the sack.

Or maybe just put her in a sack and bury her ass in the woods next to her old buddy Ray-mun-do.

Beer. He wasn't sure how much he had left, but better to get everything now while he was out and not have to go scrambling around later. He drove into Morristown and around The Green and then turned right onto Washington Street and kept on driving for several miles up into Mendham. When he got to Main Street, he pulled into the little shopping mall by the Kings Supermarket and parked the Range Rover in the middle of the crowded lot and walked over to the liquor store where he had bought beer yesterday. The store was open, and he got a twelve-pack of Stella out of the icebox and asked the guy behind the counter for another pack of Marlboro Lights and paid for it all and was walking out of the store when he looked up and saw a police cruiser slowly idling past his Range Rover. Skooley immediately turned left and ambled along the walkway, looking in store windows and casually making his way toward Kings. The cruiser drove past the Range Rover and around the next line of cars and then almost out to Main Street, but instead of leaving the lot, he parked out of the way and left the car idling. Skooley figured he could have just been enjoying a coffee and a donut or maybe setting up radar or he could have been keeping an eye out, see who got into the dark green Range Rover. Maybe that little cunt with the camera phone had followed him out of the bar last night. Maybe she saw him get into the Range Rover. Maybe she told the cops and they told the paper to keep that little tidbit out of the news story. Skooley entered a stationery store and found himself interested in the greeting cards and knickknacks that were near the window that looked out over the parking lot and waited to see what the cop would do. After about ten minutes, the cop must have gotten a call because he pulled quickly out of the lot, turned sharply, and accelerated up Main Street.

Skooley strolled over to the Range Rover, got in, put the beer on the floor in front of the passenger seat, then opened the glove box, pulled the Beretta out, and set it on the seat next to his brand-new go phone. He drove slowly out of the parking lot and turned in the opposite direction that the cop had. He drove about a quarter of a mile down Main Street and had to stop behind two other cars at a traffic light. Suddenly, the car directly in front of him gunned its engine, pulled out and around the first car with a screech of burning rubber, leaving dark black skid marks on the pavement. The car accelerated through the red light and hauled ass down the road. Schooley looked on in utter amazement. What in the hell got into that asshole, he wondered? He's gonna kill someone driving like that. Where's a fucking cop when you need one, he thought absently as he put on his blinker and then slowly and carefully turned left onto Cold Hill Road and made his way back toward the house.

THIRTY-SIX

The trip to the Mendham office had been a waste of time. Everyone had been busy, running in and out, gathering lawn signs and making copies of listing information getting ready for the Open Houses that were going on all over town that day. Loretta had smiled a lot and tried to be helpful, but no one really had the time to talk to her. She realized after she had arrived that she wasn't even sure of what to ask. She couldn't describe the property that she was interested in, didn't know where in town it was located, didn't have the owner's name or even a good description of the house. If she simply started asking random questions, people might think she was looking for leads or trying to steal clients, as Mendham really wasn't her sales territory. The real estate business was cutthroat, and with the economy being what it was, everybody was both protective of their business and wary of their colleagues. So she just told everyone that she happened to be driving by and stopped in to use the bathroom and to see if she could help in any way.

She actually did use the restroom to pee and then sat down at one of the empty sales desks and used the phone to call her own office just to check in. Then she waved goodbye and headed out toward her car.

There was a small bakery right next door to the real estate office. Her stomach was empty after throwing up her breakfast earlier and so she stopped in and ordered a coffee and a croissant and then sat at one of the small tables and thought about her morning so far.

The calls to the Mendham and Morris Plains police departments had gone well. She began by mentioning the article in the paper and about seeing the photo and recognizing him as the man who had assaulted and raped her. She gave them his name and description and the make, model, and color of the car he was driving and kept her composure throughout, embellishing her story only a bit, skipping the part about being drunk and inviting him in and instead saying that he must have slipped something into her drink because after just one glass of wine she nearly passed out. Then he forced his way into her apartment and hit her before raping her. She also mentioned the gun. That had gotten the policemen's attention, just as it had the Morristown cop's, and they peppered her with questions. But she kept to her story and once or twice came close to breaking down again, but this time that worked in her favor. She sipped her coffee and nibbled at her croissant and fantasized about meeting Ray Mundy again, thinking about what she would do to him. She bet he would think twice about even getting near her when she was sober—and angry. She was strong and relatively fit. She remembered him as being a rather slight and skinny man. Dangerous, for sure, just had to read that story in the paper again. But still, she liked her odds as she contemplated seeing him again while she sat there in the quaint Mendham bakery, the pleasant smells of fresh rolls and coffee wafting through the air.

Her cell phone rang, interrupting her reverie, and she put down her croissant and dug through her purse until she found her phone and then looked at the number, which said private caller. She answered cautiously.

"Hello?"

"Hello. Is this Loretta Taylor?" The voice had a slight Hispanic accent.

"Who's calling, please?"

"This is Detective Fernando Alvarez of the Miami Police

Department. Are you Loretta Taylor?"

"Yes, I'm Loretta." Loretta was at once alarmed and confused. Why would the police be calling her? And from Miami?

"Miss Taylor, I'm sorry to surprise you with this telephone call. I am calling about a man you met recently. He told you his name is Ray Mundy, but that is not his true name."

"How did you get this number? I didn't give this number to anyone." Loretta heard herself almost snapping at the voice on the other end of the phone. She was upset and she was scared and receiving this unexpected call made her angry.

"You called a reporter at a local newspaper recently. She retrieved your number from her caller ID."

"But I didn't give her permission to give this number out. How can she give out my number without my permission?"

"Miss Taylor, you called her with information. You did not give your name, but you never specifically directed her to not divulge your phone number. Now, please, this is a very serious matter. I am calling you as a courtesy. I can also have some men, police officers, come to your home and bring you in for questioning if you would prefer."

"To Miami?" She was not trying to be funny when she said this.

"No, we are working with local law enforcement in New Jersey. The man we are seeking, the man you know as Ray Mundy, is wanted in Miami. He is facing some very serious charges. You would do well to cooperate with us, Miss Taylor. It would be to your benefit."

"I don't want to get involved with this. That's why I didn't give anyone my name. How did you find me again?"

"Miss Taylor, if you cooperate right now, on the phone, I promise you will not be bothered again. No one will come to your house. No one will call you again. We are trying to apprehend this man. When we find him, and we will find him, he will be brought back to Miami to face charges. I will personally see to it that he is locked away for a very long time.

But if you prefer, we can visit you at your home and make this a much more official interrogation. It is entirely your decision, Miss Taylor."

She was quiet for a minute.

"What did he do? In Miami, I mean?"

She heard the man on the other end let out a soft sigh.

"May I call you Loretta?" The man did not wait for an answer. "Loretta, first off, understand that it is I asking the questions, not you. But because I know that you will be cooperating, I will tell you that the man we seek is involved in the drug business. He is wanted for drug trafficking, aggravated assault, theft, and murder. So, you see, you were lucky to have escaped him unharmed. There are others that have not been so lucky, like those two young men last night. Now, please, tell me what you know."

And so she did. She told him what she had told the other cops and the reporter. She told him about the Range Rover and the story he had told her about his construction company and about his saying that he was staying in Mendham. The detective asked some questions about the car: did she notice the license plate, the year, any distinctive marks like scratches or dents? He asked what the man was wearing, if he had mentioned any address in Mendham or if he had described the place where he was staying, if he had mentioned any other bars or restaurants that he had frequented. But she had no other information to give him. Finally, he thanked her for her cooperation and asked her to call if she thought of anything further that could help the investigation and then he hung up.

Loretta slowly put the phone back into her purse. She was a little shaken, but as she thought about the phone call and what the detective had said, she began to feel better. Ray Mundy was going to get what was coming to him. Drugs, theft, murder, maybe that cop was right—maybe she really was lucky to have escaped that psychopath with her life.

And now at least she was sure something was being done.

That detective had said that he would personally see to it that Ray was locked away for a very long time. That was truly the most heartening thing she had heard since this nightmare had started, and it began to lift her spirits.

She picked up the remainder of her croissant and ate slowly and thoughtfully. When she was done eating, she cleaned off her table with a napkin, threw her empty coffee cup into the trash bin, walked outside, and headed over to her car. She got in and started heading down Main Street toward Morristown. She would stay straight on East Main Street until it turned into Mendham Road, then into Washington Street once she got into Morristown. Next, she would cut across town to Speedwell Avenue and take that to Route 53, then follow that right to her condo in Morris Plains.

She was just about a block past the Black Horse Tavern when a Mendham Township police cruiser came speeding down Main Street heading in the opposite direction. The police car had its emergency lights on, but no siren.

Maybe that Detective Alvarez from Miami was making things happen already. Maybe someone saw that green Range Rover and called it in. The thought of Ray Mundy in handcuffs warmed her heart, and she actually smiled as she drove through town.

The post office came up on her right, and she slowed down a bit as Tempewick Road met Main Street right there, and with the strip mall coming up on the left, the intersection was always busy. She glanced to her left just as she passed the post office, and there coming out of the Kings parking lot was a dark green Range Rover. Her breath caught in her throat and her heart started racing as beads of sweat almost instantaneously began forming on her forehead. She kept moving, and the Range Rover pulled in right behind her. She reached up with a trembling hand and readjusted the rearview mirror to better see the driver behind her.

It was him, Ray Mundy. He was driving the same dark

green Range Rover that he had been driving on Friday night. She felt a sudden, all-encompassing panic engulf her. She couldn't seem to get any air into her lungs. She could actually feel the muscle that was her heart hammering away in her chest and hear the blood pulsing rhythmically past her ear-drums. The car in front of her slowed down and she almost slammed into it. She wanted to lean on the horn.

"Move, you asshole!" she said out loud, and the volume and intensity that she heard in her own voice both surprised and scared her. She looked up and saw that the traffic light had turned red. There was just one car in front of her and Ray Mundy behind her.

"Move!" she shouted even louder, "Move, move!"

She turned the wheel and hit the gas, pushing the accelerator to the floor. Her tires screeched, and white smoke billowed behind her as her car bolted past the stunned driver in front. She blew through the red light, and cars on either side of her slammed on their brakes, skidding to avoid each other. Her car gained speed down Main Street, but she wasn't even look-ing in front of her, both eyes glued to the rearview mirror, straining to see if the dark green Range Rover was in pursuit. Her lungs felt like bursting, and she realized that she hadn't drawn in a breath since she had first spotted Ray Mundy pull-ing in behind her. She took a gulp of air and kept driving, hoping to hear a siren and see the red and blue flashing lights of a police car behind her. Where's a fucking cop when you need one, she thought! She didn't slow down until she reached Morristown.

She drove straight to her condo, deciding on the way that she was going to pack a bag as soon as she got home and head over to her younger sister's house down in Toms River. She could stay there with her. Her sister would be glad to see her. Maybe hang out together for a week or so, give the police a chance to do their jobs. She wasn't sure if that murdering, rapist asshole had seen her or not, but she wasn't taking any chances. He knew where she lived. Yes, she thought, get away from here. Put some miles between herself and this trouble. That's what she'd do.

Then she looked down at her purse lying there on the passenger seat next to her. The bag must have fallen over when she accelerated past that car at the stoplight back in Mendham, and the contents were strewn all over the seat and on the floor. She saw the top half of her cell phone peeking out of the bag and remembered the conversation she had had with the detective from Miami. She picked up her phone and scrolled down to her incoming call log, found the last number that had come in, and then hit the call button.

THIRTY-SEVEN

They sat in the family room and went through the loot bag, taking an inventory of what they had found. He wasn't sure he could sell the shotgun but decided to take it with him anyway, find out if the guy wanted it or not. He didn't know how much the coin collection would be worth, but he'd let the guy in NY make him an offer on that. The watches were the genuine article: the heavy men's Rolex and the women's Piaget, those should be worth plenty. Also, all the sterling silver flatware. That could be sold or just melted down. Then there was everything they had found in Mrs. Russell's jewelry box: a lot of gold chains and bracelets and pins and pendants, assorted rings and some diamond jewelry including earrings and broaches. Again, everything was of extremely high quality as far as Skooley could tell.

He gathered up all the cash they had found and tossed it over to Esmeralda.

"Here, count this up. I don't know how much we'll get for all this other stuff. Them watches, they should fetch us a nice number, and a lot of the jewelry is top notch. But these fences, they're out to make a profit same as anyone. My friend told me this guy in New York is a friend of his and will treat us right, but I don't know. Even my friend is always cutting his number, giving me a song and dance about he's got lots of this and the markets going to shit on that, trying to screw me over—it's fucking robbery is what it is."

He smiled at his own joke, and then looked up at Esmeralda.

She was busy counting the money and seemed not to have heard. She had been quiet since he returned, almost subdued. Maybe that little threat he had made before he left this morning shook her up some. He thought about it and decided that was probably a good thing, make her behave. When the time came, might make things a little easier.

"Three thousand four hundred and twenty. That's what we have in cash," she announced.

"Here, let me have that," he said, and she handed the money over to him meekly, without saying a word.

He counted out fifteen hundred and tossed it back to her.

"That's your share. I'll keep the extra four hundred, as I gotta haul this stuff into New York. When I get back, we'll split whatever we get and decide what we do next. You keep searching the house, maybe find us that lockbox. We find that, we're golden."

He took out his wallet and pulled a wrinkled piece of paper out with faded writing on it. He put the small piece of paper on his knee and flattened it out as best he could. Then flipped open the go phone and punched in the number that was written down.

She could just make out the phone ringing on the other end from the tinny speaker of the inexpensive phone.

"Hello." A man's voice.

She watched Skooley put on his false, friendly smile and then wink at her. "Hey, how y'all doing? I'm interested in selling a few items I inherited recently from my poor old aunty, and I understand you might be in the business of buying estate items."

"Says who?" The man's voice was gruff.

"Well, I got your number from a friend of mine got a store in Florida, town called Brandon, just outside of Tampa."

"Who's your friend?"

"Fella by the name of Billings. Joe Billings. Known as Big Bill on account of his size. Man has a mighty appetite if you get my meaning."

"Yeah, what color's his hair?"

"Hair? Hell, that's a tough one. I ain't never seen his hair. Where's he keep it at, up a shelf in his closet? Every time I ever seen Big Bill, he was bald as a cue ball."

There was a few seconds of silence on the other end of the phone. Then the man asked, "What are you selling?"

"Well, we got a few watches, Rolex, Piaget, a nice coin collection, sterling silver flatware, some assorted jewelry that dear old aunty wanted me to have, all high-quality items. A few other odds and ends."

"Who's we?"

"Me and my partner; I mean my wife, you know."

"What's your name?"

This time, Skooley was quiet for a few seconds.

"Look, pal, you wanna do business, I'm going to need a name. And tell me something Big Bill is gonna know about you, so I can make sure you're on the level. Otherwise, you can go fuck yourself."

"Name's Lamar. Ask Big Bill what skinny-ass redneck can out-eat him in tacos any day of the week. And tell him I near about pissed my pants when he started choking on them hot peppers he told me he's so fond of last time we was out to lunch. Hell, I ain't never seen another human being's face turn so red as his did, his eyes crying and him sweating like that. Ask him about that, though he'll probably lie to you, deny the whole damn thing."

"I'll call you back on this number. If everything checks out, I can meet you later today. Or tomorrow if you want."

"Give Big Bill my regards. I'll wait for your call." Skooley closed the flip phone.

"Lamar?" said Esmeralda.

"It's my given name. You can see now why I prefer to go by Skooley."

He gathered all the jewelry and assorted items back into

the pillowcase.

"We're gonna need to find us a tote bag or some kind of case to carry this stuff in. It won't do for me to be wandering around New York City carrying all this stuff in a pillowcase. Might as well wear a stocking over my head with a sign on my back that says burglar. I guess that fella is going to give me an address where to meet him at. And I ain't never been to New York. Do you know how to work one of them GPS navigation machines?"

She nodded.

"Good. I'm going to take the Mercedes instead of the Range Rover. I ain't so sure that girl that took my picture on her phone last night didn't see me get into it. She could have followed me out of the bar. Maybe she didn't, but there ain't no sense in taking any chances. Don't take that truck out. Hell, just keep the fuck away from it. Don't even leave the house. Once we get the call, you can set the address he gives me into the GPS. Might be a good idea we erase it after I come back. Show me how to work that machine, too, so I can figure out how to get the hell back here after I've finished this business."

"Okay," she said, "there's some luggage upstairs in one of the closets. I saw a bag that can fit all this stuff. Even the rifle and the coin collection."

"I done told you, it ain't a rifle, it's a shotgun."

"Who gives a shit, Lamar?"

"Yeah, well, I guess obviously you don't."

"How long do you think it will take? I mean, going into the city and selling these things and everything?"

"I don't know," he replied. "I ain't sure how long it takes to get to New York. I figure it won't take but maybe fifteen or twenty minutes to make the deal. He's gonna look things over and give me a price. I'm gonna say I want more and he's gonna hem and haw and make up some excuse and then he's either gonna up his offer or he ain't. I'll try and get whatever I can, but in this particular case, it ain't me that's in the driver's seat. Big Bill told me this guy is solid and I got to take Big Bill at his word, so I guess we'll get what we get."

They left everything in the family room, and then they both stood up and started making their way upstairs. Skooley watched her fold the money he had given her and slide it into her front pocket. That had been a good idea, he thought, give her some money now like real partners, keep her quiet. Quiet and a little bit scared, that was good.

"I'll keep looking for the lockbox. It's got to be here somewhere. I'll look down in the basement. We haven't really been down there yet. And I'll make some chili for us to eat for dinner. You like it hot, right?

"The hotter the better."

"I picked up some hot peppers. I got those habaneros; they're so hot they clear out your sinuses, make you sweat. I tried them once and they actually took my breath away. I couldn't breathe. I got the hiccups and was gulping air like a goldfish out of water for like an hour. I can't eat it hot like that, but I'll make a special batch, real hot and spicy, just for you."

They were upstairs in one of the bedroom closets looking at a matching set of luggage, suitcase and garment bag and some overnight bags, deciding which one would be best for the trip to New York when Skooley's phone rang.

Skooley opened the phone and without preamble said, "So, are we on?"

"Yeah. You know your way around the city?"

"Ain't never been."

"Yeah, well that figures. Okay then, we'll make this easy. You come across the Lincoln Tunnel, head downtown toward Penn Station."

"Just a sec, I wanna write this down." He looked at Esmeralda and made a writing motion with his hand, and she scrambled around looking for a pen and some paper, and then hurried back to Skooley and handed them to him. "Okay, go ahead."

"Take the Lincoln Tunnel, think you can find that?"

"It's like a big hole in the ground, right?"

"Cross the tunnel, then get on Ninth Avenue and head downtown, find Penn Station. I'll be at the corner of Eighth Avenue and Thirty-First Street, Penn Station side. You can't miss it. Ninth Avenue heads downtown and Eighth Avenue heads uptown, so you'll have to cut across one block to get on Eighth. Penn Station is on one side of the street, and the post office is on the other. What kind of car you got?"

"Black Mercedes."

"I'll be wearing a brown leather jacket. When you get near the corner, put your emergency blinkers on. I see you, I'll wave you down, get in and tell you where to go from there. You got that?"

"Yeah, I got it."

"Three o'clock. Don't be late, Lamar."

"Three o'clock." Then the phone went dead.

Skooley looked at the silent phone for a second, then closed it and put it into his shirt pocket.

"You sure got some uptight assholes here in New Jersey," he said.

"He's not from Jersey, he's from New York."

"Yeah, sorry, that makes all the difference. I'll take that smaller bag over there. I think I can get everything into it."

They brought the bag downstairs, and Skooley started transferring all the items from the pillowcase into it. The shotgun case did not fit, but Skooley decided he'd just lay that on the floor in front of the back seat, show it to the guy, and see if he wanted it. Then it would be up to him to carry it away.

"Where do you think he'll take you?" she asked.

"He probably got himself a pawn shop or some kind of store there in New York. If not, we'll probably go to a garage or a lot where he parked his car. He can take what he wants, put it right in the trunk."

"You scared, Skooley? You think he might try and rob you?"

"Naw, he won't do nothing like that. There'd be no point to it. He's a fence; buying stolen shit is what he does. Word gets out that he's holding people up, then who's gonna be stupid enough to try and sell him stuff? What he's gotta worry about is people like me."

"Are you going to rob him?"

Skooley was quiet for a moment, then looked up at her and smiled.

"No, I ain't. I'm in a bit of trouble already, and I don't need no more. I did something like that, it'd get back to Big Bill and then everyone I know'd just turn their backs on me. I gotta try and keep the few friends I got left. But that's why that fella was asking me questions and why he even called down to Brandon, check me out with Big Bill himself. Big Bill don't give him the good word, he don't see me. It's that simple. What time is it?"

Esmeralda looked at her watch. "It's twelve-forty-five."

"That gives me two hours and fifteen minutes. Let's get this stuff loaded in the car, see if you can program that GPS to get me to that corner near Penn Station where I'm supposed to be heading. I don't believe it's gonna take no two hours to get there, but I'd like to drive around a bit, look things over before I meet this guy."

He picked up the overnight bag with all the stolen items, and she picked up the presentation shotgun case, and they headed out to the garage. He grabbed the car keys off the peg and used the remote to unlock the car. She walked to the driver's side door while Skooley headed around to the passenger's side. The Range Rover was parked right next to the Mercedes in the garage and Esmeralda happened to glance inside. There on the passenger seat was a gun. She hadn't seen a gun before. Shit, she thought, he has a gun. She acted like she hadn't seen anything and got into the driver's seat, placed the shotgun case on the passenger seat, used the remote to open the garage door, and started the car. She turned on the navigation system as Skooley opened the passenger door, moved the shotgun case to the back seat and tossed the overnight in next to it, then sat down and watched her as she punched the address into the GPS. She showed him how to find the home icon when he was ready to return, then pushed a few more buttons on the screen and told him he was ready to go.

They both got out of the car, and she started heading back into the house. He followed her up the steps.

She turned around and looked at him. "I thought you were leaving."

"I am. Just got to take me a leak before I go." He went into the half bath and left the door open while he peed. Esmeralda walked into the kitchen and then heard the toilet flush.

"I'll be back in a while," he called out to her. "Find us that lockbox, maybe we can have us a nice celebration. I put some Stellas in the fridge. Make sure they ain't all drunk by the time I get back." Then the door slammed.

She tiptoed back to the garage door and listened as she heard one car door open, then slam shut, then another door open and close. Next, she heard the chirp of a car's remote locking system. Then the garage door came down, and she ran to one of the front windows and watched the black Mercedes head down the long driveway to the road and turn left, heading back toward town.

She sprinted back to the garage and looked in the passenger side window of the Range Rover. The gun was gone. Skooley took the gun with him. Shit! She tried the car door, but it was locked. She walked back into the house, feeling scared and alone. She had tried hard not to act different around him after he had returned, not let him know how scared she felt. It had been hard, probably harder than anything she had ever done. He was smart and he was dangerous. If he found out that she knew about Raymundo, she was sure he wouldn't have left her alone. And now he had a gun. She should have known. That's probably what he used to kill Raymundo. Probably what he'll use to kill her too.

She walked down the hall and through the kitchen and sat down at the breakfast table. She had to figure out what to do. She had a few hours at most before Skooley would be back. He had given her some money. For a short time after, she actually believed that maybe they would split all the money, maybe everything would be all right. But when she saw the gun, she knew better. That's why he gave me the money, she thought, because he knew that's what I'd be thinking—maybe Skooley's not so bad; so what if he threatened me, he gave me my share—he was trying to manipulate her and it almost worked and that scared her more than anything.

She got up, walked back to the front window and just looked out for a few minutes. Then she walked back to Mr. Russell's office near the garage. She reached into a basket on one of the filing cabinets. It was filled with papers. She moved aside some spare change and few paper clips and finally grabbed a spare key to the Range Rover. Clean someone's office for a few years and you find out where they keep a lot of things. She walked back out to the garage and used the remote to unlock the doors, then opened up the passenger side door of the Range Rover. He didn't want to use this car, and he didn't want her to use it. Maybe that girl last night did see him get into it. Maybe the cops were out there right now looking for a skinny guy in a Range Rover. But why would he lock it when he left? Probably best to search it, see if maybe he had any other surprises hidden inside.

It took her all of about five minutes to find the cash under the floor mat of the back passenger seat. There was an envelope with just over four thousand dollars in it, another envelope with about two thousand, and what looked like an old leather wallet with another two thousand dollars stuffed into it. Just over eight thousand dollars in cash. Plus, he had the nineteen hundred from the cash she had counted earlier stuffed into his pockets and the money from the cookie jar and probably more that she didn't even know about. That was why Skooley locked the car. That's why he told her stay away from it. And that's why he was confident enough to give her the fifteen hundred. Even if she ran, he'd still have over ten thousand in cash until he tracked her down—if he tracked her down. She thought about taking the cash, all of it, and running. Running right now. But where would she go? Leave Morristown? Wasn't enough money under that floor mat for that. He knew where she worked—the cleaning company, the restaurant—and she still had to worry about her family. So, she left everything where it was, locked the Range Rover, and put the spare key in her pocket. She wished he'd left the gun. That would have made a big difference, give her a little hope, some peace of mind. She still had a few hours until Skooley came back. Maybe she'd be here waiting for him, and maybe she wouldn't. She had to think about what to do next. She needed a plan.

THIRTY-EIGHT

It was almost three o'clock. Skooley should be just about pulling up to the corner of Eighth Avenue and Thirty-First Street looking for a guy in a brown leather jacket waving at him.

Esmeralda was lying on the bed, thinking. She had searched the basement, but it was a mess down there. Like the garage, it was full of boxes and old furniture and tools and unused exercise equipment, just like everybody else's basement. It would take her days to sort through all that crap. And besides, it was damp and dirty down there. Would anyone leave a lockbox with their most precious valuables in a dark, dank basement? Maybe pirates would, she thought, but not a builder and his artist wife.

She had come up out of the basement after about an hour. She was disheartened and didn't really know where to look next. She decided to start cooking the chili: browning the meat, opening cans of beans and cutting the vegetables—onions, bell pepper and tomatoes—and then adding tomato sauce and the chili mix. It would take a few hours to cook. Once everything was added, all she had to do was let it simmer. She made two pots, one a smaller pot for herself. In the larger pot, she added the jalapeño and habanero peppers, careful to wash her hands after she was through cutting them, remembering the time she had cooked with them before and then rubbed her eye. It was like getting sprayed with mace, her eye burning and tearing and staying red for hours. She didn't know how anyone could eat food this hot. How could you taste anything?

After she was done and the pots were both simmering on low heat, she went upstairs and laid down on the bed in the master bedroom. She began wondering where Mr. Russell would hide his lockbox. They looked just about everywhere. Why would Mr. Russell hide money all over the house? Well, she thought, why would he? Probably he wouldn't. He hid the money in his office, but he'd need petty cash for his business, and he seemed to run things out of that small room. Mrs. Russell was the one who hid the money in the cookie jar, her pin money. Maybe Mrs. Russell is the one hiding money all over the house. She thought about where she had found the various stashes—in the dining room, in the kitchen, in assorted drawers in the bedrooms—mostly in her drawers. When she thought more about it, the money was really found in places that a woman would more likely hide it than a man would, at least in her mind.

What if it wasn't Mr. Russell's key? What if it was her key?

She thought about it more and more. She was an artist. She might have some health problems—all those prescriptions in the bathroom, they were all her prescriptions, none of them belonged to her husband. Maybe her health problems weren't all physical, maybe she had some mental problems. Hiding so much money in the house just didn't seem like what normal people would do. Except according to Skooley who said lots of people did it. But he was talking about drug dealers and crooks. Mrs. Russell was a successful artist. She had a lot of paintings here in the house. And Esmeralda knew that she showed her work at several art galleries in town, probably in New York too. She also did portraits for rich people. Maybe she worked for cash. Maybe she was hiding money from the IRS—or from her husband.

So where would Mrs. Russell hide a treasure box?

The only room that she and Skooley hadn't really checked was the art studio over the garage. Her art studio: a space that was hers and hers alone. She got up off the bed and walked down the hallway. The studio door was closed. She opened the door and peeked her head in. She saw the canvasses and the easels and the jars with brushes and was a little bit awed by the woman and her talent. She edged her way past the door and closed it gently behind her.

The studio was large and well-lit with natural light coming from both the large windows and the shaded skylights overhead. The only furniture in the room was an old wooden, paint-spattered drafting table with a small stool; two cabinets with drawers of various sizes; a few shelves covered with trays of paint tubes; and another small paint-splattered stool sitting between two easels with half completed works on them, one covered with a sheet. There were canvasses along every wall, some with sketches done in pencil, some fresh and new and white.

Esmeralda sat down on the stool in front of the drafting table and surveyed the room. Unless there was some sort of secret panel or something in the wall or under the rug, there just weren't that many places to hide a lockbox.

The first and most obvious place to look was in the cabinets. They were identical, each with a series of seven thin drawers running top to bottom, and then two larger drawers on the bottom. She went to the first cabinet and began at the top, opening the drawers one by one. It would have to be a pretty thin lockbox for it to fit in any of the top seven drawers, but she checked them all anyway, mostly just out of curiosity as to what was in them. Each of the first top seven drawers contained artists' implements and assorted tools like wire snippers and screwdrivers and a small hammer and pliers and a staple gun. There were a lot of brushes and paint and plastic burnishing tools as well.

She opened each drawer, one after the other, until she got to the first of the wider bottom drawers. This one was topped with a tray containing assorted tubes of paint. When she removed the top tray, there was another underneath, also with tubes and small jars of paint about the size of nail polish bottles. She removed that tray and found the bottom of the drawer containing more tools, rulers, plastic triangles and assorted scissors. She replaced all the trays and opened the next drawer. This one also had a tray of paint tubes, but when she removed this tray to search underneath it, she didn't find more art supplies, but instead found old photos, some very old, of different people from different eras doing different things. She found photos taken from what might have been a wedding in the 1920s. There were also old baby photos, some so old they were in sepia tones, and military photos from what she assumed was the First World War, or maybe just prior. There were also antique photos of strippers and flappers and what she could only describe as very early forms of pornography: men and women sitting or standing naked, some showed couples engaged in various sex acts, and though graphic, the age of the photos somehow made the images seem more innocent and artistic than dirty. There were some disturbing photos too, of what she assumed were prisoners, perhaps on chain gangs in the south. There were shots of young men in Nazi SS uniforms, smiling for the camera under the death head insignia of their caps. As she dug deeper, she also found old magazines from the 1930s through the 1950s, all just piled upon one another with no sense of order: *Look*, *Time*, and *The Saturday Evening Post*. She spent a few minutes looking through the trove of photos and flipping through the magazines, fascinated by the old wardrobes and hairstyles, many of the subjects looking so young and vibrant. It made her sad to realize that most of the people she was looking at were long dead, or if not, so old and shriveled and wrinkled as to be unrecognizable from the youth and vitality of these photos. She wondered briefly what she would look like when she got old. Then she thought, she might not get the chance to get much older than she was right now if she didn't come up with some sort of plan.

She put all the magazines and photos back in the drawer,

and then replaced the tray of paints on top of them. She walked over to the other cabinet and decided to start from the bottom drawer this time and work her way up. She opened the drawer and found another tray, this one jam-packed with charcoal pencils and colored pastel markers of various thicknesses and glue sticks and x-acto knives and more rulers and assorted other junk. She removed this tray and sitting far back in the drawer was something dull gray in color.

Esmeralda's breath caught and her heart almost stopped beating. She carefully put the tray that she had removed onto the floor and reached way back into the drawer and removed Mrs. Russell's lockbox.

THIRTY-NINE

He was sitting in the front passenger seat of the black Chevrolet Impala that had been waiting for them when they had arrived at Newark International Airport two hours earlier. A man met them at the gate as they disembarked the plane. He walked them out to the car, opened the trunk, and pointed to a brown paper bag containing four loaded handguns, and then he walked away

The car was now idling in a parking space on Dehart Street, just off South Street in Morristown. He had gotten the call early in the morning. One of the watchers, a computer and internet expert, had uncovered an online story from one of the local New Jersey newspapers. There was a picture. The face in the picture matched a picture they had been given by the smelly man they had interrogated a few weeks back. The computer expert said that he had a program that could match the face with ninety-eight percent certainty. He said it was the same man they were searching for, Schooley. So he and his crew had boarded the first available flight from Miami to Newark. And now the hunt was on.

And he was getting close.

It was time to report his progress. He hit the speed dial on the throwaway phone he had been given and it was answered on the first ring.

"Digame. Tell me," said a voice on the other end.

"He has been seen. I just now got a call from a woman who met him two nights ago. He is calling himself Ray Mundy.

She said that she saw him again, just a few minutes ago. He is driving a green Range Rover in a town called Mendham."

"Is she following?"

"No, she got scared and drove away."

"Where are you?"

"We are close, in Morristown, the town where his picture was taken. I spoke with the reporter from the paper. She said she got a call from someone who told her he has a job at a restaurant in a town nearby called Bernardsville. I am going there now, to the restaurant, to talk to them. I will find out what I can."

"How long?"

"Two days. Maybe sooner. I will call and report my progress."

"And when you find him, remember."

"Yes, I know. I will bring you something."

Then the phone went silent.

FORTY

The female mechanical voice from the GPS directed Skooley right to the corner of Eighth Avenue at Penn Station in New York City. Traffic getting into the city had been light until he reached the approach to the Lincoln Tunnel. Then everything stopped dead for about a mile. He was shocked and annoyed at the thirteen-dollar toll to get into the city and made it a point to tell the toll collector exactly how he felt about it, but she seemed not to have heard a single word he said. Even with the traffic, he arrived at the corner just after 2:00 p.m. He drove up Eighth Avenue for a few blocks, then turned east and came down Seventh and drove past the lit-up Madison Square Garden sign and then turned right after a few more blocks and past the corner once again where the meet was to take place. The streets were crowded, even on a Sunday. He was amazed at the height and sheer concentration of the buildings that he passed. He could see flashes of the Empire State Building from his car window and fought the urge to park the car and just walk around the city.

Just a few short weeks ago he had been in Florida, never having left the state before. Now, here he was driving a Mercedes in New York City. Made him smile. But he needed to concentrate on the task at hand. What he wanted was to park the car a few blocks downtown from the meet and then walk closer to Penn Station, maybe find a spot across the street to see if he could spot the fence arriving, see if he was alone or if someone dropped him off, but he didn't feel comfortable leaving all those valuables in the car, particularly a Mercedes, given all he had heard about the rampant crime in New York City. He ended up driving around in a circle up Eighth and down Seventh Avenue until he found an empty space on Eighth about a block south of Penn Station on the opposite side of the street. It wasn't an ideal vantage point, particularly with buses and trucks and people constantly passing in front of him, but he could make out the corner and watched as best he could.

Right about five minutes to three, a man in a short, brown leather jacket and dark sunglasses seemed to just appear on the corner. Skooley hadn't seen him arrive and hadn't noticed any cars stopping on the corner to let someone out, not even cabs which were all over the place. A bus had passed obscuring his view for just a few seconds and suddenly, there he was. He was alone, not talking to anyone, nor did he appear nervous or do anything that Skooley thought suspicious. He just stood at the corner casually watching traffic approach. At precisely three o'clock, the man looked at this watch. Skooley grabbed the small .25 Beretta from under the front seat where he had placed it earlier and slid it inside the front of his pants, then pulled his shirt out to cover it. He made his way into the center of traffic, put on his emergency flashers and slowly approached the corner.

The man in the brown leather jacket and sunglasses put a hand up like he was hailing a cab as Skooley pulled up to the curb. The man opened the door and got into the passenger seat.

"Right on time, Lamar. Head uptown to Thirty-Eighth Street, make a right. I'll tell you where to pull in."

Skooley turned off his flashers and pulled out into the flow of traffic.

"Mighty nice to meet you too," he said, looking over at the stranger and putting on his nice-guy smile.

The man had shiny black hair and a dark complexion. Skooley thought he could be Italian or Greek or even Jewish. He was glad that he did not appear to be any type of Hispanic. With those cartel guys after him, he would have been a bit spooked by that. His internal antenna was not pinging and so he relaxed a bit as he drove.

"I heard you're a wiseass, Lamar. Glad to see Big Bill wasn't lying. When you get on Thirty-Eighth, we're going to go about three or four blocks. I got my van in a garage there. I know the guy that runs the place, so we got no problems. I'll tell ya where to turn once we get close. You can call me Warren."

"Man, Warren, this city is something else. I ain't never seen so many big buildings such as this. We got cities in Florida, big ones too, like Miami, but they ain't nothing like this here, nothing at all. I ain't really been to many cities outside of Florida. Can't wait to walk around, maybe climb the top of that Empire State Building or take one of them boat rides to the Statue of Liberty. They still do that after 9/11, the boat ride, I mean?"

"You know, Lamar, I've been around this city my whole life, and I never been on that fucking Circle Line or climbed to the top of the goddamn Empire State Building, so I'm afraid I can't really help you there, partner."

"How can someone live right here in the Big Apple and not climb the Empire State Building?"

"The Big Apple? Jesus H. Christ, just what I need, another fucking asshole tourist."

"You know, that's something else I really like about this city, everybody's so nice and friendly." He looked over and smiled good-naturedly. "Say, Warren, you ever been to Miami?" he asked, feeling him out a little, turning the dials on the old internal radar a bit, searching for any noise.

"I hear it's all niggers and spics. Look around you, Lamar, what the fuck I got to go to Miami for? That's Thirty-Eighth, turn right up there."

They drove on Thirty-Eighth for a few blocks, and Warren told Skooley to turn into a parking garage located under one of the old buildings in the middle of the block. He stopped at the gate and lowered the window as Warren leaned over.

"Hey, Billy, we won't be long."

The young man in the booth simply nodded, and the gate rose allowing Skooley to maneuver between the tightly packed cars. Warren directed him up a ramp and then up another ramp and then pointed him to a white panel van with no side windows that was parked by itself at the back end of the dark enclosure.

"I got a little workbench with a light and some tools in the van. I'll take a look at what you got, see if maybe we can make a deal."

Skooley pulled in next to the van as Warren got out, took off his sunglasses, and slid them into his jacket pocket. He then unlocked the sliding side door with a key, opened it with a violent pull on the handle, and then hopped into the van. Skooley reached behind him onto the back seat of the Mercedes and grabbed the overnight bag. He then exited the car, walked around, and climbed into the van and slid the door shut. Warren was already sitting on a box in front of a small desk with a high-intensity lamp shining on the desktop. He opened a small drawer and pulled out a jewelers loupe and put it on the desk.

"Okay, sport, let's see what you brought me."

Skooley sat on another small box, opened his bag, and began handing the various items singly to Warren. Each was inspected closely under the high-intensity lamp with the loupe and then set aside on a black felt pad that was lying on top of the desk. Warren didn't actually say anything as he inspected each item, he just grunted every now and again. He looked at the watches and all the other jewelry items, then he inspected the silverware and coin collection. He brought out a small electronic scale and weighed the silverware pieces in bunches, then took out a calculator and began punching in numbers.

Finally, he looked up at Skooley and said, "Sixty-five hundred for the lot."

Skooley smiled and shook his head. "Warren, you and I both know what I brung you was some high-quality merchandise. Very high-quality. I'm actually a little hurt by your low-ball offer, being as we're both such good friends of Big Bill and all. I'm sure you can do better than that. Shit, what's he gonna think I let you take advantage of me like that? Hell, you take them watches alone for sixty-five hundred and you still end up with a tidy profit. How about ten grand for everything?"

"Look, Lamar, we're not really negotiating here. I'm doing this as a favor to Big Bill. I could be sitting on my couch right now watching a ball game or getting my dick sucked, but instead I'm sitting here in this fucking parking garage talking to some hick tourist who as I see it don't really have a whole lot of options. You're right, it is good-quality merchandise, but I already got a bunch of watches I still got to unload and all this other shit is just inventory I don't really need, see? That coin collection, that's specialty merchandise. I don't even handle shit like that. I'll give you seven grand so you can go home happy and I don't end up wasting my whole fucking afternoon, but if that don't buy it, then you can take it somewhere else, understand?"

Skooley thought for a second, then said, "Wait here just a minute, I forgot something. Let me show you this one more thing."

He reached over, opened the sliding door, and jumped out of the van. He walked over to the Mercedes, opened the passenger side door, and grabbed the case with the disassembled shotgun. He turned, shut the door with his hip and as he climbed back into the van, found himself blinded by the light of the high-intensity lamp and looking into the barrel of a model 1911 Colt .45 that Warren was holding straight out with both hands.

"Say, Warren, that's a really nice Colt you got there. I appreciate you showing it to me up close like this. Now, if you get it outta my face, I'll show you this beautiful shotgun I brung you, see if maybe this will sweeten the pot some."

Warren backed up without taking the gun off Skooley.

Skooley laid the box down and reached around and closed the van door. He sat back down on the box he had occupied before and opened the case so that Warren could look into it.

"It's Eye-talian. Just look at the quality, that stock is custom wood right there. And check out all that engraving. I admit, I don't know all that much about shotguns, but I ain't never seen something like this one here before. Museum quality, don't ya think?"

"Lamar, I'm going to have to ask you to reach into your pants and lay your piece on the floor. Do it slow and easy. Just use two fingers. Make sure you toss it close to me, okay?"

Skooley did as he was told. "You mind pointing that light away from my eyes before I go blind? Maybe drop your aim a bit too in case ya sneeze or something."

Warren reached with his foot and slid the Beretta closer, then slowly lowered the gun and replaced it into the shoulder holster that he had hidden underneath his leather jacket. Then, without taking his eyes off Skooley, he reached over to the light with one hand, bent the gooseneck, and pointed it down toward the shotgun case.

"That's a nice rig you got there, Warren. I never even seen a bulge in your jacket."

"Yeah, custom made. Know a guy who makes 'em for the cops. Look, Lamar, sorry about pulling on you. I didn't know what you had in mind coming back in like that, you understand."

Skooley smiled at him. "Sure, no problem. I'm actually starting to get used to people sticking guns in my face."

Warren looked at him for a few seconds more without saying anything, then peered into the shotgun case.

"You know, Lamar, this must be your lucky day. I actually like this gun. I shoot some, trap and sporting clays mostly, that is when I'm not shooting lowlife motherfucking tourists trying to rip me off." He glanced up at Skooley and smiled. "I was actually thinking about buying myself a new gun. Course I wasn't considering a Perazzi MX12 over/under. This is a pretty nice gun. Guess you got this from your old auntie too, huh?"

Skooley smiled broadly. "Auntie just loved this old gun. Ten grand takes the whole lot, everything I brung you."

Warren scratched his chin absently. "Eighty-five hundred, that's the best I can do."

"Geez, Warren, you're killing me here. That gun alone is probably worth that."

"Look, Lamar, you're thinking retail. I only pay a percentage and that's on wholesale. I'm taking a risk on all this shit. You can walk out of here with the cash, right now, or you can take it all back to Craphole Florida or wherever the fuck you came from. Your choice."

Skooley didn't say anything for a few seconds. He would have liked to have gotten more, but he wasn't really in any position to argue.

Finally, he said, "I guess we got us a deal." He closed the case and pushed it gently toward Warren.

Warren opened another drawer in the little desk and pulled out a stack of bills. He handed Skooley a wrapped stack of fifty one-hundred-dollar bills, pulled out another wrapped stack and broke the paper seal, then counted out fifteen hundreds, put those back into the drawer and gave the remainder to Skooley.

"Thank you kindly."

"Count it, Lamar."

"I trust you, Warren."

"Count it. Right here in front of me. I don't want any problems later. You count it now, or we don't have a deal."

Skooley counted out the money. "Eighty-five hundred, just like we agreed. You mind sliding that little twenty-five back this way. You can take out the clip if it makes you feel better."

"That little twenty-five is part of the deal. You said every-thing you brought and you brought that. You got your money, now you better get on your way." Warren's hand inched a little closer to the inside of his jacket. He wasn't smiling.

Skooley hated to leave the Beretta, but then he remem-bered Ray's revolver that he had stashed in the cushions of the couch back at the house, and he brightened up considerably.

"I hope you enjoy your new toy there, Warren, it's a real beauty. And don't let any of them little clay pigeons shit on your head."

FORTY-ONE

The lockbox felt hard and solid and heavy in her hand. It wasn't made of thin sheet metal like the petty cash box that they had at the hair salon where she helped out sometimes. This metal was thicker and weightier and much more formidable. She carried the box over to the drafting table and set it down. She leaned in close and looked at the lock mechanism and then tried to lift the lid. It didn't budge. She knew it wouldn't. She peered at the keyhole. It wasn't like a keyhole of any door or even padlock that she had ever seen. It was circular. The key they had found in the smoke alarm was circular; she remembered that it had reminded her of a roller skate key. She picked up the box and shook it. She could feel things shifting and shuffling inside, but the box made very little noise.

She carried the box downstairs, set it on the kitchen counter. The kitchen was warm and smelled of browned meat and spices from the simmering pots on the stove. It smelled like her mom's kitchen, and a sudden unexpected lump caught in her throat. She swallowed it down and looked at the digital clock on the microwave. It was 3:41 p.m. She couldn't imagine that Skooley would be done in New York yet, but even if he left Penn Station right that very minute, she should still have close to an hour, probably more, before he made it back. She found a large Macy's shopping bag with string handles in the pantry and laid the lockbox into it. She decided to take the lockbox back to her car and leave it there. She wasn't going to let

Skooley get it, no matter what. She would try and get the key from him somehow. If she couldn't, and still survived the evening, she figured she could always get the box open later, even if she had to buy an axe or some sort of drill at the Home Depot. She decided to walk back to her car instead of taking the Range Rover and went out the back door and into the woods that paralleled the driveway, and as she walked past the bikes that had brought Skooley and Raymundo to this house again, a slight shiver went down her spine.

She walked down the road until she reached her car in the Patriot's Path parking lot. There were several other cars parked there as well, probably people out walking or jogging along the path, but there was no one actually in the lot. She unlocked and then opened the tailgate of the wagon, looked around to make sure no one was watching or even driving by, and then moved the pails and mops and brushes and vacuums and laid the bag with the lockbox down. She then piled all the cleaning supplies and implements on top and re-locked the doors.

As she walked back to the house along the side of the road, a daring plan began to formulate in her head. She honestly believed she'd need something daring if she ever hoped to see that lockbox opened.

Or if she ever hoped to see anything again after Skooley got back tonight.

When she got back to the house, instead of heading right in, she went out back to the pool house and retrieved Raymundo's phone from the shelf under the bar. She handled only the edges, careful not to touch the screen, and then slipped the phone into her pocket. Finding that lockbox had done something to her inside. It was a good sign, like she was fated to find it. Also, it was she who had found that key and she who had found the lockbox, not Skooley. If she had found it together with Skooley, Esmeralda had no doubt that she would be dead already. She realized for the first time that she didn't want to be partners anymore, didn't want to have to share what she had risked so much to...well...to steal. She wasn't going to just accept whatever that psycho decided to give to her, whether it be a share of the money or a bullet to the brain. She was going to act. She was scared, but she was also determined. If it came down to money or a bullet, she knew which way things would go if it were left up to Skooley. She entered the house through the back door. She had seen a lot of what she would need and tried to remember where everything was. The place to start was the garage, then she would backtrack through the house for the things she'd need to put her plan into action.

FORTY-TWO

Skooley wanted to park the car and walk around. The city was big and crowded and exciting. When would he ever get a chance to come back here to New York City? Plus, he had a wad of cash just burning a hole in his pocket. But he knew that he didn't have the time. He remembered those Miami guys who had almost gotten him back in Bonita Springs. They had found him quickly then, and he had no illusions that they wouldn't find him quickly again now if he wasn't careful. Especially since he had been unlucky enough to not only make the newspaper, but to get his goddamn picture took. What a shit show. He wasn't going to hang around in the city. No way. Soon, they'd have people all over this town looking for him. Might have people working on it right now. It was time to boogie on down the road, and the sooner he did it, the better off he'd be.

He didn't know where he was, but he knew he was heading uptown because the street numbers were getting higher with each block. He had come out of the tunnel somewhere in the higher street numbers so at least he was headed in the right direction. He turned on the GPS system and tapped the home icon like Esmeralda had showed him and the mechanical voice began directing him toward the Lincoln Tunnel.

Esmeralda. That was his next problem. He thought about his situation as he drove out of the city and started heading toward New Jersey. What should he do with the cleaning girl? He needed to get moving. The more he thought about those

Miami guys, the more certain he was that they were closing in. They would end up at the rooming house soon. That would be the first place they would stake out. He had to stay away from there. He was glad he retrieved his property earlier. He wouldn't want to have to chance it now. Stay away from the car too. Shit, he wished he had stolen some new plates for it. Soon as they see those Florida tags, they'd know it was his. That was a good car to travel in too. Nobody noticed an old Camry. He would have liked to have gone back and retrieved his car, but it was just too late for that. Maybe he would take this car. Sure was a nice ride. The people who own it should be away for another few weeks, so nobody would report it stolen. Even if someone noticed, like if maybe one of their kids happened to come over to check on the house and found Mommy's car gone, it still wouldn't matter much. He could start heading west, leave it somewhere after a day or two and find himself a new ride, maybe another old Camry, then he would change direction, head north or south, keep them cartel boys guessing. Find someplace to lay low for a while, live cheap, then figure out how to squeeze a few bucks out of that fat pig in Miami or his bosses. Dicey game he was playing, but hey, no risk, no reward. He did a quick count of his money in his head. About eight or nine grand in the Range Rover, eighty-five from Warren, plus about another two in his pocket, what's that, about nineteen thousand? Then there's the fifteen hundred he gave the girl. That's just over twenty grand, give or take.

The girl.

He was thinking maybe he should leave tonight. What was the point in hanging around? He could stay hid in that house, but for how long? Pool guys, landscapers, maybe the old guy and his wife have a fight in their vacation house and one of 'em decides to get the fuck out and go home, what then? Not good to be anywhere near that town, hell, the whole fucking state, with them Miami folks looking for you. Not to mention the cops. The more he thought about it, the more convinced he was that the cop this morning was looking for him to come walking out of one of them stores and back to that Range Rover. Probably checking out every green Range Rover they saw. That fucking cunt with the camera phone. He wished he could meet up with her again some night. Maybe if he ever came back out this way, he'd do just that. Got to be a way to find her. He tried to remember if they mentioned her name in the newspaper article. He thought about the key in his pocket and the lockbox. If Esmeralda hadn't found it, he was going to put that key back in the smoke alarm where he found it; they'd think they was too smart for him. Maybe next summer he'd come back, take care of this business with the camera girl and find that box. The thought made him smile. I'll get that girl next year. I got another girlie to think about tonight.

Esmeralda. She had to go, no doubt about it. He didn't have enough money to keep her quiet. Hell, he'd need every fucking penny he had just to survive. Not like he could live it up too much on just twenty grand either. He probably won't have to wash dishes for a while, but he wasn't going to be eating steak dinners and fucking whores every night either. Well, maybe just a few times.

He'd have to do her. Better to do it sooner than later. He'd have to carry her out back like he did her buddy Ray, dig himself another hole. Shit. He didn't feel like digging another hole. Least he knew how to work the goddamn washing machine this time. He'd need some daylight, too. Not too much though. Maybe he'd have a little fun with her first. He wanted to fuck her last night. She shouldn't have left him at the bar after he was so nice to her, bought her dinner and all. If she'd a come back to the house, he never would have gone back into that bar. Well, maybe that ain't quite so. That big dude got what was coming to him. Still, that Esmeralda, she's not bad-looking. Maybe I can show her the money and sweet-talk the pants right off her. He smiled for a second at the thought of it, then shook his head. No, he thought, sweet-talk won't do it with that bitch. She's too fucking smart. Besides, could be she ain't never even been fucked before. Maybe she's afraid to get laid, or maybe she's one of them lesbos and don't even like dick. Don't matter. Rough her up some, bend her over, and put it to her. That's how it will go. Then get the nasty business over with, maybe use a plastic bag again, no muss no fuss, dig the hole, and get on down the road.

Twenty plus thousand, he thought. Too bad old Warren took that little Beretta. Looked like that drawer in the van was chock-full of cash. If he'd a known that from the get-go, no telling how much more he'd have in his pocket right now.

FORTY-THREE

Esmeralda was sitting at the table in the breakfast room, wondering if there was anything else she could do. She reached down with her right hand and felt the hard bump near her ankle that was the paring knife she had hidden there. Then she reached down with her left near the floor by her chair and touched the handle of the heavy flashlight she had set discreetly on the floor. The other flashlight was lying on the kitchen counter. She wanted these within easy reach if she needed them. Once she saw how things were going with Skooley, she would try and casually carry around the flashlight from the counter and keep it with her at all times, maybe act like she was looking under furniture or in closets or the basement for that box and she needed the extra light. Her stomach ached and she felt nauseous. Again, she wondered if she should just call the cops, turn them both in and see what happened. Then she thought of Raymundo, his body lying up in those woods, shot through the head or the heart and of the cops forcing her arms behind her back and putting the handcuffs on tight and of Skooley with his fake, sick smile saying it was all her idea, which technically it was since she had instigated this whole thing by telling Raymundo about the empty house and hinting about what they might find inside. She felt close to tears again and had to physically choke back a sob.

She shook her head forcefully. She had to stop thinking about it. Now that she had planned a course of action, it was too late to change it. If she didn't make it through the night, maybe it was because she didn't deserve to. Maybe it was God's decision to punish her for stealing and for getting Raymundo killed by Skooley.

She got up off the chair, walked into the kitchen, and took hold of the flashlight that was on the counter. Again, she felt its heft as she tapped it against her palm. At least she would go down fighting, she thought as she heard the garage door start to rise.

FORTY-FOUR

Skooley pulled up the driveway and stopped in front of the garage door. How should he do this? He didn't think about it too long. For Skooley, these things didn't usually take much planning; they just sort of happened. Like old Ray. What were the chances of finding a fucking can of Spam in some rich people's house? Why, it would never happen in a million years. That's because rich people don't ever eat Spam. Shit, poor people don't eat Spam less they have to. And then finding that heavy cast iron fry pan just like in his old man's house. Why his father had cooked every damn meal on that fry pan, breakfast, lunch, and dinner. Everything worked out like it was already set up for him. He didn't have to plan nothing. He just hauled off and whacked old Ray on the back of his noggin, just like he did his old man all those years ago. And digging a hole is digging a hole.

He hit the remote, and the garage door began opening and he pulled into the garage. When the car was in, he turned off the ignition, closed the garage door, and then grabbed the money and fanned it out in his hand. This was going to hold him until he could score big. In a day or two he'd be in some town in Ohio or Michigan or Pennsylvania, or maybe some other state. No point in planning too far ahead. If even he didn't know where he was heading, then there'd be no way anyone was going to be there waiting for him when he got there. First thing he'd do was get himself that big steak dinner and then go find himself a whore. He smiled at the thought of it, remembering what he had been thinking earlier about being

frugal. Hell, that was money well-spent. Make it a little celebration. There's always ways to make a little extra cash if need
be, and he began reaching under the seat before remembering
that Warren had taken the Beretta from him. Shit, should'a
popped that bastard when he had the chance. What was the
point in worrying about pissing off people in Florida if he
wasn't planning on going back there anytime soon? Then he
thought about the revolver that lay hidden under the couch
cushions in the family room. He mulled that over for a minute.
What were the chances that Esmeralda had found that revolver?
Maybe she was rummaging around in that back room looking
for the lockbox, maybe thinking it was in a secret hidey-hole
in the couch. Shit, that little cleaning girl wouldn't have the
balls to shoot him anyway, even if she did find that gun.

Still, it was something to think about.

He got out of the car and dug the key to the Range Rover
out of his pocket. He was carrying around keys to three different cars now, counting the stolen Camry. Well, he wouldn't
be needing that key anymore. He clicked the unlock button on
the key's remote, and the Range Rover chirped and the doors
unlocked and he went to the back passenger door and opened
it and looked under the floor mat and found the other money
that he had hid there. He was glad he had left that money and
glad that he had locked the doors before he left. That cleaning
girl was just a bit too smart for her own good. Something
about her bothered him, made his radar start to buzz a slight
undertone, and it made him uneasy. She was a problem that
he would fix shortly.

He took all the cash he had out of the envelopes and the
wallet and his pocket and held it all in his left hand. It made
an impressive bundle. He thumbed the money and watched
the hundreds flick by, making a sound like shuffling a deck of
playing cards. He smelled it, inhaling deeply and savoring the
singular odor of used money. Then he shut the car door and
headed up the stairs and into the house.

FORTY-FIVE

Esmeralda heard the garage door open and the sound of a car engine entering. Then the garage door began to descend, the engine shut off, and a car door opened and closed. Next came the chirp of the remote and another car door opening. He must be checking the money. She was glad she had left everything as she had found it. She didn't want him coming in angry or cautious, didn't want to have to answer any questions.

She tightened her grip on the flashlight. She would let him come in, talk nice for a while, see what developed. She had placed bowls on the table in the breakfast room, and the house smelled like hot food, comforting and reassuring. She breathed deep, trying to calm her nerves. She didn't want to appear too nervous or scared. Then the door leading in from the garage opened and even though she was expecting it, she actually jumped, her heart racing like mad. She walked around the counter slowly, the flashlight clutched tightly in her hand, held down at her side, and tried a nervous smile.

"Hey there, girlie, lookey what I brung back from the big city."

Skooley walked in, all excited with a big smile on his face, stepping briskly down the hallway toward the kitchen holding his left hand high over his head, waving a huge stack of hundred-dollar bills in the air.

Esmeralda came out from around the counter with her flashlight in her hand and her strained smile and looked up at the money he was waving high.

Suddenly she felt a startling jolt to her jaw and found herself flying backwards through the air, landing violently against a wall, her head banging and bouncing off of it, her ears ringing and her eyes tearing as she tried to understand what had just happened. She could make out the sound of something hitting the ground and smashing: a picture that was hanging on a wall or a knickknack off a shelf or maybe a wall clock that was jarred off its mooring. Or maybe what she heard was her own body smashing against the wall, her brain rattling around in her head. Her eyes registered nothing but a red haze for a second, her body not feeling any actual pain anywhere but rather just a general feeling of numbness emanating outward from her head and down throughout the rest of her body, the harsh buzzing tone in her ears seeming to get louder and louder.

"Something sure smells yummy," he said cheerfully.

She heard the words but they seemed to be coming from a distance, the buzzing tone all but drowning out all other sounds.

Skooley walked into the kitchen and looked at Esmeralda lying dazed against the wall. He kneeled down in front of her and looked her in the eyes.

"Man, girl, you got yourself a jaw like a block of concrete, you know that? Look at my knuckle! Man, it hurts like a mother." He stood up and walked to the island counter and began running the cold water over his right fist. He looked down at it again and saw a small cut oozing blood. "Geez, I'm fucking bleeding! Musta caught you one good, right on the old button, huh? Hope this knuckle don't swell up on me too much." He moved his fingers one after the other like he was waving. "Maybe I should put some ice on it."

Esmeralda blinked her eyes and felt a tear from each watery eye run down both cheeks. She tried to move but nothing seemed to work right, her arms hung loosely at her sides, her hands sort of resting on the floor. She managed to raise her head a bit and through a red haze saw the flashlight that she had been holding so tightly in her hand just a second ago lying in the middle of the hallway about a million miles from where she lay.

Skooley turned off the cold-water faucet and looked down at his fist. Then he put the money down on the counter, reached down and unclipped the go phone he had attached to his belt and put that on the counter too, then grabbed a paper towel off the roll that was hanging under one of the cabinets and delicately dabbed at the cut. He walked over to where the two pots of chili slowly simmered and breathed in deep.

"I forgot you was cooking us dinner. Might have waited until we ate before I socked you on the jaw. Why'd you cook two pots?" He grabbed the spoon that was lying next to the stove and dipped it into the smaller pot and tasted. Then he did the same with the larger pot.

"Whoooieee, that's what I call me some hot and spicy chili!" He looked on the counter and saw some diced raw onion in a small bowl and a sealed bag of processed, shredded cheddar cheese. "I see you got us all the fixings too. Good, because I'm starved. All the excitement of visiting New York City for the very first time and all, I guess I just sort of forgot about eating. Last thing I had was them donuts and coffee you brung me this morning. Did you know I saw the Empire State Building today? Drove right past her, had my head out the damn window looking up the whole time. Nearly pulled a muscle in my neck, that building was so tall. All them buildings in New York are tall, but that Empire State, man, that was something else. Warren, he was the fellow I met with, he told me he lived there in New York City his whole life and never once climbed to the top. You believe that shit? Was making like I was some sort of asshole for even suggesting it. What kind of dumbass has the chance to climb a building like that and don't do it, not even once? Unbelievable! I hope you saved me some beer." He walked over to the fridge and pulled open one of the doors and grabbed a Stella off the shelf. He looked over his shoulder at her and said, "You want one too?

Oh, I forgot, you got yourself a sore jaw. Maybe you should stay away from the beer for a bit, stay away from that chili too, I guess. That little pot, that was for your dinner wasn't it? Well, I'll dig into this hot and spicy batch first. If I'm still hungry after, maybe I'll help you finish up yours. I bet you ain't gonna feel much like eating anyways."

Skooley walked back to the counter, found the bottle opener, opened the beer, and then took a long pull on the bottle. He walked around the island, stepped over Esmeralda's legs, and went into the breakfast room. He placed his bottle on the table and picked up one of the bowls.

"Hey, Esmeralda, you set me up right where your buddy Ray was sitting when I whacked him in his head with the fry pan. How 'bout that? You realize neither you nor me have set down in this chair since we known each other? Think about it. I noticed that right away, that first time we set down at this table to talk things over, get to know each other. You wouldn't a noticed 'cause you didn't know nothing about Ray and the Spam and my career as a little league slugger. Wait, I might a told ya about the little league some, remember when I told you about me and Diggs, but you wouldn't a known about Ray."

He took the bowl from the table and walked back into the kitchen, stepping over Esmeralda again, and filled his bowl from the large pot and sprinkled some chopped onion on top and then opened the bag of shredded cheddar and put a handful on top of the onions.

"Man, this looks good."

He carried the bowl back to the table and set it down in front of the chair that Ray had once occupied and then pulled out the chair and sat down on it.

"Hey, Esmeralda, I can't see you sitting over there like that." He pushed his chair back with just his legs and stood up. "Where's my manners? My daddy brought me up better'n this."

He walked over to where she lay against the wall.

"It ain't very polite of me to eat all by my lonesome after you went to all that trouble to cook and all, me enjoying my dinner way over there and you just sitting here looking like a silly cunt staring at nothing all. Here, let me help you."

He reached down and grabbed a handful of her thick, dark hair and then violently yanked it, dragging her body off the wall and toward the breakfast room. The pain shot right to her brain, making her gasp and she reached up and tried to claw at the hand entangled in her hair, her legs kicking and trying to get some purchase to take the weight off her head and hair, and he seemed not to even notice as he continued dragging her like some cartoon caveman the fifteen or so feet into the breakfast room. Suddenly, he let go of her hair and her head crashed down and bounced off the wood floor, and she actually saw an explosion of stars in front of her eyes like they sometimes showed on the cartoons her brothers and sister watched on morning TV. She found herself lying on the floor, looking up at him through teary eyes. He looked down at her, smiled, and then stepped back and hop-skipped forward into a vicious kick that landed squarely and painfully in her side, just below her ribs. She rolled over as the breath seemed to have actually been sucked out of her body and unconsciously curled into a fetal position. She was aware of some moaning noise and realized it was coming out of her own throat.

"There, this is a lot more cozy, ain't it? This way we can see each other, enjoy a nice meal together like we done last night at the restaurant. Hey, what we got here?"

He bent down and rolled up her pant leg and removed the paring knife that she had tucked into her sock.

"Damn, girl, you're just full of surprises, you know that?"

He went back to the kitchen and tossed the knife onto the kitchen counter. Then came back to the breakfast room, stepped over her, and walked back to the other side of the table where he had set his bowl and beer bottle.

"Mmmmm, don't that just smell delicious!" He leaned over the bowl of chili and breathed deep through his nose. Then he grabbed his spoon and scooped out a large spoonful, thin strings of melted cheddar cheese rising with the spoon all the way to where it stopped near his mouth. He waited, hovering the spoon for a few seconds in front of his face, blowing gently over it. He was watching Esmeralda and thinking about the knife he had found in her sock, and then he slowly lowered the spoon back down and set it back into the steaming bowl.

Esmeralda was just starting to get her wind back. She unfurled herself, breathing shallow breaths and letting her muscles react, checking to see how much it was going to hurt before each movement. She worked her way against the wall, slowly and painfully inching her back up so that she was sitting facing Skooley. She was holding her side where he had kicked her, the pain there less intense than right after he had delivered the blow but still sore and aching.

"That feeling there in your side, that'll ease up some in a few minutes. Probably just knocked the wind outta ya. Learned that one from my daddy, only I was on your side of the boot so to speak. I knowed that dragging ya over like that by your hair would wake you up some, clear the daze outta your eyes, so I kicked ya just that once to give you something to think about while I eat my dinner."

Esmeralda tried to get up, slid back down to the floor, and then painfully tried to work her way up the wall again. Skooley took a sip of his beer and looked at her with dead, shark eyes. She finally made it to a standing position and on wobbly feet took a step toward the table. She grabbed hold of the back of the chair that was opposite Skooley's end of the table, gently pulled it out, and then slowly eased her body down.

Esmeralda tried to talk. She could only make a grunting noise at first.

"Take your time, girlie. We ain't going nowhere. Your voice'll come back in a minute or so. No need to rush yourself.

That pain in your side, that will ease up some too. Just give it a little time."

She rubbed her side gently where his foot had struck her. The pain was still sharp, but he was right, it hurt less than it had just a few minutes ago.

"What you need is something in your stomach. Settle things down some."

She tried to speak and nothing came out. Then she took a breath and started again. "I, I don't think I can eat anything."

Skooley smiled and got up from the table. "Sure you can. Look, I've been where you are right now hundreds of times. I know exactly what you're going through, and the best thing is to get something in your stomach. How about I fix you up a bowl of some of this here chili? You made that other pot for you right? I mean the little one. How about I fix you up a nice bowl from that?"

She shook her head. "I think it will make me throw up."

She looked up at Skooley, and he was no longer smiling.

"No, it won't, Esmeralda, really, you need to eat something."

She looked back down at her lap and leaned over a little, testing the pain.

"Okay, Lamar, I'll try. But give me the hot one, the one in the big pot. The last time I ate hot peppers, it made my mouth numb. My mouth hurts now, where you hit me, maybe it will dull the pain in my lip."

Skooley brightened up, his face shining like a child's.

"That's the spirit! Hey, I got an idea, how about I mix the two of 'em together, so it's not too spicy? That way you can try 'em both!"

He walked into the kitchen and she heard the pots rattling and a spoon tapping against a bowl and he came back around carrying a steaming bowl, which he set in front of her.

Esmeralda's head was spinning and she felt slightly nauseous, but she slowly grabbed the spoon and delicately stirred the chili. She saw Skooley watching her from the other side of the table. She dug into the bowl and took a heaping spoonful and hovered it in front of her mouth and blew gently on it. Skooley watched her intently, almost transfixed. Then she opened her mouth and put the chili in and chewed slowly. Skooley continued to stare at her, not saying anything. She closed her eyes and swallowed. When she opened her eyes again, they began tearing.

"Wow, that's hot," she said, "it's making my eyes water. But you know what? I think you were right, Lamar. I think it does feel better to eat something." Then she dipped her spoon back into the chili, stirred it again, brought another heaping spoonful into her mouth and began chewing.

She watched as Skooley's face broke into a big smile, and then he sat back down at the table and grabbed his spoon and took in a big mouthful himself. Once he got it into his mouth, he started bouncing up and down in his seat and fanning his fingers in front of his face. He was sucking in air and chewing intermittently, and he grabbed his beer bottle and took in a quick mouthful of beer and seemed to swish it around in his mouth like mouthwash and then he finally got the whole thing swallowed.

"Yeooow," he said, shaking his head, "but that's some good stinking chili. What kinda peppers you put in this, girl?" He glanced down at the bowl and took another heaping spoonful as thin strings of melted cheddar cheese rose with the spoon all the way to where it stopped near his mouth. This time he waited, hovering the spoon for a few seconds in front of his face, blowing gently over it. Then he carefully inserted it into his mouth, his other hand clutching the beer bottle that was at the ready on the table and chewed thoughtfully.

"Man, that's good. I just gotta ease into it is all. You remember that story I told that guy Warren on the phone? The one about Big Bill choking and crying 'cause he ate those hot peppers after he done told me how he liked his Mexican real hot and spicy? Well, that was no lie. This reminds me of that shit I ate with him that day. We was both sweating, but I honest to God like it hot. Like this here chili; the hotter it is, the better I like it. But old Big Bill, he just about coughed up a lung. I was laughing so hard, I nearly done the same."

She watched as he took another big mouthful, his cheeks flushed and his eyes watery and sparkling. He continued eating, shoveling one spoonful after another into his mouth, and she wondered again how anyone could actually enjoy eating something that hot and spicy. Then he got up, carrying his bowl with both hands like a child carrying his cereal bowl to the breakfast table and walked past her into the kitchen. She heard him fill up his bowl with more hot chili and onions and cheese and then she heard the refrigerator door open and then the sound of the bottle cap coming off and bouncing on the granite countertop and he came walking around the counter with the chili bowl in one hand and a beer in the other.

"Glad I shut off them burners after I got us those first bowls. Was so damn hot—I mean temperature wise, not spicy hot—that I almost couldn't eat it. Looks like it cooled down some. Still, better to be careful. Got a sore hand already, don't want to end up driving all night with a burnt mouth too."

Esmeralda dipped her spoon into her chili and was about to take another bite, then slowly lowered the spoon away from her face and let it rest back into her bowl.

"What's the matter, girl? You don't like your own cooking?"

"I'm not feeling so good, Lamar. My stomach, I mean. Maybe eating wasn't such a good idea."

"Yeah, well, I wasn't exactly being truthful with you before. About feeling better after you ate something. Actually, eating might not have been the best thing for you after a kick to the ribs." He gave her one of his big great-guy smiles, then got up from the table and went around into the kitchen. She heard him rummaging around and he came back with a plastic shopping bag. He set it down on the table in front of her, right next to her bowl.

"You got to puke, do in that. Don't want to make more of a mess of nice Mrs. Russell's breakfast room."

He went back to his seat and resumed shoveling chili into his mouth. Esmeralda grabbed the bag off the table and held it ready between her legs. She waited for something to happen, but the nauseous feeling subsided and she lifted her head and looked back up at Skooley.

"Why did you kill Raymundo?" she asked softly. It still hurt to speak.

"Huh?" He had brown chili sauce oozing out the corners of his lips and thin strings of melted cheddar cheese clinging to his chin.

"Ray. Why'd you kill him?"

"Ah, your boyfriend, Ray-mun-do. Wait, he ain't your boyfriend, right? I mean, wasn't. Well, that Mexican fucker was a pussy, through and through. Did I tell you he pulled a gun on me? Just 'cause I was foolin' with him a bit. Pulled a fucking gun right out of his ass, he did. Can you believe that shit? You shoulda seen him, his face sweating, his hand shaking like Don Knots in that old movie, *The Shakiest Gun in the West*, you ever see that one? Boy, that was one funny movie. I wouldn't a touched a hair on old Ray's head, he hadn't a pulled out that gun. He shouldn't a started ordering me around like that neither, treating me like I was his bitch, little-ass pussy with his shaky gun, 'we gonna do this, Skools, we gonna do that.' So, what was I gonna do? How could I trust a guy pulls a gun on me? What if he decides he wants to take everything all for himself, you know? Well, I'll tell ya what, then it would'a been me sitting there against that wall just like you were a few minutes ago only instead of just nursing some sore ribs and a cut lip, I'd be leaking blood all over this nice wood floor from being shot full of holes by the shakiest gun in the west." He laughed at his own joke.

"You're going to kill me too, aren't you, Lamar, just like

you did Raymundo."

Skooley was sweating. He wiped his brow with the back of his hand, then took another sip of beer.

"Well, yeah, you got me there, Esmeralda. I guess I am. But not like old Ray. First, I'm gonna strip you down naked and fuck you in every hole you got. I been dying to get my hands on them titties of yours since I first seen you, remember, when I was in the hot tub and you was sitting there smoking my cigarettes like they was yours? You shoulda joined me then, got outta them clothes and into that hot tub, we coulda had us some fun. Say, I was just wondering, you like dick or are you one of them muff divers? It don't matter none now, you know, but I was just wondering."

Esmeralda suddenly dropped her head down and threw up violently into the plastic bag on her lap. The contents of her stomach burned her throat as it came up and this made her gag and heave once again. She stopped suddenly, waiting to see if anything would happen. Nothing did for a second and then she dry heaved once more.

"Now that's just plain gross, Esmeralda. Good thing I don't have a sensitive stomach. On the up side, I guess you ain't gonna eat any more chili, so maybe I'll just have me another bowl." He shoved one last spoonful into his mouth and then got up and walked past Esmeralda still chewing into the kitchen for a refill.

When he returned, Esmeralda was sitting up straighter than before.

"You're right, Lamar, it doesn't hurt as much as before."

He watched her lean over slowly, testing the pain, and then, slowly, straighten back up again.

Skooley walked past her carefully, carrying his full bowl and sat down. He felt flushed and was sweating even more heavily than before. He wiped at his forehead with the back of one hand again and then rubbed the sweat off on his pant leg.

"That burned as much coming up as it did going down,"

said Esmeralda as she tied the plastic shopping bag off in a knot and then dropped it onto the floor. Then she looked at Skooley and sat quietly watching him eat.

"I don't know how you can eat things that are so hot. I mean, you can't really taste anything, can you?"

Skooley didn't answer. He just kept eating and taking sips of beer between spoonfuls.

Now that the pepper and stomach-acid taste in her mouth was dissipating, Esmeralda could once again detect the coppery taste of blood on her tongue. She delicately reached up and touched the cut on her swollen lip. Her finger came away sticky and red.

"You know what's really gross, Lamar? Sitting here watching you shovel that food into your mouth like it was your last meal. You're going at it like an animal. You don't even know what's in it. How do you know I didn't doctor my recipe a little, maybe add a little something extra, just for you."

Skooley's spoon stopped halfway to his mouth. He looked at Esmeralda and realized that he didn't like the way this conversation was going.

"I ain't too worried about that, girl. I made you eat it first, remember? I sat right here and watched you eat chili from both pots. Watched you swallow it right down."

"Yes, Skooley, I remember."

She looked down at the floor.

He smiled to himself more than at her and resumed eating.

Then Esmeralda turned her face back up at him and smiled through bloody teeth. It was so unexpected, that bloody smile, that it caught him unaware and his breath stopped short and he had a coughing fit like something was stuck in his throat. When the coughing subsided, he grabbed his beer and took several long swallows. He put his beer back down on the table, but his throat felt strange, like it was beginning to swell, like maybe he had strained something inside his throat from coughing so hard. He was sweating again and this time he grabbed at his shirt near his shoulder and turned his head and dragged the material across his forehead to mop up the moisture.

"Guess I went a little heavy on those habanero peppers, huh, Lamar? You don't look so good. You look like your friend Big Bill must have looked when he ate those hot peppers down in Florida. Maybe you ought to slow down, try not to eat so fast."

Skooley wasn't feeling right. He grabbed his beer and took another long pull.

Esmeralda leaned over again, and then came back up slowly, testing the pain some more.

"You know, the more I move, the less it seems to hurt. It hurts when I bend down, but after I sit up again, it doesn't hurt as much."

She looked at Skooley's face. It had turned bright red, and the muscles on his cheeks were beginning to tick and twitch. She could hear his breath coming faster, getting a little raspy.

"Boy, look at you, Skooley, turning all red and breathing hard like that. Big tough guy like you, telling me about eating peppers so hot you can't feel your tongue, then sitting there sweating and coughing after a few bowls of chili. What's with that? Maybe I should take a video with my phone like that girl in the bar, send it to Big Bill down in Florida, give him something to laugh at. He could share it with your new friend, what's his name, that guy in New York who won't climb the Empire State Building. Warren? Both of them have a good laugh."

She leaned over again and then straightened up slowly. She watched as Skooley's head began to hang down a bit, his facial muscles twitching more and more, a very slight froth forming at the corners of his mouth.

"Or maybe it's something else got you all hot and bothered? I guess you really can't wait to take my clothes off, fuck me in every hole, is that it, Skooley?"

He looked up at her with hard eyes, his hands clutching the

sides of the table so tightly that she could see every knuckle on each hand shining bright white.

"What you done to me, bitch?" he croaked.

She bent over again, even lower than before, this time noticing that she could move a bit faster and less painfully.

"Well, Lamar, while you were out there sightseeing in New York, I had a busy day myself. I found that lockbox, by the way, you know, the one we were looking for, then I made that delicious meal you just wolfed down, extra hot and spicy with jalapeños and habaneros, just the way you like. I even cut up a nice piece of raw onion so you could add a little zest to it yourself if you wanted. Then I decided I'd better add a few more things to that chili."

She straightened up and sat upright in her chair.

"See, all day long I was thinking about what would happen when you got back. I knew about Raymundo; well, I guessed really, I didn't absolutely know for sure that you killed him until you told me that you hit him in the head with the frying pan. But I found his phone in the backyard, in the woods. I knew he wouldn't just leave without it. I tried calling him a bunch of times and no one answered. I thought he just didn't want to talk to me, maybe he felt guilty about running off, but then I tried calling him this afternoon, from outside and I heard his phone ring in the woods out back. In the back of my mind I wondered if maybe he was dead, but when I heard that phone, I knew. I thought I was going to find the phone in his pocket, you know, on his dead body. But it was just the phone lying there in the woods. Still, like I told you, Lamar, I'm not stupid. And then later, I found something else too."

She stood up painfully and reached into her back pocket and brought out Raymundo's wallet and dropped it onto the table, then gingerly sat back down again.

"It's Raymundo's wallet," she said. "I found it in the garage. I was scared all day, Lamar. I mean, really scared. You have a gun. I saw it on the front seat of the Range Rover. I knew I had to do something to protect myself. Even if I couldn't and I didn't make it through the night, you know, if you went ahead and killed me, I decided you were weren't going to make it either, Lamar. You're a psycho. I bet you killed other people besides Raymundo, didn't you? Probably lots of people. So I started hunting around for something special to put into your chili. I knew you'd eat it, even if you killed me first, I knew you'd still eat that damned chili. I was upstairs earlier, found some nice flavorful ingredients, Percocets, some Ambien, and a few Valiums, other pills that I don't even know what they're for. I crushed them all together, every single pill I could find, added it right into the pot, mixed it in with the beans and the tomato sauce. Then I went into the garage and found that last crucial ingredient, the one I expect is giving you the most discomfort right now. Box of rat poison, Lamar, you must have seen it. You had to. Gee, isn't that funny? Rat poison for a stinking rat like you. And guess what was sitting there? On the back of the shelf right next to this big yellow box of rat poison?"

"This." She tapped the wallet that was now lying on the table.

"I was going to see how things went. No, that's not really true. I knew how things would go. You just made it easy for me, Lamar. I don't feel bad or guilty or anything. You just punched me without saying anything. But you're dangerous and you're smart; you smelled a rat because you are a rat. You found that knife I put in my sock, and then you started thinking about that chili. So you wanted to see me eat it first. You figured I wouldn't eat it if I put something bad into it, didn't you? But what you didn't realize, Lamar, is that I just didn't care. I knew that you were going to kill me. I knew it all day long. So what if I ate that chili and died? So what? At least you'd be dead too, Lamar. That's was I was thinking when I put that poison into my mouth and swallowed it down. But then maybe I'm not going to die after all."

She reached down and picked up the knotted plastic bag that she had vomited into earlier and then set it onto the table.

"As for you, well, you don't look so good. I guess this is going to spoil your plans. Remember how you told me you were going to strip me naked and fuck me and then kill me? You are an animal, Skooley. You're a rat, and you deserve to die like a rat."

His body had started convulsing, the foam around his mouth getting thicker, making him look rabid. The table moved violently to one side and Skooley stood up, weaving from side to side. He made his way toward Esmeralda, one hand bouncing along the table, helping to support his weight as he lunged toward her.

Esmeralda stood up quickly and, just as he reached for her, her hand came around from behind her back, swinging the heavy flashlight that she had placed by the chair earlier and caught him square on the side of his head. He fell over, heavily knocking one of the chairs over as he went down, landing at her feet, his face just inches from her foot.

Esmeralda's heart was racing again and her ribs ached with every breath she took and she thanked God that she had thought to place that flashlight where she had. She had grabbed it just a few seconds earlier and held it in her hand under the table as she talked. She hadn't expected Skooley to lunge at her like that. She had watched him—the facial tics and muscle spasms and the sweating and foaming at the mouth—and she hadn't taken her eyes off him and he looked like he was going to just fall over, right there in his seat. It had shocked and surprised her when he got up. If she wasn't already holding the flashlight, she didn't know what would have happened. As it was, she hadn't even thought about what she was doing; she just reacted, swinging with all her might.

But he was down now, and she didn't think he would be getting up too quickly. Still, she stepped away from him, not wanting to be within reach of his grasp.

She looked down at the flashlight in her hand and saw that it and her hand were both trembling. She was about to put the flashlight down but then thought better of it and carried it with her into the kitchen. She went to the fridge and took out a beer and put the flashlight down and then used the opener to pop the cap and picked up the bottle with one shaking hand and picked up the flashlight with the other and walked back to the breakfast room. She put the beer down on the table and then dragged one of the chairs away from the table, far away from Skooley and went back and picked up the beer and then walked over to where she had dragged the chair and sat down. She took a sip of beer and then for some reason she started laughing and she couldn't seem to stop and she laughed for a full minute or so and then the laugh sort of transitioned into a sob and she sat and cried hard for a good fifteen or twenty minutes, the beer and the flashlight never leaving her hands.

FORTY-SIX

It was about 7:30 p.m. She sat on the edge of the couch in the family room in darkness and looked out and up into the sky over the backyard. The sun had gone down over an hour ago, but she could still see the last traces of light tingeing the sky overhead. She had been sitting here on the couch for quite some time, not sure of what to do. She got up and checked on Skooley again. He hadn't moved much. He was still lying where he had fallen. For a time he had rolled over onto his side, then onto his back, now he was on his side again. The ticks and muscle spasms seemed to come and go; his eyes were closed now but they had opened for a while before and the pupils inside his eyes had enlarged almost to the size of quarters, his eyeballs protruding out of their sockets like two golf balls. She was hoping he would just die. She figured he would, but she didn't know how long it would take. She had been trying to formulate some kind of plan for what to do with him. It took a while, but as before, she came up with an idea and decided to just go with it.

She got up and walked over to where Skooley lay. She held the flashlight, raised in her hand ready to strike, and began reaching into his pockets. She pulled out a handful of keys, several sets including the keys to the Range Rover and the Mercedes, and one loose circular lockbox key. She held it up and looked at it closely. Maybe it would end up being the key to her dreams, she thought as she slid it into her pocket. Next, she pulled out another key ring from his pocket with two

235

flash drives attached. Shit, she thought, had to be property of the Jumbo cartel—the flash drives he said he had returned to them. Just like the money he had returned. This Skooley was something else. No wonder these people from Miami were after him, why he seemed so anxious and so eager to be on his way. What had he said, something about driving all night? He was going to kill her and then take off. She corrected herself in her head: fuck me first, then kill me. Shit, she'd rather die than let that animal touch her. She searched his other pockets and found the small leather codebook as well. She just shook her head.

"Skooley, you were dead-set on getting yourself killed, weren't you? If you didn't eat that chili, hell, those guys from Miami would end up catching you eventually and cut your fingers off, one by one. Probably your penis too, after they found those flash drives and that codebook in your pocket. You really think you could have blackmailed them? They make you look like a choirboy." She kept the keys to the Russells' cars but returned the Toyota keys, flash drives, and the codebook to his pockets. She didn't want anything to do with those, nothing at all. She was already in enough trouble.

She stood up and carried the Russells' car keys through the kitchen and down the hall, replacing them on the key pegs in the mudroom. Then she walked into the kitchen, found a plastic bag, pulled all the knives out of their holders, and then went through all the kitchen drawers placing whatever knives she found into the bag. When she was satisfied, she grabbed her flashlight and went back to check on Skooley one final time. He was just as she had left him, facedown on the floor.

The house was getting dark, so she turned on the light over the stove, confident that no one could see it from outside, and used her flashlight to make her way into the garage. She placed the bag full of knives under the rear of the Mercedes, then went out the back door and into the backyard.

She walked down the middle of the driveway, knowing she

could jump into the woods if she saw the lights of an oncom-
ing car. She didn't see any cars at all the entire way back to
the lot at Patriot's Path. There was one other car still in the
lot besides her own and she was glad, figuring if there were two
cars still there, one would not look suspicious to any policeman
that might have driven past. She took her car keys out of her
pocket, unlocked the doors, and got inside. She got out again
almost in a panic, ran around to the back and opened the tailgate, moving the cleaning implements around until she saw
the Macy's bag. She poked it with her finger, feeling the hard
metal case, and felt instant relief. She was tempted to use the
key to unlock the box and take a quick peek inside, but resisted.
She closed the tailgate and got back into the car again, reached
into her pocket and slid the lockbox key onto her key ring,
then started the car up and began driving back to the house.

She drove slowly, keeping an eye out both ahead and behind for any signs of car lights. When she got to within about
a hundred yards of the driveway, she turned off the headlights
and tried to guide the car in without having to hit the brakes.
She had to brake once before she made it to the garage and
then she slammed the car into park and turned off the engine.
She flipped the switch of the overhead lamp so that the light
wouldn't turn on when she opened the door and got out of
the car.

Once she was around the garage, she turned on the flashlight and slowly crept to the back door that led into the garage.
She edged her way up the rickety stairs as quietly as she could,
turned the knob silently, and eased the door open. The house
was dark except for the dull light that she had left on above
the stove in the kitchen. She walked on her toes as quietly as
she could down the hall toward it. She almost tripped over the
flashlight that had fallen out of her hand when Skooley had
punched her in the jaw, and she picked it up to hold as a
weapon, just in case.

She fought the urge to whisper his name and shined the light ahead of her and into each room as she passed it: the mudroom, the half bath, the small office, and finally into the kitchen. She poked her head in first, flashlight club at the ready. Everything seemed quiet. She shined the light into every corner, then slowly made her way around the center island expecting Skooley to jump up and grab her at any minute like some horror movie monster.

But there was no one in the kitchen. She peeked into the breakfast room and shone the light to where she had left Skooley.

Only Skooley wasn't there.

Her heart started pounding again, and sweat seemed to just turn on like a faucet, dripping from her scalp down her temples and her forehead and into her eyes causing them to burn and blurring her vision. She fought the urge to run back out of the kitchen the same way she had just come in and jump into her car and go home to her mother and her brothers and sister and just sit on the couch and watch TV and hug them all.

She continued slowly into the breakfast room, moving the light ahead of her as she entered the room. She heard a sound, like a metallic click, coming from somewhere up ahead. She stopped, realizing suddenly that she could have just clicked on the lights when she first got back, but now she wasn't sure where the light switch was and didn't want to take her eyes from up ahead where she had heard the sound. She shown the light into the family room and thought she could make out a leg. Skooley must be sitting on the floor with his back to the couch, facing this way. She moved slowly and cautiously.

"Lamar?" she said, her voice soft, almost a whisper. "Lamar, are you okay? I got something here to help you. I looked on the computer when you were passed out. I found something to counteract that rat poison you ate. I just got back from the drug store. You hear me, Lamar? I've got something that's going to help you."

She could hear him breathing up ahead, raspy and rough like a wounded animal. Just what he is, she thought. And just as dangerous.

"Lamar, can you hear me? I'm coming in, okay? I'm going to help you."

She worked her way to the far side of the breakfast room, around the table and chairs, keeping as much distance between her and the leg that she saw sticking out of the family room as she could. As she edged closer, she could make out more and more of him. He was sitting with his back propped up to the couch, one of the cushions was off and lying on the floor next to him. His head was lolling to one side. He had foam and spittle around his mouth and a string of thick saliva hanging down his chin and sticking to his chest. His eyes were rolling back in his head.

"Skooley?" She worked the light slowly up his legs and to his chest and finally to his face. He turned away from the light for just a second. Then slowly raised his left hand to shield his eyes from the light. As he did, he eased his right hand out from under the couch cushion on the floor next to him and slowly waved a gun in her direction. A loud explosion erupted from the family room and something slammed into the wall right next to her head. She was momentarily startled, and then she stood up furious and walked quickly and decisively over to where he was sitting, screaming as she walked, "Why don't you just fucking die, you fucking psycho?" And she swung the flashlight she had planned to use as a weapon with all her might and hit the feeble hand that was waving the gun and she heard something fly across the room and hit the wall and then she backswung the flashlight connecting with the side of his head and he fell silently over onto his side.

She was standing over him, breathing hard, waiting to see if he moved. She had the beam of one flashlight trained on him and the other raised over her head. She was ready to hit him again. She would keep on hitting him too until there was nothing left of him; all he had to do was fucking move. But he didn't move. Not a muscle. Finally, she directed the light onto his head and then down to his face. There was a large cut on his forehead where she had hit him with the flashlight. Blood was trickling down from the cut and pooling in his eye socket and then running down his nose, producing steady drips onto the rug. He was still breathing, but his breath was now much more shallow, not the heavy, raspy animal breaths she had heard before.

"You're something else, Skooley, you know that? You're not even fucking human, you piece of shit!" She heard someone shouting in a high shrill voice and realized that it was hers. It was her that was shouting, and she stopped, the absolute quiet suddenly taking over the dark room, making just as startling an impact as the loud shot that was fired just a few seconds ago. She was still standing over him, and she felt the strain of her arm muscles and lowered the flashlight slowly that she held raised above her head and stepped back away from him, keeping her eyes on him the whole time.

She shown the flashlight around the room and saw a small lamp in the corner that she hadn't even noticed before and walked over to it and flicked the switch on, bathing the room in soft, warm light. She saw the gun near the wall on the far side of the room where it had landed when she knocked it out of his hand, dropped the flashlight she had used as a club, and walked over to the gun, picked it up, and with her finger on the trigger, pointed it at Skooley. She made her way cautiously past him again and back into the breakfast room and then into the kitchen where she put the flashlight on the counter and then turned on the tap of the island's faucet and using her cupped hand took a long drink of cool water.

Her throat was parched, and the water felt like heaven going down.

When she'd had enough, she turned the water off and walked back inside and sat at the table, putting the gun down delicately. She put both of her elbows on the table and then rested her head wearily into her cupped hands.

She was calmer now, and as she breathed deep and steady, she realized that she wasn't afraid of him anymore. She wasn't afraid of Skooley. Not because he was poisoned and hurt, it wasn't that at all.

She just wasn't afraid.

Now all she had to do was get rid of that fuckhead once and for all.

FORTY-SEVEN

She got some wet paper towels from the kitchen and cleaned him up as best she could, wiping the blood and foam and spittle from his mouth and face. She cleaned the cut on his head as well, though it continued to bleed some, but the blood was starting to congeal, staunching the flow.

Her plan was simple. Drive him over to his car in Bernardsville, put him in the driver's seat, and leave him there. She had put a lethal mix in that chili, she was sure of it. She also had Raymundo's wallet. And his cell phone. Probably best to shove his cell phone somewhere behind the seat; the cops will find it when they find Skooley. Let them chase a ghost. No, wait, she had called his phone from her phone. Shit. But she had his wallet too. Maybe slide the wallet down behind the seat like it fell out of a pocket. It felt obvious, maybe too obvious, but at this point she didn't really care. She went over to the table and picked up Raymundo's wallet and wiped everywhere that she had touched with clean paper towels. Then, carrying the wallet in the paper towel, she walked back to Skooley and put the wallet in his hand making sure to get his prints all over it, let the cops sort it out. Then she took the phone out of her shirt pocket and slipped the wallet with the paper towel still around it in its place. She walked with the phone out to the backyard and crushed it with a rock. Then she brought the broken pieces back into the house and threw them into the garbage. After she was done with Skooley, she would return to the house and clean the place.

Cleaning up, she thought, was something she was good at.

It wasn't easy, but she dragged Skooley outside and got him seated in the passenger seat of her station wagon. She brought the flashlight with her as well. She walked back inside and grabbed the money and the phone that Skooley had left on the kitchen counter and then retrieved the revolver that she had left on the breakfast room table. She would bring it with her, then maybe wipe it down and leave it in the car with Skooley for the cops to find. Or maybe just keep it. She went back outside with the money and the phone and the gun and then opened the tailgate and put them into a cleaning bucket and then stuffed the bucket with dirty rags and sponges. She tried to think of what, if anything, she had forgotten to do.

She couldn't think of anything, and so she got in the car and started it up.

It was about 9:15 p.m. She wished it was later, but then figured where Skooley was parked in that lot near the rooming house would probably be fairly deserted now as most of the people who lived there were kitchen help and would most likely be working. Also, Skooley had parked in the back corner of the lot. As long as no kids were parked there making out, and no cops decided to come cruising past the lot just when she was unloading Lamar, she should be fine.

She drove down the driveway with the lights off, and then turned left onto the road for about a hundred yards before turning her lights on. She was scared, and she gripped the steering wheel so hard that her hands ached. She drove slowly and carefully, watching each car that she saw, praying she wouldn't see any type of emergency lights indicating that the driver was law enforcement. Every time a car came up from the rear, she expected to see red lights flashing on its roof and from its grille, and her head ached and her mouth was dry. Skooley sat next to her, head lolling to one side, eyes closed. She wondered if he would die, or if all that stuff she had put into his food might not have been as potent as she had thought. Maybe cooking it had somehow weakened whatever effects they had on the body. But she had put a lot in. She once had to take Percocet when she had broken her wrist playing soccer in high school. It was a painkiller, and she remembered that every time she took one, she ended up falling asleep for a few hours. She had stopped taking them after that first day because she just didn't like the way they made her feel. She couldn't remember how many of those she had crushed into the chili, but those along with the Ambien and assorted other pills, not to mention the rat poison, had to be lethal. Shit, if the cops pulled her over, how would she explain Skooley? She tried not to think about it and concentrated on driving carefully.

She got onto Main Street in Mendham and drove past the strip mall by the post office and turned onto Tempe Wick Road and followed that for several miles past old farmhouses and fields and then through Jockey Hollow Recreational Park. There were no streetlights on the road and the night had gotten dark and she was extra careful to look for the glowing eyes of deer or other animals in the woods along the side of the road. Tonight of all nights she did not want to take a chance on hitting a deer. Only a few cars were on the road in either direction, and she was glad for it.

When she got to Mt. Kemble Avenue, she turned right and headed toward the town of Bernardsville just a few miles to the south. She panicked for a second, thinking maybe she had forgotten the keys to Skooley's car, then remembered that she had put them back into his pocket.

She drove into town, turned left, and crossed the railroad tracks and then left again and down the street toward the old rooming house. She stopped about a block away and pulled over to the curb.

"Hey, Lamar, how you doing?"

His eyes opened and the lids fluttered for just a second, then they closed again, head to the side, labored breathing.

"I'm just going to reach into your pocket, get your keys.

I'll help you to your room, call an ambulance if you're not feeling better. How's that sound?"

She patted one pocket and then the other. She felt keys in the right-hand pocket and decided it would be easier if she got out, walked around, and reached in through his door. The interior light switch was still turned off, so she kept the car running and quickly walked around and opened the passenger door and Skooley would have fallen right out of the car if she hadn't belted him in and she struggled her right hand into his pocket and pulled out his keys and shut the door as quietly as she could and quickly ran around the car and climbed in and began driving slowly toward the parking lot of the rooming house.

The lot was dark and almost empty. She drove in and made a slow loop, trying to look into the few parked cars to see if anyone was inside. She didn't see anyone, so she drove to the end of the lot and parked on the driver's side of the dirty white Camry.

She shut off the engine, got out of the car, and looked around again. Nobody. She closed her door quietly, then took Skooley's keys and unlocked the driver's side door of the Camry. The interior light turned on, so she leaned into the car and reached up and moved the switch to the off position, returning the car to darkness. She sat in the driver's seat and fumbled her hand around under the seat and found the lever and then slid the seat back as far as it would go.

She got out of the car, leaving the door open, took a quick look around again and then opened Skooley's door and undid his seat belt and started dragging him out of the car.

"Come on, Lamar, see if you can stand up. I've got you; I'm going to help you get into this other car." She dragged him out, and he was virtually unresponsive. She managed to lean him against the Camry and started working his backside into the seat.

"How you doing, Skooley? See if you can sit."

His eyes opened and his head lifted up and her face was right next to his and he said something low and she could smell his fetid breath and she had to turn her face away.

"What was that, Lamar? What did you say?" She worked his feet into the car.

"I'll...fucking bitch."

She got him all the way in and closed the door, then she went back to her car and leaned in and found the flashlight. She closed the door quietly and then walked around to the passenger side of Skooley's car and got in.

His head was down, chin on his chest, and she reached over and grabbed his seat belt and brought it across his body and clicked it home.

She looked at the keys in her hand and found the Toyota key and put it into the ignition, the two flash drives dangling, and she thought for just a second about taking them off and putting them back into her pocket, then dismissed the thought. She just wanted to leave. She reached into her shirt pocket and retrieved the wallet that was still wrapped in the paper towel and she dropped it on her lap and she turned on her flashlight and then very carefully, using just the end of the paper towel, she stuffed the wallet as far down into the seat as it would go. She turned off the flashlight and was just reaching for the car door lever when lights illuminated the entrance to the parking lot and a car entered.

Her hand froze. The car turned away from her, and she watched as it made a slow loop around the lot and then headed for the corner where she was and pulled up right behind the Camry and the headlights were shining through the rear windshield and the car was illuminated with a light so bright it hurt her eyes.

Then suddenly the light went out.

She heard one car door open, then another. Shit, cops! She scrunched down in her seat, gripping the flashlight tightly and almost screamed when a flashlight beam hit her full in the face from the window on her right and then someone yanked open the door.

A hand reached in and grabbed her wrist and pulled her out of the car so violently that her feet couldn't grab purchase, and she was dragged on her butt to the back of the car, still clutching the flashlight, legs kicking and scrabbling behind her.

The hand let go, and she found herself at the feet of a tall man wearing neatly pressed tan slacks and dark red pointy cowboy boots that were polished to a gleaming shine.

"Who are you?" His voice was low and calm, almost kind.

She didn't say anything, and she got a light kick to her backside from the man who had dragged her out of the car, not from the pointy cowboy boots.

"Alejandro!" This time, his voice was not kind.

"Who are you," he asked again. "What are you doing here?"

She heard the door to the Camry open again.

"My name is Esmeralda."

She could just make out low conversations in Spanish coming from behind her, from inside the Camry, but she couldn't hear what was being said.

"Get up, Esmeralda. What were you doing in the car? Who is that with you?" The man had only the very slightest Hispanic accent.

"He...he tried to rape me. That guy in the car. His name is Lamar. Lamar Skooley."

"How do you know him?"

"We work at the same place sometimes. At the Lion's Head Inn. It's a restaurant. He washes dishes there. I'm a hostess."

"And he tried to rape you?"

She let out a sob. She wasn't faking either. She was scared and she was tired and she couldn't help it.

"Are you the police?" she managed to ask, looking up into his face. "Are you going to arrest him?"

One of the men who had been rummaging in the car came over and, without saying a word, handed a little black book and car keys to the man with the red boots. He smiled, then slipped the book into his jacket pocket and began removing the two flash drives from the key ring.

"Take him," he said with authority, and two men pulled Skooley out of the Camry. She watched as they roughly dragged him past her and shoved him into the back seat of the large sedan that was now sitting directly behind the Camry with the engine still running. "Alejandro, you follow us." He tossed the Camry's keys to the man who had dragged Esmeralda from the car.

"Tell me what happened here, Esmeralda. He don't look so good, our friend, Skooley." He reached his hand under her chin and raised her face gently. "You don't look so good, either."

She took a breath and tried to compose herself.

"He asked me if I would go out with him, have a drink somewhere. He was new and didn't know anybody, and he seemed nice so I met him here. That's my car, right there." She pointed to the station wagon. "Well, it's my work car. They let me use it sometimes." She sniffed and raised the hand without the flashlight to wipe at her eyes. "I clean houses too, that's my other job. Anyway, we went out and had a few drinks. Then he took these pills, like a whole handful, I don't know what they were, he tried to give them to me too but I wouldn't take any and I told him to bring me back here and when I tried to get out of the car, he grabbed at my...at my breasts and told me he was going to...you know...and he wouldn't let me out and I fought with him and he hit me in the face, in the mouth." She touched at her swollen lip gingerly. "And then he hit me some more and I tried to fight back." She stopped and took a deep breath.

"Then I grabbed this flashlight." She held up the flashlight for him to see. "It was right there, sitting on the floor of his car right at my feet, and I hit him. I hit him hard and he stopped. Then I hit him again."

She looked down at the dirty ground of the dark parking lot.

"I was scared that maybe I killed him because he stopped moving. I was going to leave, get in my car, and go home just when you pulled up. That's all."

She sniffed again, still looking down at the floor. "I just want to go home."

The man with the pointy red boots didn't say anything. One of the two men who had grabbed Skooley and placed him in the large sedan walked up to him.

"Que quieres hacer con ella?" What do you want to do with her, he asked.

"Get in the car. I'll be right there. Tell Alejandro to follow us," he told him in English as he grabbed Esmeralda's hand and led her over toward her car.

"Give me your keys," he said. She reached into her pocket, took out her keys, and handed them to him.

"What's this?" he asked, holding up the key to the lockbox.

"That's a roller skate key," she said. "I've had it since I was a little girl."

"You still have the roller skates?" he asked with a smile.

She shook her head. He reached down and put the car key into the lock and turned it, but the car was already unlocked.

"It's not locked," he said.

"I must have forgot."

He opened the door and looked into the car.

"Good thing nobody came and stole your mops and brooms."

He handed her the keys. Then he reached into his pocket.

"Your friend Skooley, he's not a very nice man. We're going to take him with us. His uncle is looking for him, worried that he might get into trouble. We'll take him home with us. His uncle will be happy to see him again."

She watched him reach into his pocket. She still held the flashlight and her grip tightened again. If she saw a knife or a gun come out, she was going to hit him with it, try to run.

He pulled out a thick wad of bills held tight with a large silver and gold money clip. He pulled the clip off and peeled two one-hundred-dollar bills off the wad.

"It would be good if you forgot about Mr. Skooley and what he did to you." Then he peeled off two more hundreds. "It would be good if you forgot about me and these other men you saw here tonight." Two additional hundreds came off the wad of money. "Best if you forgot this whole night."

He slipped the six one-hundred-dollar bills into the pocket of her jeans. "And, Esmeralda, if you ever start remembering, ever talk about this to anyone, I will find out. Then you and I will meet again. Do you understand what I'm telling you?"

She nodded her head.

"Say it," he said.

"I understand."

"Okay, go home now." He turned and walked back to the large sedan, opened the passenger side door, and got in. The headlights came on with a harsh glare and the car backed out and the Camry with the man named Alejandro behind the wheel started up and she watched as the sedan left the parking lot with the dirty white Camry following close behind.

FORTY-EIGHT

There were about twelve or so people sitting on folding chairs facing a small, portable wood pulpit in the basement of the old church. Against one wall were tables upon which were a few open boxes of Dunkin' Donuts. Stale cigarette smoke hung thick in the air like a fog. Just about everyone in the audience was drinking coffee out of white Styrofoam cups. The people in the room, for the most part, looked haggard. Men and women, young and old, some dressed in business suits and dresses, some in ripped and tattered jeans, all with somber faces and sad, tired eyes. An undercurrent of sour body odor could be detected floating right alongside the unmistakable scent of Chanel No. 5.

The speaker, a disheveled-looking young man with a scruffy beard wearing dirty tan chinos, a stained sweatshirt, and old work boots had just finished talking. A smattering of weak applause followed and continued until the man had shuffled back to his seat.

Once it was quiet again, the moderator, a balding priest in his late forties got up from a chair in the front row and walked up to the pulpit. He was slightly overweight, his black shirt stretched tight against the buttons running down his chest and stomach, his white clerical collar stained with perspiration.

"Thank you, Bob, for sharing your story with us. I see some new faces here tonight. I just want to say that all are welcome. I invite each of you who are new to our gathering, or perhaps just visiting us tonight, to introduce yourselves and come up and say a few words if you're so inclined. Understand that sharing is totally voluntary, and we do not want you to feel pressured in any way."

The priest looked into the crowd and with a warm smile said, "You, sir, in the back. Would you care to tell us your name and maybe share with us your story?"

The man was sitting in the last chair in the last row wearing a dark, expensive suit and was staring at the floor between his feet. He glanced up for just a second, almost startled, and looked directly and intently into the priest's eyes, and then looked back down at his shoes again. One foot began rhythmically tapping up and down.

He said in a voice that was barely audible, "My name is Ryan."

The group answered in unison, "Hi, Ryan."

There was no sound from anybody for a few seconds. Then the man in the back row took a deep breath and said softly, "This is my first time here. I think, I think I will just listen today."

The priest smiled warmly and said, "Welcome, Ryan. We are glad that you came tonight. Each of us, everyone in this room, myself included, has sat where you sit now. Each of us, in his or her own time, has taken this first step. It is a big step, Ryan. It is a start."

The priest's eyes roamed the audience once again and came to a stop on an attractive woman with dark red hair. She was dressed business casual in a brown pants suit and light blue blouse. A colorful silk scarf was tied jauntily around her neck.

"And you, miss. I haven't seen you here before. Would you care to introduce yourself and maybe say a few words?"

The room was quiet. The only sound that could be heard was a very light tapping from the man's foot in the back row. And then the woman slowly got up from her chair and made her way to the pulpit. Her high heels clicked off the tile floor and echoed through the silent room as she made her way up front. The priest walked up to her, smiled, shook her hand, and then walked back to the seat in the front row, which he had vacated earlier.

The woman stood at the pulpit and looked over the audience. Her eyes were red, her mascara a little smudged as though she'd been crying. She didn't say anything as she glanced around the room and took in the small, silent audience. Then she looked down at the pulpit as if reading a speech, and as she was about to begin speaking, she stopped and cleared her throat, then began again.

"I'm sorry, this is very difficult for me," she said. "I am visiting my sister here in Toms River. That's her over there." She nodded to where her sister sat in the chair right next to the one she had just left. Nobody looked over at her sister, who was smiling bravely, her eyes wet and shining.

"I have been here for just over a week now, and I came here tonight because...because I think..." Here she stopped and cleared her throat again, the tears now streaming freely down her face. She composed herself and started again.

"I am here because something terrible happened to me recently." She looked up once again as if gauging the audience, deciding whether or not she was going to continue. Then she looked back down again and continued softly.

"I was, ah, I mean someone bad, an animal really, he, uh...he, uh." She stopped when she heard a sob from the audience and knew without looking up that it was her sister. The sound of her sister crying opened up something inside of her and, without really being able to control herself, she let out a sob herself and then cried silently, her eyes shut tight, her mouth slightly open as her body seemed to shrink in on itself, her shoulders shaking.

She stood in front of that audience, alone, and cried for about a full minute before taking a deep breath and composing herself once again. She wiped tears off her cheeks with the back of one hand like a small child might.

"And the, uh, reason I'm here tonight is that I'm beginning to think, no, that's not right, it's because I have come to realize…" Here she cleared her throat again. "…that alcohol has become a problem for me."

She glanced up just for a second and saw her sister sitting in the audience with her face buried in her hands, shoulders heaving, and had to look away. She lowered her eyes back down to the pulpit again and stared at small scratch in the dirty wood.

"I know this isn't coming out right, but, well, you see, the truth is, this bad thing that happened to me, well, I don't really, you know, remember all of it." Her voice got softer, so much so that it was hard for some in the audience to hear. A chair leg scraped across the floor as someone shifted in their seat, leaning forward in an effort to hear better.

"You see, I was drinking." Her voice cracked, going slightly higher in tone. "It was happy hour, after work. I sometimes go with my girlfriend Robin, but she couldn't make it. I didn't mean to drink so much." The words started coming out faster. "I had a few glasses of wine…and wait, I smoked a joint too, no, half a joint…and then he bought me a few more…and, you know, I got a little wasted and decided to…ah, go home… alone…and then…and then he followed me home…and I let him in…and then I opened another bottle of wine…and then, and then…"

She couldn't finish.

She cleared her throat and started again.

"So, you see, if I wasn't so drunk…if I wasn't so goddamn drunk, then…then that fucking animal, that fucking piece of shit lowlife would never have been able to…able to…"

She shook her head from side to side. "I just can't believe it…I can't believe I let this happen to me…" Then she dropped her head even farther down so that her chin was almost touching her chest and said in a barely audible whisper. "…again."

There was no sound in the room. Even the rhythmic foot tapping from the back had stopped.

The woman looked up at the audience. She ran a sleeve across her face to clear the moisture off of her cheeks and out of her eyes.

"So, that's it. That's my story."

She took another deep breath.

"My name is Loretta," she said, "and I'm here because I am an alcoholic."

FORTY-NINE

She drove to the bank, the one on South Street in Morristown, just past the Rite Aid and right before the highway and told the teller that she wanted to get into her safe deposit box. One of the managers came over and asked for her key and made her sign the logbook as usual. She came into the bank about once every two weeks or so. She was familiar with the procedure by now, and the bank people recognized her and smiled and were very helpful and then left her to her business.

She rented one of the larger boxes. Large enough to accommodate the money she had found in the lockbox all those months ago. Forty-five thousand dollars in cash. There was nothing else in the lockbox. She had also placed the roughly twenty-thousand dollars that she had gotten from Skooley, as well as the go phone and the revolver that he had tried to kill her with, into the bank box.

After those Miami guys took Skooley away, she drove back to the house and gave it a thorough cleaning. She retrieved the knives from under the car and replaced them in their holders and drawers, wiping their handles well with a rag. She was methodical, just as she was taught at her housecleaning job. When she was done in the house, she wiped the cars down inside and out, then went to work in the pool house. She wasn't too worried about leaving fingerprints except in areas where she shouldn't have been. Like Mrs. Russell's painting studio. She was on the cleaning crew after all and so it would be logical for her prints to be in some places. But still, she wore the rubber gloves she used when scrubbing toilets as she wiped and cleaned all surfaces including all the doorknobs and electrical outlets and sockets. She cleaned the kitchen, making sure all the tainted chili went into a plastic bag and cleaning the pots and bowls and sinks and counters. She wiped the smoke alarm where they had found the lockbox key and screwed it back onto its base on the bedroom ceiling, this time using a ladder from the garage to reach it. She gathered whatever garbage she could find including the empty beer bottles and went through the entire house emptying any garbage pails that she found. She put all the trash into two big plastic garbage bags and loaded them into the back of the station wagon.

Then she drove home and carried the lockbox and the cash and the phone and the gun that she had retrieved from the cleaning bucket up to her apartment and went into the bathroom and locked the door and then opened the lockbox and counted the money. Her money.

She looked down into the bank box. She had started with over sixty-five thousand dollars when she first rented that box almost seven months ago. But then she had bought a car. A 2006 Ford Fusion with ninety-six thousand miles on it for just over five thousand dollars, then she had to pay insurance and gas. She bought the car to get her back and forth to cosmetology school. Even with the financial aid that she had managed to qualify for, it was still going to end up costing her close to ten thousand. Five she paid up front. She still owed the rest. Plus, she had to give up her housecleaning job during the day so she could attend classes. Luckily, she was able to work weekends at her office cleaning job. Sometimes she got an extra shift one or two nights during the week if someone called in sick or quit unexpectedly. She quit working at the restaurant too. She just couldn't go back to work there. That meant that she had to take money from the box every other week or so, usually about a thousand dollars, just to pay bills.

She had started with sixty-five thousand dollars: a fortune, she had thought. Now she was down to about forty.

She grabbed another thousand to put into her checking account at the other bank. Down to thirty-nine. Not really a fortune any longer.

She locked the box and left the bank and sat in her car and thought about Skooley.

She had read a story in the *Star-Ledger* not long after that night about a dead body being found in a car in Newark, a body with hands that were missing all of their fingers. The body's head was also missing. She thought those missing items might be sitting in pickle jars in a fancy condo in Miami. There was a person of interest in the case, a Hispanic man named Raymundo Enrique Sandoval, whom authorities were trying to locate for questioning. She had heard that the cops had come to the restaurant where she and Raymundo had worked, but she had already left by then. Still, she felt sad whenever she thought about Raymundo.

She didn't feel sad about Skooley at all.

She never read anything in the newspapers about a robbery in Mendham. She stayed away from the Russells' home and for some reason decided to drive by today, just to see it. She was a little nervous as she drove over to Mendham, afraid for some reason that one of the Russells might see her drive by, remember her as one of the girls from their old cleaning crew who no longer worked for their cleaning company, put two and two together, and then call the police.

Silly, she knew, but she still put on sunglasses and a hat before she drove past the house and wasn't surprised at all to see a brand-new fence surrounding the property. She could see cameras mounted on the stone pillars that guarded the locked, gated entrance to the driveway. Signs along the fence warned of the property being protected by some high-tech security system.

She guessed no one else was going to be breaking into the Russells' house anytime soon. She wondered if they would still go away for a month every summer. She hoped they would. They were nice people, and she was sorry that she had robbed them. But she realized too that they wouldn't really miss the money all that much. Sixty-five thousand dollars wasn't such a fortune after all. They probably spent more than that installing their new fence.

She drove on past the house further into Mendham. She looked at the beautiful, stately homes as she passed them and thought about her dream of opening her own business, The Starlight Salon and Spa. She had spent over four years cleaning rich people's homes just like these, as Skooley had said so insightfully, scrubbing out their toilets. Maybe one day she would be able to live in a big house in Mendham, hire people to come and scrub her toilet.

She thought about the ratty salon where her friend worked and knew that she herself would have to start as a shampoo girl again, probably in another ratty salon, and she thought of her job cleaning offices on weekends and of the box at the bank that held her dream and of the quickly disappearing cash.

Then she remembered something that suddenly made her stomach flutter and her heart speed up a bit in her chest and her hands begin to sweat on the steering wheel.

It was something that Skooley had said to her, something he had asked her when they had first met, that first day. She remembered it clear as a bell. She could picture him in her mind, there by the pool, that blond, unruly hair and his shark eyes and his face with that sick, scary smile and she could see his skinny white body and hear that soft southern twang in his voice. She remembered sitting at the table in the breakfast room, dealing hundred-dollar bills into piles like playing cards.

"Let me ask you something," he had said, holding that green bottle of whatever beer it was that he always drank, "you happen to know about any more houses get left empty by dumbass rich people?"

ACKNOWLEDGMENTS

Anyone who's tried knows that writing a novel is hard enough. But getting one published is an even more daunting endeavor. I want to thank my love, Susan, for her encouragement, editorial assistance, and the occasional kick in the butt that she provided when needed. I could not have done this without her. Also, I need to thank the very talented crime writer Charles Salzberg whose enthusiasm, advice, and invaluable assistance has helped push this novel forward. Charles, you are the best. Lastly, I have a cadre of trusted readers, some who are literary professionals and some who are simply fans of fiction, who were kind enough to review the initial versions of this story and gave me the confidence to keep at it. I want to thank you all.

Steven Max Russo has spent most of his professional career as an advertising copywriter and agency owner. He got interested in writing fiction after one of his short stories was accepted by an online literary journal in 2013. After that, he caught the bug and began writing seriously. His first novel, *Thieves*, has garnered praise from renowned crime and thriller authors from around the globe. Steve is proud to call New Jersey his home.

StevenMaxRussoBooks.com

BOOKS

On the following pages are a few
more great titles from the
Down & Out Books publishing family.

For a complete list of books and to
sign up for our newsletter,
go to DownAndOutBooks.com.

Harbinger
The Ania Series
Frank Zafiro and Jim Wilsky

Down & Out Books
December 2018
978-1-948235-43-3

On the sunny Gulf Coast of Florida, lifelong friends and fishing charter boat partners, Boyd Tomlin and Hicks Ledoux, are in desperate need of money. They consider smuggling drugs as a solution. Then they meet two beautiful sisters who will change everything—a young Ania and her sister Karolyn.

Boyd and Hicks are quickly embroiled in romance and danger, with violence lurking around every corner.

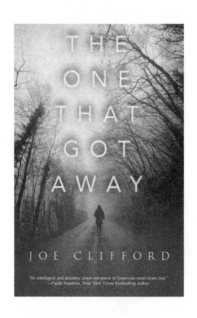

The One That Got Away
Joe Clifford

Down & Out Books
December 2018
978-1-948235-42-6

In the early 2000s, a string of abductions rocked the small up-state town of Reine, New York. Only one girl survived: Alex Salerno. The killer was sent away. Life returned to normal. No more girls would have to die.

Until another one did...

Repetition Kills You
Stories by Tom Leins

All Due Respect, an imprint of
Down & Out Books
September 2018
978-1-948235-28-0

Repetition Kills You comprises 26 short stories, presented in alphabetical order, from 'Actress on a Mattress' to 'Zero Sum'. The content is brutal and provocative: small-town pornography, gun-running, mutilation and violent, blood-streaked stories of revenge. The cast list includes sex offenders, serial killers, bare-knuckle fighters, carnies and corrupt cops. And a private eye with a dark past—and very little future.

Welcome to Paignton Noir.

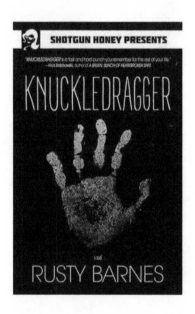

Knuckledragger
Rusty Barnes

Shotgun Honey, an imprint of
Down & Out Books
978-1-946502-07-0

Hooligan and low-level criminal enforcer Jason "Candy" Stahl has made a good life collecting money for his boss Otis. One collection trip, though, at the Diovisalvo Liquor Store, unravels events that turn Candy's life into a horror-show.

In quick succession he moves up a notch in the organization, overseeing a chop shop, while he falls in lust with Otis's girlfriend Nina, gets beaten for insubordination, and is forced to run when Otis finds out about Candy and Nina's affair.